Copyright © 2019 Olivia Hayle

All rights reserved. No part of this publication may be distributed or transmitted without the prior consent of the publisher, except in case of brief quotations embodied in articles or reviews.

All characters and events depicted in this book are entirely fictitious. Any similarity to actual events or persons, living or dead, is purely coincidental.

The following story contains mature themes, strong language and explicit scenes, and is intended for mature readers.

Edited by Stephanie Parent
www.oliviahayle.com

arrogant BOSS

OLIVIA HAYLE

1
EMILY

"*Relax.*"

"I am relaxed!"

Denise raised an eyebrow. "As if. I can practically feel the tension radiating from you across the table. Tomorrow's going to go *great*. Both you and Turner have prepared for this for weeks."

"I know. But—"

"No, stop thinking about it. A night of fun will do you good."

I took another sip of my fruity, wildly overpriced mocktail. "Okay, okay, I won't think about it. You're right."

"I always am. It'll go great, Em."

"I don't even know what you're referring to."

Denise grinned. "That's the spirit. The only things you should be concerned about tonight are drinks, dancing, and dudes."

"Dudes? Since when do we refer to men as *dudes*?"

"It was an alliteration. I know how you like slogans and catchy titles. Oh! My co-workers are here."

Denise waved at a group of women making their way from the bar. They were dressed to the nines, in sky-high heels and matching clutches, and looked far more used to this scene than Denise and me.

We were in a packed club in the Financial District, a place with a massive waiting list, all to impress Denise's new colleagues. She'd been made a full-time writer at the online platform Yas.

Yes, exactly like that—Yas. We both thought the name was a bit silly, and the platform vapid, but Denise was a brilliant writer and this was just a stepping-stone to world domination.

As the supportive friend I was, I had come along to celebrate her promotion—even if that meant going to a too-expensive club, putting on a pair of uncomfortable heels, and breaking out a red lipstick I've worn too few times to justify the price.

The music was a pulsing beat and bodies were writhing out on the dance floor. The club was packed. Just finding a table for the two of us had been hard enough, and I had no idea how we'd fit three more people here.

Despite my promise to Denise, I wanted to glance at my watch. Tomorrow was a big day for my brother, and I had to be sharp…

"Emily." Denise snapped her fingers in front of my face. "They're approaching. Look alive."

"Sorry!"

Denise stood. "Hi guys! I'm so glad you could make it."

"Me too," the blonde ringleader said to Denise. "We were ecstatic to hear that you're joining Yas permanently."

"Just *ecstatic*," a brunette repeated from behind. I shook hands with all three of them and wished I could hear their names over the pounding beat. Their eyeliner was perfect, and I ran a hand through my loose hair self-consciously.

The blonde took a seat next to me. "What do you do at Yas?" I asked.

"I cover holistic beauty and experimental health."

"Wow. What does that mean?"

"Trying a lot of funny-smelling products," she said with an enviably raised eyebrow. "What do you work with?"

This was where I *wished* I had a better answer than the truth. "I work in press and marketing."

"No way!"

"Yeah."

"For what company?"

I cleared my throat. "For Pet and Co."

She frowned. "I haven't heard about that."

"It's a pet and grooming business. Not really too exciting. I think it's—"

"Guys?" Elisa, the brunette, shot us all a secretive grin. "Have you seen who's in the VIP section tonight?"

Blondie next to me leaned back. "Do you mean the launch of *Viper*?"

"Yes. Did you know?"

She looked superior. "Why do you think we suggested this place?"

Denise and I shot each other confused glances. "What's Viper?"

"Some new app." She waved her hand dismissively. "That's not important. Who is in attendance, however, is. Some of the hottest names in tech are here. Rafe Christensen, Danny Stephens, and of course… Julian Hunt."

"Hunt is here?"

"I *swear* I just saw him."

"It wasn't confirmed if he would attend or not."

The three of them craned their necks, trying to see across the club to the VIP section. Even from this distance, I could see the polished suits, the flowing bottles of champagne.

Denise sidled closer to me. "That's where we should be."

I snorted. "Right. Doing what? We know nothing about tech."

"Which is why they would love us! They'd find it refreshing."

"Aren't you dating that blogger?"

"No, that was ages ago! You have to keep up."

I grinned. "You're impossible to keep up with, Denise."

"Come on, girls," the blonde declared. "Let's dance." I grabbed my half-finished daiquiri and joined them on the dance floor.

Nearly an hour later, I was done. I was so, so, so done.

I could party with the best of them. But the business meeting

3

for my brother's potential contract was at ten o'clock the following day, and despite my promise to Denise, there was nothing more important.

I grabbed Denise and gave her a quick hug.

"I have to go," I spoke into her curly red hair, hoping she could hear me over the pounding bass. "I'll talk to you tomorrow."

"Thank you for coming. Good luck tomorrow! Tell Turner I'll be thinking of him."

"I will." I grinned at her. "Don't go *too* crazy tonight."

She gave me an innocent little smirk. "Who, me?"

I shook my head at her in mock disapproval. If there was someone who could handle herself, it was Denise. Party until five and then up at nine for work, and do a damn good job as well. It was very unfair, but she'd always been like that. Too much energy for one person to contain.

I made my way through writhing bodies, my clutch tucked tight under my arm and the last of my daiquiri in my hand. I needed to find a place to leave the glass.

Too many people. Too loud music.

An arm wound its way around my waist and I twisted away. A man leered at me, a drink glued to his hand as his other reached for me.

"Dance with me, sugar."

I frowned. *"Definitely not."*

This, too, reminded me why I didn't go out too often. Denise kept pushing me to go out with more men, and while I agreed that my semi-celibate status wasn't exactly enjoyable, you don't find your soul mate in a club.

I was by the exit when it happened.

I heard a snap, and then I was airborne and tumbling. My hands reached out to try to steady myself and I fell straight into a passing stranger.

A strong arm reacted but it was too late, and I hit the club floor with a crash.

Embarrassment flooded through me and I scrambled onto

smarting knees.

"Are you all right?"

I pushed my hair back and looked up to find the owner of that deep, rumbling voice.

Cheekbones. Expensive suit. A concerned expression.

No no no. I recognized this man.

"I'm fine!"

He reached down and strong arms fitted themselves under my shoulders. I was lifted to my feet like a child, only to find that I couldn't stand properly. He frowned and looked down.

I followed his gaze. "Oh. My heel broke."

"Occupational hazard." His voice was smooth, polished. Dark. I cleared my throat and slipped out of my pumps. Barefoot, I only just reached his chin.

Julian Hunt.

Of all the men in the world, why did I have to trip into him?

My eyes traced down the long column of his throat, his white shirt, the top button undone to expose just a hint of tan skin, a giant pink stain on his shirt…

I clasped my hand to my mouth. "Oh my God. I am so sorry, that was my drink, wasn't it?"

Julian Hunt looked down. "I think so. Strawberry daiquiri, was it?"

"Yes. I'm *so* sorry." My cheeks were on fire. "I'll pay for the dry-cleaning."

He smiled—actually smiled at that. "Certainly not. I'm just happy you weren't injured in the fall."

I blinked. "No. No, I wasn't injured. I… where is my bag?"

We both looked at the dark club floor in silence. We were by the exit, so there was more light, but still not enough. I was also looking at it far closer than I would have liked, being barefoot on this disgusting surface.

Julian found it first, grabbing the navy clutch hidden along the dark baseboard. "This it?"

"Yes. Thank you again."

"Anytime." He cocked his head. "Did you have a good time tonight?"

For a long moment, all I could do was stare into the curious green eyes looking back at me. Julian Hunt—billionaire playboy, America's tech sweetheart—was prolonging the moment. Making conversation with me.

"Yes, it was all right."

"That's not exactly a ringing endorsement."

Maybe it was the fall, or maybe it was the teasing glint in his eyes, but I surprised myself with my answer. "I don't know if you heard, but there was a launch party tonight for an app. A bunch of rowdy Silicon Valley types were making a lot of noise from the VIP section."

His eyebrows shot up. "Is that so?"

"Yes. Sort of ruined the mood for the rest of us, to be honest." I bent forward, and dear God, I was *flirting* with him. "Don't let them know, if you see one."

Julian's smile turned crooked. "Oh, don't worry. I stay far away from that crowd."

My heart was beating fast. This was too much, and I was too inexperienced at this. This wasn't a college guy fumbling around. This was a man, a man who was experienced and wealthy and used to perfection and by God was he handsome. I wetted my lips.

"Thanks again for finding my bag."

Julian looked amused. "One of my lesser talents."

"Very impressive."

"I'm sure." He looked out toward the parking lot. "Were you heading out?"

"Yes, I was planning to. My car is parked here."

"But now you can't."

My eyes widened. I couldn't leave? Because now I had met him?

But then he glanced down at my bare feet. "Because you have no shoes."

"Oh. Right. I don't."

He shrugged. "There's only one thing to do then."

Before I could register what he was doing, Julian Hunt bent and put his arms around me. I was lifted up with a very unflattering screech.

"What are you doing?"

"You can't walk barefoot out of a nightclub," he said, not looking winded in the least. "There might be glass on the pavement."

"But… this is weird." I was being carried by a veritable stranger—a famous stranger—and I hadn't been carried like this since I was twelve.

His crooked smile was back. "I've never been bothered by 'weird.'"

Julian Hunt smelled good. Too good. My arm wrapped around his neck as an employee opened the front door for us.

"Valet stand?"

"To the left."

People were lingering outside, some in line to get in and others just out for a smoke. All of them watched us walk across to the valet stand. My cheeks had to be on fire, that's how hot they felt.

Julian didn't put me down when we arrived, just looked at me expectantly. So did the valet worker.

"Oh, right! Let me just find it." I clawed through my bag in search of the ticket. Seemingly unable to stop myself, I rambled on. "My heel broke, by the way. That's why… that's why he's being chivalrous."

The valet worker accepted my ticket with a grin. "I'm sure, miss."

He disappeared to fetch my car and I glanced up to see Julian grinning too. He was far too close like this—it was impossible to ignore just how excruciatingly handsome he was. He always had been, on the magazine covers and online interviews. But weren't famous people supposed to be, well, just *less* when you saw them in person? Shorter than you expected, or less attractive? They were not supposed to be *more* good-looking.

"You can put me down now," I said. "This will take a while."

In a smooth movement, Julian let me slide down. My feet touched the cold pavement and I pulled my jacket tighter around me.

"Stand in your shoes?"

I nodded and slipped them on, mismatched heights and missing heels and all. "Thanks for carrying me."

"Just being chivalrous," he repeated with a smile. "I have to say, I've had a lot of women do interesting things to get my attention, but fake-falling is new."

My eyes snapped to his face. "What?"

"I'm complimenting you on your ingenuity. The drink was a nice touch."

For a long moment, all I could do was stare at him. Julian Hunt might be handsome, but he was surely not humble.

"You're serious," I said slowly. "How arrogant do you have to be to believe I willingly tripped just to get your attention?"

His lips quirked at my tone, and the fact that he was enjoying my outrage only made me angrier. "You're unbelievable. Do you think I snapped my heel on purpose? Waited for the right moment when you passed by the exit?"

Julian's dark eyes were alight. "You have a temper."

"I do when I'm being accused of… of… I'm not even sure what to call it."

"Entrapment?"

"Yes. That."

"Are you OK driving yourself home?"

I blinked at him. "Um, yes. Of course."

"Are you sure? I could drive you home, if not. My Porsche is parked just over there." He nodded to the front.

I couldn't help myself—I laughed. This man was unreal. "Was it really necessary to mention the car brand in that sentence?"

His smile turned bashful, and then a bit teasing. "No. I'm bragging, aren't I?"

"I think you are."

"Damn." He ran a hand through his admittedly very thick hair. "You really didn't fall on purpose, did you?"

"Absolutely not. It was humiliating."

"How much have you had to drink tonight?"

"I fell because my heel snapped, not because I'm *drunk*."

Julian glanced down at the stain on his shirt that appeared to prove otherwise, but I was quick to correct him. "That was virgin."

"Oh?"

"Um, yes. The drink."

"Thanks for clarifying."

My cheeks flushed again. This was going all wrong, he was infuriating, and I needed to get home. I pushed my long hair back and saw his eyes follow the movement.

"I don't usually fall on strangers."

His grin was back. "I'm honored that I was the chosen one tonight, then."

The valet boy still hadn't returned with my car and I tugged my jacket tighter. Julian didn't seem remotely bothered by our odd interaction or the sudden silence. He looked just as serenely calm as in the photos of him, jawline screaming masculinity and competence and power.

Arrogant man.

I was not like him—the uncomfortable silence was unbearable. "Do you come here often?"

"As a matter of fact, no, I don't. Only when apps are launching and there's rowdiness to be had."

I bit my lip to keep from smiling, despite myself. "Of course. A favorite past-time, is it?"

He shrugged, powerful shoulders stretching out a perfectly fitted suit jacket. The man had held me for near on three minutes without a change in his breathing. "It's practically a national sport in my circles."

"Are you heading home now too?"

He nodded. "Yes. But I'm—"

A voice called out from across the parking lot. "Julian, my man! Are you coming?"

A blond man stood across the parking lot, his arm around a brunette in strappy heels. They were standing next to a Hummer with music blaring.

"Duty calls?"

He ran a hand through his thick hair, a faintly embarrassed look on his face. "I don't go to a lot of launches. This isn't my scene."

"I'm sure it's not. Just like you don't have a lot of experience with women fake tripping just to catch your attention." I rolled my eyes and his lips quirked up again.

"Because of your shoes," he said softly and caught a flyaway strand of hair. Gently, he tucked it back in place behind my ear, and I stopped breathing.

"Can I call you?"

Definitely not breathing.

I found myself giving a shallow nod. "If you don't insult me again."

The eyebrow quirked again. "I'll be on my very best behavior. Promise."

The sound of an approaching engine cut the intimacy as my car pulled up next to us. It looked small and ordinary suddenly, standing next to the magnificence that was Julian Hunt.

The valet got out and left the car in idle. "All yours, ma'am."

"Thank you." I slipped out of my shoes and handed him a tip. "I guess this is it. I'm sorry about your shirt again."

Julian leaned against my car and held the door open for me. "I'll forgive you if you tell me your name."

"Emily."

"Emily?"

"Emily Giordano."

The mischievous look was back in his eyes. "Is that so?"

"Yes."

"Huh." Julian bent so that we were eye to eye. "Well, I'll be in touch, Ace."

A shiver ran down my spine. "Ace?"

"You could have barreled into anyone tonight, but you hit me." He winked. "You have excellent aim."

I opened my mouth to protest the sheer arrogance of his statement, but he shut my door with a grin and took a few steps back. With shaky motions, I put the car in drive and pulled out of the parking lot.

What the hell had just happened?

I had met Julian Hunt. He had strong arms and a crooked smile and he smelled *amazing*. I had probably never been so instantly attracted to a man before in my life.

And then he asked if he could call me.

Things like this—meeting men like this—didn't happen to me. It never did and it never had.

He likely had no intention of calling me, and I wasn't even sure I would pick up if he did. He was arrogant and obnoxious… and funny. Besides, he hadn't even asked for my number!

I shook my head at my own musings. I would never see Julian Hunt again, and that was probably for the best. I couldn't start comparing regular men to his standard or I'd be single for life.

I ignored the small part of my brain that wanted to think of *maybes* and *what-ifs*.

Julian Hunt was not for me, and I was certainly not for him.

2
JULIAN

At every launch, there were two types of assholes.

The first were the ones who went all-in at every event, who drank as much of the free champagne as they could. They handed out business cards and smiles like currency and stayed until closing, posting the whole thing on their social media. There might even be a livestream sometime during the evening.

The second type of asshole arrived late, posed for the requisite photos, said hello to everyone with a practiced handshake and left in time to get their sleep and workout in.

I was in the second category.

Yesterday's launch was as run-of-the-mill as they go. I figured Viper would last maybe five to eight months. I saw versions of the same story all the time; poorly developed apps with an innovative interface and a slick promotional campaign. Investors inevitably backed them, like they did anything out of the Valley, despite the software being mediocre at best.

Nothing I would ever invest in. Hell, Rafe and I had placed bets on how long we thought Viper would last. My press secretary, the one I had left, had correctly pointed out that going to the launch and getting photographed would cause a buzz. With our new launch up and coming, Hunt Industries needed all the buzz it could get—so I went. But for all other intents and purposes, the night had been a bust.

I'd been more than ready to head out and leave the polite small talk behind when a young woman quite literally tripped into my arms.

She'd come out of nowhere.

I grinned just thinking about it. As soon as I saw her, I knew she would fit me perfectly—I could imagine pulling her close, bending my head down, having her reach up. Her body had been soft when she crashed into me.

I had replayed the image of her flushed cheeks the entire morning, wondering if I could get her like that by other means. Long black hair, shiny down her back. Eyes that had seemed just as captured by me as I had been by her.

And when I carried her… she smelled divine. If my body had called the shots rather than my brain, I would have carried her straight past the valet and to my car, taking her home and making her mine.

She had seemed sweet and shy—until I made the comment about her attempts at entrapment.

She'd been so angry at me, her eyes flashing as she scolded me for my presumption. Pushing her buttons was surprisingly amusing. I wanted to see her flash like that again—call me out and tease me.

Emily Giordano.

The name had been familiar, but it had taken me nearly an hour until I'd made the connection. That was just my luck, wasn't it? She just happened to be *Emily Giordano.*

As in, the sister of Turner Giordano.

The boy genius my HR rep was meeting with today to discuss a potential starting contract. He'd sent over information, and I was well aware of the young man's talents. It was why I wanted to hire him in the first place. David had made it clear, though, that the way to the boy was through his older sister.

A very beautiful, very feisty older sister. An older sister who might or might not despise me.

This could be very fun.

I called David and he answered on the first signal. "Mr. Hunt, what can I do for you?"

"I want an update on the meeting with Giordano."

"I'm preparing for the meeting now." I heard the sound of rustling paper in the background. "They'll be here at ten o'clock."

"They? Is his sister accompanying him to the meeting?"

"Yes. She was his legal guardian for several years and Turner made it clear that he wanted her to participate in the negotiation."

I thought of her flashing eyes and her outrage. "The older sister can't be bought."

He was quiet for a moment. "Have you been reading the information I sent over?"

"Yes." I hadn't, but I would the second I hung up. "I'll be at the meeting too."

This time David's silence was incredulous. "I didn't think you had the time, but of course. The CEO being here when they arrive shows just how seriously we take Turner's potential. We need to charm them into accepting this."

I tapped my fingers against the desk. "We need to meet their demands and make them an offer they'll feel happy about."

"That too. I think one of his mentors at MIT wants a word with us too. It might be the key to convincing him; the opinions of those he respects."

"And his own opinion."

"Yes, yes, of course."

"Text me the location and time."

"Will do."

I hung up. Pressing down the buzzer on my desk, I phoned my secretary.

"Yes?"

"Clear my schedule for the coming hour."

Tim's silence was also shocked. "Okay. Absolutely."

14

I leaned back in my chair and pulled up the file David had prepared on Turner Giordano and his family.

I skimmed the section I knew by heart—about the coding prodigy. The things Turner could do had already made it possible for him to attend online classes at MIT, professors taking a special interest in him. It was only a matter of time before one of the big tech companies snapped him up with the promise of a big salary and unlimited bandwidth.

I was damn lucky that I was still friendly with a high school buddy who was on the faculty, and that we'd heard of Turner's potential first. My friend had spoken excitedly about a quiet kid who could write legions of code that magically sped up nearly the entire system of course registry.

In his spare time.

Coding like that could make my company *millions*. It could change the technology landscape entirely, if properly harnessed.

But it was the section labeled *Family* that I focused on most.

All of Turner's communication goes through his former legal guardian and older sister, Emily. Age twenty-five, educated media strategist with a major in marketing. Currently works for Pet and Co.

Attached was Emily's resume. I grinned as I read through it. Straight As, community college. Had risen quickly in the ranks. I saw her flashing green eyes in front of me again and the way she'd protested when I'd lifted her up. Hell, I couldn't remember the last time I'd carried a woman like that. There was just something about her…

Below her dossier, David had added a handwritten caveat. *Emily will likely need to be convinced that her brother should bypass college and begin working for us.*

College… I remembered what a hell that had been for me, when all I wanted was to be let out of the gates and try my own hand at the world. To be misunderstood. Expected to behave one way and failing to live up to that. To want to test your wings right away. From reading Turner's bio, I had a feeling that might be what he needed.

I wasn't so certain, however, that Emily Giordano would be

as easily convinced—particularly when she realized who owned Tech José.

Hunt Industries.

And who owned Hunt Industries?

I did.

I made sure to arrive at the meeting a few minutes late, giving David time to butter them up with small talk. I grinned at the thought of seeing her blush again.

The conference door was half open when I arrived, and I heard clear voices coming from inside.

I paused and waited for a cue. Anticipation curled in my stomach at the thought of seeing her eyes flash in agitation.

"I was led to understand we would only interview with you," a familiar voice said.

David spoke. "Yes, well, I will also be here. But the CEO has expressed a particular interest in Mr. Giordano and wanted to be here himself as well."

"David, what company owns Tech José?"

I grinned and stepped forward.

3

EMILY

Ten minutes earlier

"He should be here by now."

I glanced at my watch. "It's exactly ten o'clock. Let's give him a few minutes."

Turner twisted his ring around his finger, a habit to calm himself, and gave me a short nod. The lobby we were seated in was *huge*. Vast expanses of glass and white marble floors, tall palm trees in massive pots. No receptionist, however, and no names. It all seemed to be done with key cards. Probably some fancy new prototype.

I'd lived in Palo Alto for twenty-five years, but this was the first time I'd really come face to face with these giant billion-dollar companies.

A man with a pleasant smile and short blond hair hurried toward us from the elevators. "Hello, and welcome! You must be the Giordanos. It's a pleasure to finally meet the both of you in person. I trust you've not had to wait long?"

"We arrived ten minutes ago," Turner said in his usual blunt fashion. He didn't look David in the eyes, focused instead on the sharp lines of his shirt.

"Ah. Great. Well, my name is David and I'm the head of recruitment here." He extended a hand to Turner.

My brother hesitated only a moment before he grasped David's hand in a firm grip. "Hello."

"Hi. And this must be your sister? Emily, is it?"

I shook David's hand. "Yes. I'm his older sister."

And you're going to have to go through me.

"Let's head upstairs, this way."

Turner and I followed David through the blindingly white lobby. This place was easily as big as our entire house, and we were only on the first floor. David used his key card to call down one of the sleek, chrome elevators.

"I like how this place looks," Turner told me.

I smiled at him. "Of course you do. It's all clean lines and free from clutter. Exactly your style."

He shot me a small smile without looking at me. He was turning his ring around and around again.

"You know exactly what you are going to say," I told him quietly. "You've rehearsed this."

He nodded and while the fidgeting didn't stop, I thought it mellowed slightly.

The elevator arrived and we followed David into the space. He attempted some small talk on the way and I handled it for us. *No, it hadn't been difficult to find parking. Yes, it was unusually warm today.*

We walked down an open hallway. Windows opened up into wide landscapes of desks with people working at computers. A large tree grew in the middle of a courtyard surrounded by white desks. People didn't look up as we passed. I saw energy drinks and at least two Rubik's Cubes. Good God.

Turner would fit right in.

David gestured to the office. "These are some of our coders and software engineers. They're junior associates."

Turner cleared his throat. "Would I also receive a desk out here?"

"Potentially, yes. But it might be possible to get you your own office."

Turner's shoulders relaxed somewhat. I knew that was on his list of demands.

The rows just continued. "Tech José looks like a big company. I was under the impression that it didn't have more than forty employees."

"You're quite right. But we are a subsidiary of a bigger company, with holdings in several industries."

We were shown to a beautiful meeting room, with bottled water and muffins displayed on the table. They had really pulled out the big guns for this meeting—but then again, I knew Turner was considered valuable in their eyes.

Turner and I took a seat as David opened his folder. "As I was saying, we are a subsidiary company. That gives us a lot of the resources we need but also allows us considerable freedom in terms of direction. We function like an in-house incubator, to use jargon." He gave a small laugh, but neither Turner nor I joined him. "Our mother company recognizes your potential just as much as we at Tech José do, Turner, and what you could accomplish here. The CEO will actually join us here today as well. He should be here in a minute or two." He smiled at us like this was a brilliant revelation.

I frowned. "I was led to understand we would only interview with you."

David looked taken aback by my lack of thanks. "Yes, well, I will also be here, of course. But the CEO has expressed a particular interest in Mr. Giordano and wanted to join us himself."

I leaned forward. "David, what company owns Tech José?"

But it wasn't David who replied.

"That would be Hunt Industries," a voice said from the doorway.

And leaning against it, an infuriating smile on his face, was Julian Hunt.

I just stared at him in shock.

If he'd looked mysteriously handsome last night in the dark, he was blinding in daylight. Thick hair, a smirk, a perfectly fitted suit. No tie.

Damn it, Emily.

I should have done better research. How had I never realized that Tech José was a subsidiary branch of Hunt Industries? There was no way I would have come along today if I had known. After yesterday… my cheeks flushed with humiliation. He had known. He had known right away, as soon as I had said my name.

I shut out the small part of me that was thrilled at seeing Julian in the doorway. It couldn't be helped—he was an intensely attractive man, objectively speaking, and I wasn't *blind*.

He stepped into the room. "I'm Julian Hunt. You must be Turner Giordano?"

"I am, yes."

Julian moved around the table and extended a hand to my brother, who looked at me briefly before shaking his hand. If Julian was curious as to why Turner didn't meet his eyes, he didn't show it.

I cleared my throat. "I'm Emily. His sister."

Julian clasped my hand and I looked straight into his dancing green eyes. "Emily. What a beautiful name."

"Thank you."

"When David informed me that you had agreed to a meeting, Turner, we were all very excited." Julian took a seat, long legs stretched out in front of him.

He took up too much space in this room, too much *air*. I glanced nervously at my brother. He hadn't prepared for this eventuality. Hell, neither had I.

Turner put his hands palm-down on the table. "Let's begin."

David looked down at his papers. "Absolutely. Well, Turner, we've been lucky enough to see a sample of the code you've written recently. It's great. You're young but clearly very capable. We'd therefore like to offer you a position here at Tech José. It's unusual, considering your age and lack of university education, but we think you have great potential."

So that was how they were going to play it, I thought.

Great potential. Turner had great potential, of course, but the way David phrased it made it sound like they were doing him a favor. I didn't know much about code, but I knew my brother, and Hunt Industries would be lucky to have him on their team.

"First and foremost, I am high-functioning autistic," Turner said. "So I'm not as adept with interactions and social cues as you're likely used to. Therefore, if you want me to do or not do something, it would be efficient for all of us involved if you just say so directly. I will do the same with you."

Julian gave Turner a solemn nod. "Thank you for telling us that. We'll make sure to keep all communications as clear as possible."

"Thank you. Now, if I am to agree to work here, I have a number of demands."

I saw that David's eyes widened in surprise, but Julian regarded Turner with something quite different. It looked like respect.

"We're listening."

"My code is great," Turner said. "I know it's just as good as what your competitors are working on, because I've been comparing, and I have a lot more potential in me. Given the resources and time, I could do great things for a company of your size. I could also, of course, take my code and skill to another company who would gladly hire me. But I chose to come here first."

Julian nodded. "We appreciate that. We'll try to accommodate you, within reason."

"I want my own office. It doesn't matter where it is or what it looks like. But my own space without people distracting me."

"Consider it done." Julian leaned forward and braced strong forearms on the table, looking for all the world like the consummate young CEO. This morning, I'd debated whether to have cereal or toast, and now I was participating in a negotiation over my brother's future with America's favorite boy billionaire. *What was my life?*

Only, he was very much *not* a boy—that had been clear from the moment he lifted me yesterday. From the faint stubble on his cheeks to his deep voice.

My brother continued with his demands. "I don't want to be…micro-managed. Poked and prodded every day. I know what I'm doing and I will do it."

David opened his mouth to speak, but Julian cut in. "Done. Having seen lines of your code, I don't think that will be a problem."

"I want to be exempt from team-building exercises and any other obligatory company outings or events."

"You're welcome to join company events at your own discretion, or not," David said. "We understand."

I had to give it to the two men opposite us—I had not expected them to be so accommodating. While I'd always thought so, seeing them watch my little brother with such respect made me realize just how impressive Turner's skills must be.

"And my final demand. I want to have a mini-fridge in my office that is always stocked with soda."

I saw the corners of Julian's mouth begin to curl. This had been Turner's final demand, and the one he'd fretted over the longest. He'd asked me if I thought they could grant it, and quite frankly, I said it was the least they could do.

"There's a communal fridge in the lounge room," David said. But Julian shook his head and shot both me and Turner a blinding, practiced smile. "One stocked mini-fridge, coming up. I can't help but notice that you haven't mentioned any salary demands, Turner."

Turner turned to me. "I don't know what an adequate salary is. I've done some research, but nothing conclusive. Emily will tell you if what you are offering is acceptable or not."

I squared my shoulders. This was why I was here. Not just to act as moral support, but to double-check all of the contracts before Turner signed anything. He was only nineteen. I'd been working for the past six years, had experienced both good and bad employers. No one was going to exploit my baby brother on my watch.

Julian watched me with those dark eyes of his. "Of course. We're offering a starting salary of 52k a year, with a generous health insurance package and yearly bonuses. Your salary would be revisable upwards during quarterly performance meetings."

"Here's a draft of the contract." David pushed a piece of paper across the table at us. "Feel free to take a look."

52k. I struggled to contain my expression as I looked over the contract. It was a massive salary for someone without a university education. I'd always known that these places were practically flowing with money, but still. With that money, Turner could have a proper savings account by the end of the year. He was a saver by nature, and he would be able to pocket so much for the future.

Some of my nerves lessened.

But I kept re-reading the line at the bottom of the contract: *Any line of code written during the employee's time on Tech José property will be considered the intellectual property of Tech José.*

I didn't know if Turner was going to invent anything, but it certainly wouldn't surprise me. And if he did, it would be entirely out of his hands.

"You don't look convinced," Julian said. "What are you concerned about?"

I cleared my throat. "Line 27, regarding intellectual property rights."

"Yes. A standard part of any software design contract."

"I'm sure it is. But if my brother takes this job, he will not go to college. He will be learning and developing on the job. I don't want this company to end up taking advantage of any code he might write or software he may invent."

"We understand that." Julian nodded. "But that clause is applicable only to things written using Tech José equipment and software on the property grounds. I also want to assure you that we have a very generous bonus structure and program. Turner will be well-compensated for his efforts in accordance with their reach. All employees of Hunt Industries are well-treated."

I glanced down at the contract. It wouldn't stop bothering me, I knew. But the job was arguably a good one, and they had agreed to all of Turner's demands. I had been proud of him this entire meeting. My baby brother, growing up. Getting a job. Finding his place.

It had always been a matter of time before the world realized what a genius he was.

I knew I had to let go some time or another, and this was the place Turner had said he wanted to work. I sighed, resigned to the prospect, and looked across the table at Julian and David.

I opened my mouth to agree, but Julian raised his hand.

"Before you object, Ms. Giordano, I have a suggestion." He leaned back in his chair and looked with dark eyes between me and Turner. His gaze was speculative.

"You're a media specialist and you come highly recommended. We also happen to need a new press secretary for our press and marketing team for Hunt Industries. Both David and I understand your reservations, but to put your mind at ease, I'd like to offer you a position at our company as well."

My face was a mask of shock.

What?

He could not be serious.

Judging from the way David glanced at him, this was not something Julian had discussed with anyone. A spur of the moment decision, then.

And I was to entrust my brother to these men?

"But you haven't even seen my resume," I spluttered. "You don't know anything about me."

Julian leaned forward again, bracing his powerful arms against the white table. Squared like that, with the thick hair pushed away from his forehead, he looked like a force of nature.

"We've seen your LinkedIn profile. It's impressive, and I believe you'd be a good fit here. Look at it this way—working at Hunt Industries will let you see firsthand what type of company we are. You'd be part of our team, a member at hand who could influence the direction of the company. And you'd be working two floors above your brother's office, only a stone's throw away. There could be no better place for you."

He'd managed to tap into my concerns right away. But I'd essentially become Turner's plus-one, shoehorned into a company that didn't actually have a need of me. I didn't believe for a second that they happened to have a marketing position conveniently *available*.

They were tacking this on as an addition to the salary benefits and health insurance and free chocolate muffins and all the other things they were using to woo Turner.

"Thank you, Mr. Hunt. But I'm very pleased with my current position, and I don't think this type of buy-in would be suitable."

Julian gave a small smile, like I was reacting exactly as expected. I met his eyes with an annoyed glare of my own.

Turner turned to me. "But Emily, you've been complaining about your current job for months. The odds of this job being worse than the one you're in aren't very high. It could be a good change for you."

His calm gaze was sincere, but I cursed inwardly. He was right, of course, like always. And now the others knew how much I hated Pet and Co.

I turned back to the two men. David quickly smothered his smile, but Julian did nothing to hide his.

Asshole.

Turner looked straight at the space between them. "If you hire my sister, you're going to have to double her salary in comparison with what she's currently making. She's good at her job and she deserves it. That's my final condition for the job."

My heart nearly broke.

Oh, Turner. My amazing baby brother, who remembered all too well the financial difficulties we had faced.

"It's a deal," Julian said. He looked straight at Turner as he spoke, seemingly unbothered by the fact that Turner didn't return his gaze. "I respect a man who stands up for his family like that. And I have no doubts regarding your sister's skills. If you agree, we'll draw up employment contracts for the both of you, containing your conditions in writing. There is no pressure to sign. Both of you may take the evening to read it over and get back to us tomorrow. How does that sound?"

It sounded damn good, and I was sure he knew it, judging by the satisfaction on his face.

I'd have to quit my job.

Turner wasn't looking at Julian or David, but rather tracing the edge of the table with a methodical finger. But he was smiling, small and true. "It sounds good to me," he said. "My sister and I will read it and let you know tomorrow."

Now he was speaking for the both of us. Being his own man. He wanted this—I could tell. Given nearly unlimited resources, a steady salary… he would grow so much from this. I knew he'd been concerned about finding somewhere to work that would suit him, and frankly, so had I.

I would have to work for Hunt Industries.

We rose and shook hands with both men. Julian held my hand a heartbeat longer than strictly professional—his dark eyes and brows startling against his fair complexion. His voice was pitched for privacy when he spoke.

"Happy to see you got home okay."

I pulled my hand out of his. "Goodbye, Mr. Hunt."

"It's been a pleasure." His eyes danced again. "I look forward to hearing from you tomorrow."

4

EMILY

Turner and I said yes.

Of course we did. It was hardly even a discussion in the car ride home, and by that evening, we'd both signed.

When I called Denise and told her the whole story, she squealed so loud in my ear that I'd had to hold the phone away from my ear until she calmed down.

Turner would be given free rein and practically unlimited resources; we'd both get a salary increase substantial enough to make our lives easier.

But best of all? I could quit my job at Pet and Co. Three years in a field that didn't interest me one bit had finally come to a close. I'd been looking for a way to get out of that job for a long time anyway, and Hunt Industries represented the big leagues.

The evening before my first day, I spent half an hour watching Hunt promotional videos to get a feel of the dress code. It still took me nearly the whole evening to pick out the perfect outfit for my first day.

I know. *I know.*

I was judging me too.

But when I walked into that massive lobby in a pair of well-fitting suit pants and a silky blouse, I felt like I'd struck just the right balance between forgettable and sophisticated. I wanted to stand out because of my ideas, not my outfits. It was a style that should get its own genre: invisibly chic.

I had no idea what to expect from this arrangement. It wouldn't surprise me if someone popped up and shouted "psych!" as if this had all just been one big joke. Was that show *Punk'd* still on? Because any minute now, I'd have to go back to creating ads for dog food.

Turner and I said goodbye at the elevators. He walked away with his head held high and a lunch bag in hand, not showing any of the nervousness I knew he felt. My stomach was in knots, half of it for me and half of it for him. My grown-up little brother.

But as he disappeared, I squared my shoulders and ran a hand down the silky material of my blouse. *Let's do this, Emily.*

I was greeted as soon as I stepped off the elevator by a tall woman with a massive smile.

"Emily?"

"Yes, that's me."

"Right on time! I'm Rachel. Let me just start by saying that we're *so* happy you could start on such short notice."

I blinked. "Hi. Yes, so am I. Thank you for taking me on."

She shook my hand in a firm, business-like grip before handing me a stack of folders. "Here's all the information you might want on Hunt. It's a bit of a welcome package, so to speak. I have to tell you, we've been working with one position empty for nearly a month and it hasn't been easy, so you're a godsend."

"You have?"

"Kamal was unexpectedly headhunted. He left us for London two days after he got the call." Rachel pressed the button for the elevator. "I was of course happy for him, but it left us one man short in the middle of an expansion and rebranding."

"I understand." I gripped the folders tight in front of me. Her eagerness was intoxicating, and suddenly I wanted nothing more than to become a member of this dynamic team. I might not have liked how I ended up here, but here I was, and I wanted to make sure that I pulled my weight.

"Let me show you to your office first, and then to the break room. We usually have coffee or tea around ten thirty with the entire marketing and press team."

"You work jointly here?"

"Yes." Rachel shot me a wide smile. "I'm guessing there were more clear-cut divisions at your last job?"

"Yes." Very strict ones, in fact, that had often seemed ridiculous to me.

"That's not really the way Hunt Industries operates. You'll see soon enough for yourself, but we have more of a collaborative work environment here."

"One of those tech firms," I said with a smile. "Do you also have arcade games and beanbag chairs?"

"Yes," she deadpanned. "We do yoga during our lunch breaks. It's a company-wide policy"

I gave a startled laugh. "Really?"

She grinned. "No. But you're welcome to petition Mr. Hunt for that. Who knows? He's had weirder ideas before."

Rachel showed me into an open office with floor-to-ceiling windows. "It looks a bit bare now, but feel free to fill up the bookshelves and the desk with anything you might need. IT will be up here in a bit to set up your company laptop and cell phone. Let's go meet the team."

The team, as she so collaboratively put it, was making a lot of sound in the break room when we approached. Rachel stopped in the doorway with her hands on her hips.

"We're meeting a new team member today. Is this really the way to introduce yourselves?"

A motley crew of five looked up from the game of Hungry Hungry Hippos they were playing. My look of surprise and bafflement must have been clear on my face, because they all broke out into laughter.

Rachel gave me a chagrined look. "It's not like this often, I promise."

"Hi everyone!" I gave a small wave. "I was looking for the

press and marketing team? But I see now that I've must have gotten lost. Is this the kindergarten?"

Thankfully, they laughed at my stupid joke. A thin man with a kind smile got up and extended a hand.

"I'm Trent. It's nice to meet you. I'm sorry about this—I brought one of my kid's old games in here today. We figured some of the junior software associates down at Tech would have fun with it during their breaks."

"But we had to test it out first," a dark-haired woman called out. "You know, to make sure it works."

Rachel shook her head good-naturedly. "These idiots will be your new colleagues. This is Trent, Veronique, Josef, and Sasha. Together with the two of us, Emily, we all make up the marketing and press team."

"It's great to meet you all."

Sasha smiled. "Likewise. Would you like a cup of coffee?"

"I'd love one, thank you."

"But more importantly," Josef said, leaning forward, "would you like to join the game?"

I smiled. "I thought you'd never ask!"

I ended up back in my office with a spinning head and a huge, goofy grin on my face, settling down to read through all the information on Hunt Industries. I had a lot of catching up to do and would try to stay late if I could.

Rachel and I were more focused on traditional press roles, while Trent and Sasha handled marketing. Josef and Maria were copywriters and illustrators, and really talented too, if Trent was to be believed.

This would be *nothing* like working for Pet and Co, but I had the feeling I would love every day.

I lasted until eleven before I sent Turner a text.

Emily: How is everything so far?

Turner: Good. They've just installed my mini fridge and I've had to reboot the computer they gave me twice. I'm planning on rebuilding it tomorrow.

I smiled at the text. He'd have unlimited resources here to really explore the limits of what he could do. I'd seen him tug at his restraints for years. Plus a job, with co-workers… and somehow he'd managed to score a job for me too.

I knew how lucky I was to have a brother like him.

I'd nearly reached the end of my introductory information on Hunt Industries when there was a knock on my door.

I looked up, expecting Rachel.

But no such luck.

Julian Hunt leaned against the frame, his hands in the pockets of a pair of perfectly tailored slacks. He wasn't wearing a suit jacket this time and his white shirt fit snugly over a wide chest and broad shoulders.

"I had to swing by and check up on the newest addition of staff."

I cleared my throat. "Wouldn't that be Turner?"

Julian strolled into my office and took a seat in the chair opposite me, arms tracing the length of the armrests. A swath of wavy hair fell casually over his forehead and my hand itched to push it back.

"I just came from the eighth floor. He was doing well. Ripping one of the company's computers to shreds, but I have no doubt he'll be able to rebuild it."

"He will. It'll likely be faster and better, too."

Julian grinned. He had perfect teeth, I saw, except for a barely noticeable chip in one of his front teeth. Somehow that little flaw made him *more* handsome and not less. The world wasn't fair.

"You think the world of him."

"He's my little brother. Of course I do." I put my hands on my desk and fought to regain the upper hand on my emotions. "Mr. Hunt, I want to apologize again for the other night."

"Call me Julian, please."

"Julian. Thank you again. I'm…" I fought the flush in my

cheeks at the strictly unprofessional memory. "I didn't know that—"

He interrupted me again. "It was my pleasure."

"You knew who I was as soon as I said my name."

"Maybe I did." Amusement was clear in his eyes.

"And that my brother was considering working for you."

"Yes."

"Tell me something. Was there truly a space available on the press and marketing team?"

Julian crossed his long legs. "Do you think I'd manufacture a fake absence for you *just* for the purpose of acquiring Turner Giordano's prodigious brain?"

The frankness in his gaze made me bold. "You don't become a billionaire for nothing, Mr. Hunt." I held up the prospectus I'd been reading on the conglomerate. Exhibit A.

He tsked. "Millionaire, if you would be so kind. There are only five hundred billionaires in the country, give or take, and I'm not quite there yet."

"Sorry."

"Common mistake." He smiled again, flashing that charming tooth. "Have you enjoyed reading my CV?"

I looked back down at the prospectus, titled *The History of Hunt Industries and Its Holdings,* and back up at him. This man truly needed to be knocked down a peg.

"No. It's honestly not that impressive."

"No?"

I leaned forward, as if telling him a secret. "Someone told me that the owner, this Hunt fellow? He's not even a real billionaire."

Julian's smile sank deeper somehow, connected with his eyes. He looked at me like we were friends. Like he knew me.

"There was a position free. One of our former press secretaries up and left three weeks ago. We've been on the hunt for one ever since."

"And if you could leverage that into getting what you want…"

"Then that's what I'll do." Julian shrugged. "Seems to have worked out well for all of us, no?"

"So far so good."

He leaned back with an infuriatingly smug expression. "What do you think of your new place of employment?"

"You mean judging by my four hours of experience?"

"Yes."

"The others in the marketing team seem like hard-working, nice people. This company seems... unconventional."

"How so?"

I raised an eyebrow. "The CEO is sitting in a lowly employee's office at noon on a Thursday, having an almost entirely unprofessional conversation."

"Yes, well, I like to be involved."

"And your employees like to play board games in the break room."

"Really? Seems I've been missing out. Perhaps I should spend more time down here."

"Perhaps you should. Now, shoo. I need to get back to reading about this company if I'm going to be able to handle its marketing and press needs."

I didn't know how I got the confidence to speak so boldly to him. Perhaps it was my nerves, or the infuriating smirk he wore.

He rose out of his chair. Really, men that tall and broad shouldn't *also* be able to move gracefully. "Yes ma'am. Your dedication to Hunt is noted and appreciated. Tell me one last thing—did your former employer mind the quick end of your contract?"

I thought of the satisfaction I'd felt when telling my former boss that I was finally quitting. I was so done with being wing-clipped, all my ideas for expansion and growth shut down.

"Yes. They minded," I said. "But I didn't."

His grin turned dark. "I think we'll get along famously, Emily."

5
EMILY

I raced through the lobby as fast as I could on my heels. I could not be late. Not when it was still my first week, and *especially* not when there was a damn team-building exercise scheduled first thing in the morning.

I pressed the button to the elevator several times in rapid succession, shifting from one foot to another. If only I'd heard about the construction work earlier, maybe I wouldn't have gotten stuck in traffic.

I hit the elevator button a couple of times again.

"I hate to break it to you, but that's not really how technology works."

Of course.

I turned to see Julian, a wide grin on his smugly handsome features. I pressed the button an additional ten times and ignored the irrational shot of adrenaline that coursed through me.

"You're the expert," I said, "but I'm innovative."

The scent of his aftershave hit me like a tidal wave. This close he was tall, nearly a head above me even in my bestest and blackest of pumps—their heels still intact.

The doors opened smoothly before us.

"Would you look at that?" He waved me ahead. "Your method worked."

I stood as far away from him as the confined space would allow, clutching my bag with both hands. His presence was too big. It was sucking all the air out of the elevator, and all the rational thought out of me. I wasn't sure which would end me first.

Julian leaned against the opposite wall. I forced myself to meet his gaze with a cool one of my own.

He looked at me with far more familiarity than the situation warranted. Like we weren't practically strangers.

"Tell me how your first days have been."

"They've been great. This company demands some serious press and marketing strategies."

He nodded. "It's a dynamic work environment. I know the press team is also very open to suggestions and input from all. There will be plenty of opportunities to make your mark."

I looked away, staring intently at the number of floors passing us by. It annoyed me that he had figured me out so completely and so quickly. That he knew I'd felt trapped at Pet and Co.

It made me feel on edge. Particularly considering the fact that he was so... enigmatic. As charming as they come, but in a practiced way.

The elevator slid to a smooth stop.

And it didn't start back up again.

"No. No, no, no. This *cannot* be happening right now."

Julian uncrossed his arms and bent to inspect the control panel. "Don't worry. I'm sure we'll be out of here in no time. Are you claustrophobic?"

"No. I'm late."

Julian gave an infuriating little chuckle, like he thought I'd said something witty. The yellow button was flashing and I hit it, holding it pressed down.

"Someone will be with us soon. This qualifies as a valid excuse, you know, regardless of where you're rushing to."

I sighed. "Rachel has a team-building session scheduled this morning."

Julian burst out into laughter, infectious and loud. It was exactly like him: larger than life itself.

"With trust falls and egg-and-spoon races?"

"God, I hope not. Although I was told to bring comfortable footwear and a shirt I didn't mind getting dirty."

He was still grinning at me. "By who? Josef?"

"Yeah. And Sasha."

"I can see that. Well, I had a busy day scheduled, but you just made me consider skipping all that for a chance to join in on some team building."

"You already know the team!"

"Do I, though?" He raised an eyebrow. "There's one new member I don't know very well at all. Yet."

"Well, the key to getting to know me is most definitely *not* trust falls."

"Really? That's practically how we met, Ace."

I shot him a furious look. There were so many things I wanted to say, but I couldn't—he was my boss now.

"Not on purpose," I ground out. "And I don't think it increased trust."

He still wore that infuriating smile. "Hmm. How do I do that?"

Was he flirting with me? I bit my lip and fished out my phone, trying to avoid the power of his gaze. The man was a walking neon sign of sexiness. It wasn't fair of him to flirt with me. He'd recover, but I'd come out permanently blind from the light.

"The key to gaining my trust is to make sure I get out of stuck elevators on time."

"Right. Well, let me call service. They should already be alerted, but just in case…"

I watched as he called someone named Tim and gave a few short orders, explaining our situation.

"It'll be fixed in five minutes."

"Five?"

"Yes." He cocked his head. "I have complete faith in my personnel."

"Even those you hire without an interview?" The words came by their own accord, and it wasn't until they were out that my mind registered what I'd said. I owed this man so much—my brother's job, my own—and a significant increase in both of our salaries.

But Julian Hunt just laughed. This close, I saw that his eyes were a deep green, a comforting and warm color. They were eyes you could lose yourself in.

Ones I should stay far away from.

"*Especially* the ones I hire without an interview," he said. "That means the decision was based on intuition, and those decisions always turn out to be the best ones."

"You have high expectations?"

"For you? The highest. Just make sure you get a few back-to-back bonding exercises under your belt, and you'll be up and running here at Hunt in no time."

"Right," I murmured. "I will. Can I ask why you hired me though? I'm not Turner. I don't have—"

An electronic voice cut through the space. "Mr. Hunt? The elevator is fixed. It'll start moving shortly."

"Thank you. We were heading to the eleventh floor."

"Sending you there now."

The elevator began its smooth ascent again and the attendant clicked off. Julian glanced at his watch.

"Three minutes. And to answer your question, I think I have good people-reading skills. And I read you the second I saw you, Ace. You have fire."

I was caught in his gaze, steady and intense on mine. How do you respond to something like that?

A smile broke across his lips. "This is your floor."

I swallowed. "Right. Thanks."

Julian gave me a wink as I stepped out of the elevator. "Good luck today."

"Thanks. I think…" I trailed off, the elevator doors already shutting behind me, and he was gone. So I cleared my throat, squared my shoulders, and hurried down the hall.

———

Turner and I carpooled home that day, just like we did most days. The house we'd inherited from our parents was only a fifteen-minute drive from the office.

My car was nice, but it was in need of a bit of a service. I would for sure treat it to a bit of pampering with my fancy new salary. It was right up there with *paying off my student loans* and *buying a few sets of matching bras and underwear.* Not that I was currently dating anyone who saw me undress, but a girl could hope. The image of Julian smiling came back to me, and I pushed it away firmly. *No, Emily.*

Anyone else would do.

Turner was quiet the entire drive.

"What are you thinking about?" I asked him as I pulled up on our driveway.

"What I should do first thing tomorrow morning."

"And what's that?"

"They have an inferior code structure for how they handle mail communications. The servers' response time is too slow, and I know what the problem is."

We double-checked that I'd locked the car before making it to the front door. I smiled as I dug around in my purse for the house keys, hiding in the bottom. "That place is going to be ten times better once you're done with it, Turner."

"Maybe more like twice as good, Emily. That's more realistic." He hung his backpack on the designated hook in our entry. "It's my turn to make dinner tonight."

"I know. I'll be downstairs and ready at seven o'clock."

We'd operated on a standard schedule every week for the past four or five years, a whiteboard calendar in the kitchen making it easy to plan for each coming week.

Turner enjoyed punctuality and regularity, and Mom had installed that calendar when he was just shy of ten. Each Sunday we would all fill it out and then act accordingly. I had to give it to Mom—it had done a lot to boost my own punctuality and productivity as well.

I retreated into Dad's old study while Turner busied himself in the kitchen. I'd spent the entire day reading up on Hunt Industries and all former ad campaigns. Rachel had given me copies of their progress in formulating new ones, with sketches of branding options and color schemes. My head spun in the best of ways. I couldn't *wait* to get back in tomorrow and brainstorm with the team.

It had been a long time since I'd felt like that.

Coincidentally, it had also been a long time since I'd been around a man as attractive as Julian Hunt.

My hands flew across the keyboard as if of their own volition. I'm all for dogs, but Google really was man's best friend.

An unsmiling image of Julian came up immediately. He was dressed in a tux and posing at a charity event for water purification technology for the developing world. He looked imposing and unreadable, nothing like the smiling man in the elevator.

I scrolled down and clicked on the Wikipedia page dedicated to him. Thirty-four years old with one younger half-brother. His father, the late state senator Arthur Hunt, had remarried after the divorce with his first wife.

Julian spent his college years creating software that he later sold for a record-breaking figure and used the money to set up his own company. They had now expanded into app development, software programming, technological advancements and start-up incubation.

I sighed. I really would have to learn all that tech stuff if I was going to effectively market Hunt.

I clicked on the section labeled *personal life* with apprehension. I had no idea what I'd find. Was he also a well-known connoisseur of blow-up dolls? Did he own and operate forty ice-cream trucks?

Had he been married for twelve years?

Did he have five illegitimate children?

The internet had very little information to share with me. A few brief relationships with people of note, a couple of models and one B-list celebrity, but other than that nothing. He'd never been married.

I scrolled back up and was met again by the image of his tux-clad, ridiculously handsome form. Even seeing it on a screen sent my heart into overdrive. Men shouldn't be allowed to be so attractive, particularly not ones who poked fun at themselves in elevators and smelled of sandalwood aftershave. It wasn't fair.

This job was fun.

It was exciting.

And I knew I couldn't jeopardize it for this man, particularly not when any interest he had in me was for, without a doubt, something short-lived and temporary.

Men like Julian Hunt didn't end up with women like me—that much was clear. I couldn't delude myself that he would.

I glanced down at the time. 6:58. I closed the computer and followed the scent of spaghetti carbonara to the kitchen. Tomorrow I'd prove to everyone that I was kick-ass at my job—and I would prove to myself that my foolish attraction to Julian Hunt was only due to a dry spell, and nothing more.

6

EMILY

Pet and Co ran about ten marketing campaigns a year.

Hunt Industries ran about a hundred, and that was only in the continental US.

Any fears I might have had about Julian's motivations behind hiring me were dismissed by the veritable mountain of projects Rachel dropped on my desk.

"We're planning on launching seven new products in the coming thirteen months. I know this looks like a lot, and that's because it is." She grinned at me. "But it's also going to be a lot of fun."

I smiled back at her. "I'll read up on this right away, and hopefully I can take on a more productive role tomorrow."

"Sounds awesome. Tomorrow's meeting will start around eight thirty in meeting room C, by the way." She rolled her eyes. "Josef claims he's going to bring homemade bagels for everyone, but I wouldn't trust him."

"I'll make sure to eat breakfast before."

"Good. But if he asks…"

"I didn't hear it from you." I pretended to zip my mouth shut. She gave me a wink and left my office, her bright skirt swooshing around her legs.

The camaraderie at this office was a complete one-eighty

from Pet and Co. There, the best I could hope for was the occasional encouraging thumbs-up from the receptionist. That was it. No other socialization took place, neither at work nor outside of it.

I threw myself into the world of app creation and software developing. *Taking art as a subject in high school really helped me with this,* I thought sarcastically. The most advanced thing I'd ever done in this field was rebooting my computer when it occasionally crashed. Did that count?

I'd made it halfway through the information folder on a new data storage technique when a knock on the door interrupted me.

I kept my eyes glued to the spot where I was, so as not to lose it. "Yes?"

"You don't even look up now when you have visitors?"

I closed the folder.

"Mr. Hunt. To what do I owe the pleasure?"

"I'm glad you think of my presence as a pleasure."

I resisted the urge to roll my eyes again. I hated that he managed to look both rich and casual, powerful and lazy, leaning against the door in a suit that was doubtless Italian in origin. It had to be the undone top button.

The lack of a tie.

The infuriating smirk.

I hadn't seen him around for the past week. Not because he wasn't an active participant in the company—he seemed to be highly involved in everything Hunt Industries did—but rather because he was always so busy.

"I'll add that to the list of figures of speech to avoid using around you."

He raised an eyebrow. "You're catching on. Well, get up and let's go. I'm here to take you to lunch."

"Lunch?"

"Yes. There's a restaurant on the first floor of this building. I want to make sure you're settling in all right."

"Is that's the CEO's job?" Surely that should be HR's role.

"David outsourced it to me."

"Because you're so underworked?"

His eyes glittered with mirth. "Notoriously so. Come on, let's head out."

A few people turned heads as we walked down through the corridor. Some eyes touched on me briefly before skating off again, no doubt wondering what I was doing with him, alone.

"Do you often take your employees out for lunch?"

"Yes. I like to make sure I know what's going on in all departments." He pressed the elevator button. "I regularly meet up with Rachel and Trent, for example."

Some of my initial apprehension and nerves settled. Not entirely, because I was still very aware that I was in a confined space with a man who could easily place in the top ten of *People* magazine's list of the world's sexiest men.

Getting used to him would take time.

I honestly didn't know how others did it. The only way I managed was to pretend he was a nobody, someone who didn't intimidate me. Someone I could be snarky with.

Julian straightened his suit jacket. "Tell me more about yourself."

"I thought you already knew my life story, you know, considering my LinkedIn profile was so *comprehensive*." People in the lobby gave us a wide berth, their gazes circling back to land on Julian several times. He walked on as if it didn't bother him.

I supposed he'd grown used to it.

"I know you're twenty-five and I know you went to City College. I also know that you're incredibly hard-working. There's hardly a month unaccounted for in your employment history." He held the door open for me as we entered the busy lunch restaurant. Without waiting to be seated he directed us to a table along the back, next to tall windows.

"I also suspect that you felt stagnant in your last position. You'd been there for nearly three years and had climbed your way up to become the chief marketing officer and press strategist. But Pet and Co is a small company, and you're a person with big dreams."

"I am?"

He gazed serenely back, the picture of competent ease.

"You'd written that you won an award for a creative writing class in college and that you graduated summa cum laude." Julian's smile turned smug. "Shall we say that like recognizes like?"

I opened the menu. "Seems like you already know all about me."

"Oh no. I have plenty of questions to ask."

"Professional ones." I met his green gaze again. It was almost painful to look at him this close, with clear-cut cheekbones and thick hair. I didn't have lunch with men like this. Men like this didn't have lunch with me.

The waiter arrived to take our order. I chose the first thing I saw on the menu—pasta primavera—and a bottle of still water. How did people relax around him? I didn't think it was possible. Maybe that was how he was so successful. It was physically impossible for anyone to be lazy when around him. My nerves were on hair-trigger alert, ready to respond to anything and everything he might throw my way.

"Professional questions, yes, but I also want to know other things about you. Like—"

"No, I didn't have a Julian Hunt poster on my wall growing up."

His laughter was surprised. "Emily, you're in danger of becoming my favorite employee."

"Is that a dangerous thing to be?"

Julian nodded with mock sadness. "Kamal was before you, and look where he ended up. Shipped off to the Old World, never to be seen again."

"A job he took *voluntarily*."

"Tomayto, tomahto." Julian waved a hand. "Tell me about how your first days have been here at Hunt. I want to hear about the team-building exercises."

So I told him, trying and failing to relax. He still felt far too intimidating to be around, just by the sheer power surrounding him. His name was on all my documents—it was on my security badge!

Our food arrived and I bent forward to breathe in the scent of parmesan and basil.

Julian watched me. "You're a foodie?"

"Sure. Who isn't?"

"There are some really great restaurants in this area."

"I'm sure there are," I said. "I haven't been to that many, but there's a new Korean place down the block I've been wanting to try."

"Really?" He took a bite of his lasagna. "I imagine a woman like you would spend every other night being asked to dinner."

I looked down at my food. Did he just give me a compliment?

"Sometimes. Not quite as often as you do, I'd wager, Mr. Hotshot."

He grinned and looked like he was going to say something witty or sarcastic, I was certain, but I cut him off. This was dangerous territory. "What did you think about the marketing suggestions we brainstormed yesterday? I know Rachel CCed you the email."

He closed his mouth and watched me with amusement, like he was perfectly aware of what I was doing.

Retreating to safety.

"I liked them. Particularly the one about rebranding Hunt Digital Security as something geared toward the average person. I've been playing around with developing a sub-division that deals more with individual consumers and not just the corporate clients, so that could go hand in hand."

I nodded and took a sip of my water. "I think we could bundle it with some of the other more user-friendly software applications the company has been working on. Make it into a must-have software package when buying a new computer—regardless of the hardware."

"That's a really good idea."

"You think?"

"Yeah, I do." Julian leaned back in his chair and regarded me in silence. His eyes were speculative.

"What are you thinking?"

"Damn. You really, *really* care about this job, don't you?"

I felt like a child again at school, called out by a classmate for actually liking a homework assignment.

"Um, yes. I hope I've made that clear. I'm committed."

"Like I feared." He shook his head and took another bite of his food.

I narrowed my eyes at him. "What do you mean?"

"I'd been planning to ask you out. You know, maybe not right this second, but in a week or so. But now I already know what you'll say." Julian shook his head again, a sad expression on his face.

"That it would be entirely unprofessional."

"Exactly. But it's such a shame."

I stared at him. This man was impossible. No—he was flat-out insane. And he deserved to be knocked down a peg.

"What makes you so sure I'd even accept becoming one of your wham-bam-thank-you-ma'am's?" I asked him. "Theoretically speaking, I mean, if I wasn't committed to my job."

He raised an eyebrow. "First and foremost, I never implied my intention was a one-night-stand."

I rolled my eyes again. "Sure. Well, what makes you think I'd accept?"

"We have chemistry," he said, holding up a finger. "We are great at verbal sparring. Surely you've noticed that as well? Or do you talk this freely to everyone?"

"Lenny, our mailman, and me are like this." I held up two intertwined fingers.

Julian laughed. "All right, so it's me and Lenny. I can handle a bit of competition. And thirdly… well, you're the most beautiful woman I've seen in a long time. I think we'd be good together."

"These are all hypotheticals."

"They're very real arguments, Ace. But since you're committed to your job, you can't possibly accept me." Julian put a hand over his heart. "Leaving me eternally disappointed."

I rolled my eyes at his silliness, trying to play it cool despite my racing heart. Julian had asked me out, even if it was in a joking manner. *Julian Hunt.* I remembered the feel of his arms around me, how he'd carried me without missing a beat. The masculine scent of him.

But I knew how this would play out if I accepted.

And I was not going to be the girl who had a fling with the boss early on and who was then transferred to a different department only a month later. No. I wasn't going to give people the chance to gossip about me at the water cooler.

"I'm sure you'll find someone else who can lick your wounds, Julian," I said. "You won't even remember my name next month."

"I wouldn't bet money on that. But don't worry—I won't expose my fragile ego any more by asking if you might have gone out with me, had I not been your boss."

I snorted. "Fragile? I've never met a more self-confident man."

Julian grinned and waved at the waiter for the check. "And you never will, Ace."

7

JULIAN

She'd said no.

It didn't come as a surprise—from the moment I saw Emily Giordano's gorgeously flushed face in that club, I knew I'd met a force to be reckoned with.

She stood up for the people who mattered to her, had played an honestly pretty shitty hand of cards in life really well, and was smart as a whip. The fact that I never knew what would come out of her mouth made her damn near impossible to stay away from.

Wasn't that just typical, though?

You meet an amazing woman and before you really, truly understand *how* amazing she is, you go and offer her a job which makes you the only man in the world she will categorically *not* date.

I hadn't thought that one through properly.

It had been a long time since I'd met a woman so responsive. *Passive* was not in Emily Giordano's vocabulary, and she didn't try pandering or flattering me. She even had the balls to openly question my decision to hire her, a decision that undoubtedly worked out well for her.

I didn't have a good answer.

Offering her the job had been a spur of the moment idea, a

brilliant one at that. I knew it would bring Turner over to us, but more than that, it'd ensured her eyes lit up with agitation. She enjoyed a challenge, all right.

Taking her out for lunch had been a… stretch. I hadn't lied—I did sometimes go out for lunch with employees to pick their brains on a project or another.

Occasionally.

Perhaps once or twice a year.

But knowing I was only three floors away from seeing her beautiful eyes sparkle as she called me out on my bullshit was enough to break my willpower.

But then she thought I'd offered her the chance for a one-night stand or some cheap fling.

She thought her job would be in jeopardy if we became better friends.

In retrospect, *of course* that's what she assumed. Hell, that must have been what she thought I was doing at that idiot club with Rafe—womanizing and schmoozing.

I had my work cut out for me. I had to ensure she started seeing me in a different light, like a man she'd consider spending time with. It would be a challenge, but I had never backed down from one before.

"Sir?" My assistant's head popped through the half-open door.

"Yes?"

"It's your mother's birthday next week. I just wanted to ask if you've prepared anything or if I should schedule a flower delivery?"

I sighed. "Schedule a flower delivery."

He nodded and shut the door behind him. Honestly, he was the best assistant I had ever had—no one was more organized—but sometimes I thought he followed my life so closely it left no room at all for his own.

As if summoned by the mere mention, my phone lit up with my stepmother's name.

With a sigh, I decided not to answer.

For a while my mother was living with her sister in Florida, my stepmother was still in California. And she was driving me *insane*.

To say that we had different views on life would be an understatement. More than that, though, were our different views on Ryan.

My little brother meant well, but he often got himself in all kinds of trouble. Some of that trouble might leave rather permanent dents one day if he kept it up—he was getting older. Being bailed out by your brother worked at twenty-one, but it wouldn't look so cute at twenty-five.

I'd had this discussion with my stepmother a thousand times already. No doubt she wanted to schedule another screaming match. Everything was dragged up; my father's legacy, money, the future.

A problem for another day. For now, I needed to ensure my app launch would go smoothly.

I needed to meet a reporter for a two-page spread.

And I needed to figure out a way to date Emily Giordano.

8

EMILY

"Emily?"

"Yes?"

Josef leaned against the door to my office, Sasha peering around his shoulder. "A bunch of us are heading down to Shoots and Hoops after work."

"You should come!"

"Are those for our meeting later?" I nodded at the big box of donuts Josef was holding.

"Yep." Sasha leaned down and took a whiff. "Honey-glazed."

I could basically feel myself salivating. "Have I said how much I enjoy working here?"

"Yes. Repeatedly." Josef grinned. "Anyway, the entire team is going for drinks after work, and that includes you. No excuses, Giordano."

I bit my lip. I wanted to. I knew that Turner wouldn't mind, and he was an adult now. *Technically,* I didn't need to be home every evening anymore. But it didn't feel right to leave my brother alone—and not when it was my night to cook dinner.

But I had to let go someday.

Last week I saw that he'd circled a few ads for apartments for rent in the newspaper. If he decided to move out—which he could, with his ample salary—I'd have to adjust.

"Sure. Of course, I'll join you."

"Awesome! We head out around six."

I shot Turner a text and received, predictably enough, a positive response. He'd pointed out more than once that he didn't think I spent enough time with friends, not in comparison to what he perceived to be normal in others. Yeah, I know. High standards to live up to.

Shoots and Hoops turned out to be a pool and dart bar, and I had to give it to the place, the marketing was on point: their logo was a bullseye.

The beer was served in German-looking glasses, the music on full blast was old, and the barstools all wobbled.

I loved it.

"Cheers to a damn good month!" Trent declared as we toasted. My glass was filled to the brim, so full I couldn't stop some from running over the rim.

"And to the newest addition to the team," Sasha added and tilted her beer toward me in acknowledgment. A solid mouthful gushed out and over Trent.

"Shit!" He scrambled to wipe at the stain on his jeans as Sasha turned beet red. I handed them a few napkins and thought, not for the first time, that something had to be going on between them.

"We're still waiting for one person." Rachel glanced over her shoulder. "*If* he even shows up."

Josef frowned. "Who? The whole team is here."

"Bossman said he'd swing by after whatever event or dinner he's attending tonight."

"Yeeeeees!" Trent gave a victorious fist pump. "I need a chance to exact revenge."

"Revenge?"

"Yes, in darts. He won last time we were here, but I've been practicing since then."

"Good luck with that," Rachel snorted.

Josef wiggled his eyebrows suggestively at all of us. "I wonder what hot date he's been out on tonight."

The others broke out into laughter and I forced myself to join. I'd seen it when I googled him; images of Julian Hunt in perfectly made suits with beautiful women on his arm. I had no doubt he regularly turned those eyes and that smile on anyone who caught his interest.

"We can't live our lives waiting for the boss," I said. "Come on. Next round of shots is on me."

The group responded with hollers and shouts, and for a moment I just grinned. I'd never really had a group of friends like this. During my time at community college, I worked part-time and was busy taking care of Turner, who'd only been fourteen when our parents died. It was high time I made sure to take every opportunity that came my way to have fun.

That included learning how to play darts, which Trent was apparently a self-proclaimed expert at.

"The key is to balance the dart perfectly between your two fingers, like this…" He demonstrated with a feathered dart. "You keep your eye glued to the bullseye… and then you throw."

He missed it with a solid two inches and let out a suffering sigh. "Sometimes you hit. Sometimes you don't."

Rachel laughed beside him. "And you call yourself an athlete!"

"I most certainly never have."

"Sure you have," she pointed out. "Last time we were here you said you could have gone pro if you hadn't suffered a knee injury."

Trent rolled his eyes at her and handed me a dart. "She remembers *everything*," he told me in a hushed whisper. "Avoid her at all costs."

I laughed and watched as he threw another dart. This time he only missed the bullseye by a hair.

"Damn!"

"So close," I told him. "Let me try."

I held the dart carefully in one hand, shifted my weight to my right leg and did as Trent said—I kept my eye glued to the little red dot in the middle of the board.

It went wide, landing along the green outer rim, only scoring me a measly ten points.

A familiar, husky laugh rang out behind me. "I think you all need to be taught how this is done."

Trent grinned. "Glad you could make it. I need that rematch."

"You can have a shot at it, at least," Julian said. "I won't give up the title as reigning champion without a fight."

I glanced in his direction and then back at the dart board. Dressed in a pair of gray slacks and a white shirt, he'd rolled the sleeves up to his elbows and undone the top button. No tie, no blazer, and his hair curled down over his forehead in a deliciously thick wave. Men shouldn't be allowed to walk around like that without a goddamn warning label.

I handed the darts back to Trent without acknowledging our boss standing right there beside us. "I'm heading back to the table. Good luck!"

"Thanks." Trent grinned. "I'll make sure our team wins."

I felt Julian's eyes on my back as I headed back to our table.

Keep it together, Emily, I told myself, despite the fact that my stomach had descended into a knot of nerves the moment I'd heard his irritatingly smug voice behind me. I didn't think I'd even be able to handle another sip of my drink from the way my stomach clenched. My useless attraction to him was getting inconvenient.

I slid into the seat next to Josef and Sasha. As we spoke, I found out that they'd both worked at Hunt for about two years. The entire company seemed incredibly young.

"Hunt has really been growing exponentially the past couple of years. I'm guessing you joined the team just as it was starting to pick up steam?"

Sasha nodded. "Yep. There were no shoes to fill, which I liked. It's really a great workplace since we've been able to build something from scratch. We've gotten to try all the new crazy product ideas the company has come up with."

"You mean what *Julian* has come up with." Josef nodded to where the CEO was throwing darts. He had a wide-legged stance and was facing the dartboard with a look of deep concentration. His bicep curled once, twice… and then he threw the dart. I swallowed and looked away.

"Hey, judging by the size of our last Christmas bonus, I'm not complaining. The man is a machine."

"But he still goes out with you all like this?"

"Sometimes." Sasha nodded. "Doesn't happen very often though. He's busy. You know how it is." She waved a hand in dismissal, and I could see it—all too well. Julian at events and galas and meetings with foreign investors.

Josef grinned. "Look, Trent is in the lead. Seems like it's only by a few points, though."

We all glanced over to where they were facing off. Trent wore a smug expression.

Julian was throwing, his powerful body leaning slightly forward. He had three darts in one hand and threw first one, then the second… His smile grew wider by the second.

Trent said something to Julian that we couldn't hear, but Julian's response was clear to all—a raised eyebrow. Then he threw his final dart straight into the bullseye.

"No way!" Trent exclaimed.

Sasha laughed at my side. "He's going to be insufferable now."

"Julian?"

"No, Trent. Won't shut up until he gets a rematch."

I watched Julian's smile, all glorious victory. He was a man who loved to win, it seemed, but not to gloat. Both of them ambled over to us, Trent audibly complaining, and joined us at the table.

Julian slid into the seat next to me. I was aware of the palpable heat of him beside me, the warmth of his body as our thighs touched.

"Hey," he said.

"Hi."

"You didn't say hello to me earlier."

"Didn't I?" I took a sip of my beer, trying to stave off the nerves in my stomach. "I must have forgotten."

He gave a husky laugh. "I'm sure, Ace."

"Congratulations on your victory."

"You saw that?" There was a trace of smugness in his voice.

"Yes. I'd say it was comparable to Gettysburg or Waterloo."

"Mine was far more legendary." He reached over and grabbed my drink. "What are you drinking?"

"Lager."

He took a sip. "God, but that's light."

"I'm sorry, Mister-I-only-drink-aged-whiskey."

He eyed his own highball glass. "I had a beer earlier. I just prefer ones that aren't, you know, *water*."

"Funny," I said dryly. His hand rested on his thigh, distractingly close to mine. It was broad and tanned with square nails.

I sighed. It only seemed natural that even his hands had to be the epitome of masculinity.

"Something bothering you, Emily?"

"No."

"I'd hope not. Especially not now that I've graced you all with my presence."

I glanced meaningfully at my co-workers around the table, engaged in laughter and conversation of their own, and Sasha and Rachel over by the dart board.

I turned back and gave Julian a pointed look. "Yes, *clearly* we are all basking in your glow."

He laughed again. Relaxed against the worn leather of the sofa like this, his handsome features seemed entirely human. His brown hair gleamed under the low lights and for a moment I could imagine him as anyone. Just an ordinary man, with no Amex cards or scheduled *Forbes* interviews.

"Where were you before this?"

His eyes softened. "Why do you want to know?"

"Just making conversation," I said, forcing myself to look away from his dark-green eyes. I kept a hand glued to the table to keep myself from vaulting at him. How could the others act normal around him? He seemed to set my every nerve ending on fire.

"I had dinner," he said quietly. "Not that far from here."

I took another sip of my watery beer and thought of the model he'd surely been wining and dining. "Was she pretty?"

His smile was back, teasing and quick. "Emily, why are you asking me that?"

"You're impossible." I rolled my eyes, trying to hide the flush of embarrassment already creeping its way up my cheeks. He leaned in closer and I could smell him, the light cologne of musk and smoke.

"Yes. She was very pretty."

My stomach dropped. "Awesome."

"But too old for me. Plus, she happens to be my stepmother. My little brother was there too."

I shook my head at his dancing eyes and the crooked grin on his face. *Asshole.*

But Julian only laughed at my obvious irritation. "I think your jealousy is cute."

"I was *not* jealous."

"Mhm. Sure."

"Whatever."

He took a sip of his whiskey. "Do you know how to play pool?"

"Yes, a little."

"Great. I have a suggestion." He held up a finger in warning. "You and me, pool table number three, in five minutes."

I laughed. "*No.*"

"Why not?"

"Because you're competitive as hell and I want to keep my job." I crossed my legs on the high stool but didn't miss the way his gaze flicked down, observing the movement.

"Oh, you think you might actually win?"

"I set high goals for myself." I shrugged. "Sometimes I achieve them. What can I say?"

"Then we'll make it interesting. We'll play for stakes."

"I'm not betting money on this," I scoffed. Whatever I lost would be proportionately huge in comparison to what it would be to him.

He grinned. "Don't worry, nothing so mundane as that. No… if I win, we have a standing dinner appointment every week."

"What?"

Julian shrugged, a wide shoulder brushing against mine. "I find you interesting and I want to get to know you better. Dinner every week would allow us the time."

"You want *dating me* to be conditional on your win?"

"No." He raised a finger at me and put on a mock stern voice. "As you told me—you want to be professional. So this is professional. Consider it… the beginning of a blossoming friendship."

I narrowed my eyes. "Right. Well, if I win, I want to drive your car."

"Which one?"

I rolled my eyes. "The one you *bragged* about the first time we met. Your Porsche."

"You're not planning on crashing it?"

"I promise I won't. I just want to… take it out for a spin."

Honestly, it was the first thing that came to mind. But the more I thought about it the better it sounded. I had never driven anything that ran as smoothly as that car would.

It felt like poetic justice.

"Deal." Julian stretched out his hand and I hesitated only slightly before grasping it. It was warm and dry and fully enveloped mine.

"Well? Shall we?"

"Ladies first." He grinned and grabbed our drinks from the table.

None of the others seemed to notice our departure—Josef and Rachel were deep in conversation on some new movie or another, while Trent and Sasha were battling it out at the dart board.

The pool tables were nearly abandoned. Soft indie music played from the stereo as I grabbed a billiards queue from the wall. I didn't know if I wanted to win or if I wanted to lose—both outcomes were equally tempting.

"Do you want me to show you how to hold it?"

I had to bite my lip to keep from smiling. "No. I want to start. Eight-ball?"

He shot me a crooked smile and moved to line up the billiards balls in the triangle frame. The low lighting played beautifully over his strong forearms and capable hands and I forced myself to focus on the game. *Porsche. You'll get to drive a Porsche.*

"So confident. Well then, go ahead."

I bent over and lined up my shot. He was gazing at me with hooded eyes, no doubt expecting me to fail and for the white ball to bounce uselessly against the side.

I hit the triangle dead center. The formation broke apart and three billiard balls rolled into separate pockets.

"Whoops."

"Damn, Ace."

"I'll take stripes." I lined up my next shot. As I bent over to set up the move, I shot him a sly look through my lashes. "What? Don't tell me you expected this to be an easy win for you?"

The smile he shot me felt as intimate as a kiss. "No, I never underestimate a beautiful woman."

I smiled and focused on the pocket I wanted the purple 4-ball to enter. *Beautiful.* He'd called me beautiful.

I pocketed two more balls before it was his turn. "Wow," I remarked as he stalked around the pool table, searching for angles. "Awful many solid balls out there."

Julian raised an eyebrow at me. "Most women would prefer them to striped."

I rolled my eyes at him, but he only grinned, unrepentant.

He pocketed two of his own in rapid succession. There was something beautiful in watching him move, his strong arms handle the queue, the way his forearms and biceps flexed.

I was so entirely and irrationally attracted to him. Although to be fair to myself, I figured that any straight female with eyes would be—and it seemed like he was well aware of it.

Julian missed the next shot and cursed under his breath.

"My turn now. Perhaps you should spend some quality time with the keys to your Porsche, because they'll be in my hands soon."

"I'm only getting warmed up," he said. "Don't worry, your Thursday evenings will be mine. Tell me, where'd you learn to play?"

"My father." I lined up another shot. The striped one I'd been aiming for rolled into the pocket perfectly. "He loved this game. I had a queue in my hand from the age of six."

Julian leaned against the pool table next to ours, putting him right next to where I was planning my next move. He crossed his arms over his chest and I looked away from the way his arms bulged.

"Are you as good as him?"

"No." I never had the time to reach his level, because he died when I was eighteen, and since then… well, I haven't been practicing. "Where did you learn?"

"College."

I shot and missed, sighing. "Right. Your Ivy League college experience."

"Have you been reading up on me, Ace?"

"It's part of my job."

"Is it?" His voice was deep and speculative. "I wonder if you know all the truly important things."

"Such as?"

"What's my favorite color?"

"Um, white? Black?"

He grinned. "Just because I'm wearing those two colors? Your mind works in very obvious ways. No, it's yellow."

"Yellow? That's an awful color."

He looked momentarily affronted. "It's the color of the sun."

"Is it? I was taught never to look directly at it."

Julian shook his head at me. "You're impossible. And clearly, you need to get to know me better for your job, if nothing else. I should win this game just to give you the ability to pick my brain. I'd be doing you a professional courtesy."

I pursed my lips. "How do you manage to walk with all that weight?"

"I don't follow."

"With an ego that big?"

There was a gleam of interest in his eyes. "Ace, trust me, it's not my ego that's the biggest—"

"No. Don't finish that sentence." I held up a hand to stop him. "You're really making me question whether I even want to drive your stupid Porsche."

He laughed, delighted, before he sank another ball. The tables were quickly turning and we now had the same amount of solids and stripes left.

It was time to really show off. I pocketed the remainders of mine in quick succession, and before long, there was only the eight-ball left for me.

"Damn. I hadn't expected this."

I hid my smile against my shoulder. "Clearly."

But as I leaned over and lined up my final shot, I thought about the demand. I wanted to win. It would be fun to drive a car like that.

Dinners with him were a bad idea. It wouldn't lead anywhere and might jeopardize my job.

But maybe, just maybe, I'd had enough of being sensible.

I missed the shot.

Julian tsked. "Rookie mistake."

He proceeded to pocket his final balls in rapid succession. I leaned against the wall and watched him move. A dinner a week. He'd likely be bored after the first two, but I couldn't find it within myself to dread that prospect. Any time spent with Julian Hunt felt like time spent gloriously alive.

He glanced up at me before he lined up the eight-ball. "Have you cleared your calendar, Ace?"

I gave a long-suffering sigh. "I *think* I can pencil you in, if I must."

He leaned forward in concentration, and I could see him biting the inside of his cheek to focus. High cheekbones and a perfect jawline, just faintly illuminated under the low lights. How was he real?

He made the perfect shot. The eight-ball rolled in a perfectly straight line, hitting the pocket with a satisfying thud.

Julian grinned up at me in triumph. "Once a week you're mine, Giordano."

"As long as it's only once a week, Hunt."

He murmured something barely audible under his breath and turned away to put his queue back in the stand. I watched the ripple of back muscle through the white of his shirt.

I couldn't have heard that right? It sounded like he'd mumbled *"yeah, to begin with."*

I was so far in over my head.

9

EMILY

Denise, who had stuck with me through thick and thin, turned out to be surprisingly unsupportive.

"You agreed to do *what* with him?"

"Only dinner, though. And only once a week."

She grinned at me. "Damn. I hate to give it to him, but the man is good. Getting you to date him on a dare."

"It's not dating, not really."

"But you want it to be. Don't you?"

I frowned. "He's my boss."

"But he's hot."

"God, yes. But what am I supposed to do? This situation has me so far out of my depth."

"Eat dinner, flirt a bit." She shrugged. "Do lots of nasty, dirty things together between the sheets. You know the drill."

"I can't do that."

"I don't see why not." Denise raised an eyebrow at me. "You're long overdue for a bit of romance."

I couldn't disagree with her on that. "Yes, but the fallout would be terrible. I'd have to sit through meetings with him at least once a week—that's unavoidable. And the way this office works, I'm not sure I could hide it from the others. They're like bloodhounds when it comes to gossip. Last week one of them found out a software engineer was pregnant just from a two-second glance at her browser history."

Denise poured another cup of broth into the risotto she was making us for dinner. "It sounds to me like you're creating problems."

"Really?"

"When was the last time you were *properly* out on a date?"

I raised a finger in warning. "No, don't make me say it."

"Emily."

"Two years, as you very well know. But I just never meet anyone! Besides, I can't exactly take a man home to the house I share with my baby brother. It's not like I have time, either—I've been far too busy with my career."

Denise pointed at me in accusation with a wooden spatula. "I counted *three* separate excuses in that response."

"Congratulations," I deadpanned. "You can count."

"Deflect all you want, but we both know this is the first time in a long time that you've expressed an interest in anyone."

"True, but it's not just *anyone*. I wish you could see him. You'd see why. Anyone with eyes would express an interest in Julian. It's effortless."

"I wouldn't."

"No? Have you developed a sudden aversion to chiseled jaws?"

"I've actually developed a strong preference for one man's jaw in particular. There is no one else for me now."

I grinned. Every time I met Denise she had a new crush or fling. "I have a fourth excuse. Your incredibly active dating life means I can just live vicariously through you."

She tutted and shook her head so vigorously that her reddish curls bounced. "That's the easy way out. You're going to have to take a chance sometime, Emily."

"But what if I lose my job?"

"What if you gain love? Or at least wild, crazy sex you'll remember forever?"

I sighed. "Tell me about your new man."

She smiled so widely I could practically see her molars and launched into a description of the new cook over at El Vino, an Italian Michelin-star restaurant in the nearby town. They'd already met up twice and he was going to take her to meet a few of his friends next week.

"Which means," Denise said pointedly to me, "that you're next."

"Me?"

"To meet him. If all goes well."

"Wait, hold up. When was the last time you let me meet one of your flings?"

She blushed. "I don't know… I just don't feel like this is a fling."

"Really?"

"Really."

"Well then, I'd love to meet him! And who knows, perhaps he has some cute friends."

"Yes! That's the right attitude. Either you get with Julian or with someone else, but you're not allowed to be lonely all your life. I won't allow it."

She was teasing, but a part of me realized the truth of her words.

I was twenty-five. I did want love in my life, despite the things I might say to the contrary. And while Julian was *undoubtedly* not the right candidate, he had certainly made me remember that men existed.

And that some were very, very, very charming.

He was also very good at reminding me that *he* existed—there was a text waiting for me when I got home from Denise's.

Julian: 14 Rosso Blvd at 0700 on Thursday.

That was all he'd written—an order.

I googled the place. It was a fancy French restaurant, with photos of white linen cloths and candles. It looked… intimate.

Emily: No way. That's far too romantic. What if someone recognizes us? Or rather, you?

Julian: *You'd rather we share a meal at some fast food restaurant along a highway? You're killing me, Ace.*

Emily: *I have a better suggestion. Kalispera. It's a Greek place with an appropriately friendly atmosphere.*

Julian: *I'll hold you to that.*

Nerves settled in my stomach.

I could almost see it: Julian's powerful suit-clad frame and manly appearance in that small, homely place, all folded up on a wooden chair. Long legs stretched out in front and a smirk on his face. I'd force him to eat tons of tzatziki and dolmades and make sure I got to know my boss better.

For *professional purposes*, of course—but there was no lying to myself. I would enjoy spending time with him.

The prospect of telling Turner where I was going was impossible. He was going to ask questions, require an explanation, and I could hardly explain it to myself. It would make it real, real in a way it certainly wasn't, not yet. Besides, Julian was Turner's boss as well—not just mine.

So with guilt and nerves churning in my stomach, I said I was going out with Denise for dinner.

Turner didn't even look up from his book. "Meeting her again so soon?"

"Yes."

"Good. You need friends." He turned a page and continued reading. My kind, beautiful brother. Of course that would be his response. "That's actually perfect because some of the software engineers want to go out for a drink on Thursday evening, and I debated whether I should join them. If you're not home I can go."

I frowned. "You're nineteen. No way you're going out."

Turner glanced up at me with all the exasperation of a younger sibling. "Emily, it's not a club. It's a bar frequented by coders around the corner from work and I hear they don't check IDs. I have no interest in trying alcohol. I will order a diet Pepsi and I plan on staying for an hour, maybe even an hour and a half if the conversation is interesting."

I met his calm gaze. I had no reason not to trust him, and he was an adult now. With his own job, with colleagues who invited him along to drinks *after work*. For all intents and purposes, I should be pleased— he was fitting in. He was socializing with people who liked tech as much as him. But I felt like he'd grown up a little too fast, all of a sudden, when faced with the reality of it.

"You're right. I hope you have fun."

"You too."

He turned his attention back to his book, but I couldn't quite let him slip away from me yet. "Will you make us spaghetti carbonara on Friday for dinner?"

"Sure, if you want."

"Thanks," I said softly.

What do you wear to a semi-casual, semi-professional dinner with your billionaire boss? Google was surprisingly unhelpful on the topic.

I tried on a smart gray suit and looked at myself in the mirror. I looked professional. It was a look that could easily transition from day to night. But I looked like a lawyer.

Two pencil skirts and four blouses later, I pulled out the blue and orange sheath dress I'd bought years ago but been too afraid to wear. It was gorgeous, a dress that demanded people's attention. I'd bought it for the woman I dreamed to be—not the one I was.

But today I needed all the confidence I could get, so I zipped it up

and brushed my hair until it was gleaming. I looked fun and flirty. A woman with personality, but with a sophisticated side. It wouldn't raise any eyebrows in the office, but I hoped it would raise one person's eyebrows—tonight.

I didn't want to fall into bed with Julian, to be wooed like one of the countless women I imagined that he'd pursued, but I couldn't stand the thought of him looking at me and glancing away. I wanted his attention.

At work that Thursday, I threw myself into planning the launch strategy for an upcoming product launch and prepared the Monday pitch with the team.

Despite the busy day, my mind couldn't help spinning like a dryer stuck on the last cycle, round and round and round.

I thought about whether or not this dinner was a good idea (it wasn't), if I could back out with my dignity intact (unlikely) and if I'd ever been this excited by a non-date before (I hadn't).

My phone buzzed around five o'clock and my heart leaped in anticipation.

Julian: I'm flying in from out of state and we're thirty minutes delayed. I have to push our dinner back to 7:15. I'll make it up to you.

A million different responses flashed through my mind before I finally settled on what I thought was the right amount of teasing and fun.

Emily: That's fine, I guess… Though, if you truly valued punctuality, you'd just step up and fly the plane yourself.

Julian: It crossed my mind, but I don't feel like getting arrested today.

Emily: How are you going to make it up to me?

Julian: What a wealth of answers I could give to that question. But what I have in mind will have to wait for more of a face-to-face situation, so to speak.

My heart made pathetic little double-beats, ignoring the orders my brain issued. He's your *boss boss BOSS!* Clearly, my fingers ignored them too, typing out a flirty response as if on their own accord.

Emily: Sounds ominous.

Julian: Don't worry, I can be gentle.

Heat pooled in my stomach and I closed my eyes against the images his words conjured. His tall, powerful frame behind me, pressing kisses to my neck. Feeling the strength of him against me, the reach of his hands…

Keep your head in the game, Emily. I couldn't fold like a house of cards at the first little gust of wind.

Emily: Threatening everyone's safety by texting while flying? That's a scandal if I've ever heard of one. Please don't give us press secretaries more work than necessary, Mr. Hunt. Thank you.

Julian: There's wifi in first-class. But I'm very flattered that you're worried about my safety.

Asshole. I was just about to slip my phone back into my bag and away from my unruly fingers when another text came through.

Julian: I'm looking forward to tonight.

Me too, I thought, smoothing a hand over my dress. Despite all my reservations, decisions and plans, I felt more electric and alive than I had in months. I'd made the decision to play with fire—I just had to ensure I didn't get burned in the process.

10

EMILY

I arrived at Kalispera exactly on time. The place was just as cute as I remembered it from my previous visit, then with friends, celebrating Denise's birthday. Julian wasn't there, but the waiter showed me to a table in the back, right next to a beautiful stone wall.

Looking around at the rustic decor and the charming details, I quickly realized that I'd made a mistake. There might not be white linen cloths at this place but it was stupidly romantic anyway. Two tables over, I saw a couple quite literally holding hands on the wooden table, illuminated by candlelight.

Could I ask them to, you know, leave? Maybe tell the waiter to turn up the dimmed lighting?

I smoothed a hand over my dress and felt incredibly brave and incredibly foolish at the same time.

My phone buzzed.

Julian: So sorry, but I have to cancel. Rain check?

My jaw hit the floor so hard I might need stitches. What? How dare he, when I was here and waiting?

Husky, masculine laughter rang out behind me. "I'm sorry, Ace, but I just had to see what your reaction would be. You looked genuinely disappointed."

"*You*."

Julian raised his hands placatingly and slid into the seat opposite me.

"Whoops." He hung his gray dinner jacket over the back of the chair and methodically rolled up the sleeves of his shirt, revealing tan arms and a thick silver watch. It was like I saw him relax in front of my eyes, go from the imposing CEO to a normal man.

"How long were you watching me?"

"Just for a few minutes." His smile brought an immediate softening to his features. "You look great, Ace."

I grabbed one of the menus. "Anything for Hunt Industries."

"I envy my own employees for getting to spend the entire day with you looking like that."

I shook my head at his exaggerated flattery. "Look at your menu, idiot. I'm hungry."

"No, ma'am. You're the food expert and this restaurant was your idea. So you order whatever you think we'll like."

"Really?"

"Sure." Julian ran an absent hand through his thick hair, mussing it up and away from its neat wave. "I trust you."

I dove into the menu with the fervor of someone being asked to choose a college major. When the waiter came I rattled off a list of my favorite Greek dishes and some new ones I'd always wanted to try, making it clear that we'd be sharing them all.

Julian watched me in silent amusement, eyes sparkling.

"What?"

"You're cute when you're passionate."

I bit my lip and looked away from his playful eyes. Somehow, comments like that hit much harder than the hyperbolic compliments about my beauty.

I cleared my throat. "The deal was *professional* dinners."

"No, they weren't supposed to be intimate in nature. But they're definitely going to be personal."

"Personal?"

His voice dropped in volume. "We're not here to discuss business, Emily."

I swallowed at the warmth in his voice. "Then I want to know more about you."

"I'm at your service," he said and opened his arms wide, revealing a strong frame and a chest that practically begged to be slept on. "Ask away."

"Where were you today?"

"That's professional."

"Come on. I'm genuinely curious."

"Both you and Rachel have access to my calendar."

"I want to hear it in your own words."

"I was in Atlanta. There's a new start-up I'm thinking of acquiring, and their offices are there. Well, office is a bit strong of a word—it's two young women working out of their college dorm, but they very ambitiously called it an office when they invited me." He snorted good-naturedly. "I approve."

"What are they developing?"

"A program designed to encourage young women to code. There are tons of organizations like that already, but I haven't invested in any yet and would like to add more of the equality mindset to Hunt. They're on to something unique as well, with their interface."

I softened as I watched him talk. He truly was passionate about his work. He had more than enough money to be idle for the rest of his days, but that didn't seem to interest him at all.

He wanted to build, to create, to contribute something worthwhile.

"That's really cool. Both for its own sake, of course, but also because we could really spin that for marketing and press purposes."

Julian laughed. "Are you always this cynical?"

"Realistic," I corrected. "And that's what you hired me for."

"Unfortunately, yes." He grinned. "But sometimes I find myself wishing you'd be a little *less* realistic."

I ignored the thrilling current that shot through me at his comment. "Why did you start Hunt Industries?"

"No."

"No? What kind of answer is that?"

"No, it's my turn. How's your brother settling in? I know how much that mattered to you."

"Better than I could have hoped. Your connection speed is excellent, apparently, and after he put the computer back together it's now able to process more code than before. Honestly, all of this is like a different language to me. I don't understand it, but it's clear that he's enjoying his work."

"David tells me he's basically taken the software department by storm. Coders drop by all the time to pick his brain for adaptions to any single line."

I smiled, picturing Turner trying to explain things that came so easy for him to those with less cognitive function. God knows I'd been on the receiving end plenty of times. "He's out tonight with a few of the other coders, so it seems like they're a good group."

Julian looked thoughtful. "Is that difficult?"

"Is what difficult?"

"That he's now an adult, and out on the town tonight."

"A bit." I rubbed my neck, the skin warm from the heavy weight of my hair. "I don't know if you know this, but I've been his legal guardian since he was fourteen."

His eyes gentled. "I heard."

"Our parents died in a car accident. Hit straight on."

"I'm sorry, Emily."

"Thank you." I cleared my throat. "It is what it is. But that's why I'm sometimes… a bit overprotective. With the exception of our grandparents in Louisiana and a few cousins in New York, Turner and I are all the family we have."

"And now he's grown."

"And now he's grown," I echoed. "All is as it should be, only I don't feel like I've necessarily caught up. How about your brother? He's about Turner's age?"

"He's twenty-one and causing me no end of trouble."

"Oh?"

The waiter arrived and interrupted whatever potential

response was coming with a large platter of dishes. It smelled heavenly—plates of souvlaki, a bowl of pita and moussaka. When the table was nearly covered with dishes, the waiter placed a single long-stemmed rose in a thin vase in the middle and lit a candle.

He smiled at both of us before he left. "There we go! Have a nice meal, you two."

I frowned at Julian. "Don't say it."

His eyes danced with silent mirth as he looked from the flower to me. "Good thing you chose somewhere non-romantic."

"It's just a flower. And a candle. It doesn't mean anything."

"You're right," Julian responded with a straight face. "Because romance is about chemistry, and not details. We could be in a dumpster and I'd still be swooning."

"It's such a shame that you happen to be my boss, then."

"If only there was an easy solution to that?"

"You could quit," I said with a straight face. "Give it all up for love, grand gestures and so forth."

Julian's face split into a wide grin that somehow only made him *more* handsome. "Yes, I'm sure that *Hunt* Industries would thrive without me."

"Hey, I don't make the rules."

"Well, in here you do, Giordano. Tell me what these dishes are because I'm starving."

Slowly, my defenses fell. He was charming and funny, and not once did he seek to cross some line like I had been expecting. We had more in common than I had anticipated, but in some ways, our differences were practically irreconcilable.

"You really haven't been to the movies in years?"

"No, not that I can recall."

"*Years,* Julian. You can't be serious."

"I can see whatever I feel like at home." He shrugged. "I just don't get around to going to an actual movie theater."

"That's just sad."

"No, sad is someone who doesn't want to order dessert." He

gave a pointed glance toward the untouched dessert menu between us.

"I'm full! Stuffed! I'm like one of those dolmades," I told him, "and I couldn't possibly eat another bite."

Julian looked at me through hooded eyes. "All right. You got to make the rules regarding food, but that means I get to decide on drinks."

"Julian, we have work tomorrow."

He called the waiter over and promptly ordered two small glasses of ouzo. "We won't have more than one each, don't worry."

The chilled glasses of anise-flavored liquor arrived not two minutes later. I looked down at mine in distaste. I knew it was traditional, but it was damn strong and I'd never been fond of licorice.

"Eyes up here, Ace." He grinned. "Let's cap off the night with a round of Never Have I Ever."

I couldn't help myself—I laughed in astonishment. "The game you play in high school?"

"Yes. You drink if you've done something, and you don't if you haven't. Simple as can be." Julian's face was teasing, as if he didn't really think I'd agree to this.

But I'd never lacked courage. I raised my glass high and touched it to his. "It's on, Hunt."

"Ladies first."

"All right. Hmm… Never have I ever started a company."

He rolled his eyes. "Come on, Ace. These are tiny glasses. We don't get many chances here. Isn't there anything else you *really* want to know? I promise complete honesty."

"Never have I ever been kicked out of a club," I said—and didn't reach for my glass.

Julian sighed and took a small sip of his ouzo. "It was college, all right? You have to remember that I'm older than you. I have had more time to make bad decisions."

"You're not older by much."

"Eight years." His reply was instant. He'd calculated the age difference between us, just as he had known about my parents.

"That's not much."

His smile grew. "I agree. All right, it's my turn. Never have I ever stolen anything."

I took a sip of the burning liquid, but Julian didn't touch his glass. "Come on! Everyone's taken something at some point. You really haven't?"

"No."

"Not even, like, a piece of gum when you were a kid?"

"Nope." His smile was angelic. "Not me."

"Probably because you never needed to," I grumbled.

Julian rolled his eyes. "Right. Now tell me about your great crime story."

"I stole a small beaded bracelet from a grocery store. I was six or seven and just wanted to see if I could. I felt so bad I told my mom and we drove back to return it."

Julian shook his head. "I've hired a thief. I guess I should be happy she has a remorseful heart, at least."

And a very deceitful one, I thought, thinking about how it regularly sped up around him despite my decision to be professional.

"Your turn." He looked at me with a challenge in his eyes, eyebrows slightly raised, as if he knew exactly what kind of thing I'd say. He was probably expecting something cutesy and fluffy. So I raised my chin and gave him something else.

"Never have I ever had a one-night stand."

"Damn, Ace." Julian raised the glass to his lips and took a sip. "You're making it hard for me to show you what a catch I am."

Not letting my eyes drift from his, I slowly raised my own glass to my lips and took a burning sip.

"And here I thought I had you all figured out," he murmured. His gaze flicked down to my lips and I wet them unconsciously. Heat raced through me, and the air grew thick.

Julian's voice was husky. "Never have I ever thrown a game

of pool because I wanted an excuse to spend time with someone I'm interested in."

Shit. "That's really what you're going with?"

"Yes."

"Hmmm." I made a show of reaching for my glass, slowly lifting it up. His eyes lit up in triumph as I drank.

"I knew it."

"Don't flatter yourself. I don't get out much."

"Then I'm happy to be of service." He leaned back, toying with the small glass in his hand. "It's your turn."

"Never have I ever been unfaithful," I said. Neither of us touched our glasses.

He smiled. "Never have I ever said 'I love you' just to get laid."

Again, neither of us touched our glasses. Julian raised an eyebrow. "Looks like we have some things in common after all, Ace."

"If we keep going at this pace we'll be here all night."

Julian leaned forward and let his hand rest on the table. My own ached with the desire to reach out and feel if his skin was as warm as it looked.

When he finally spoke, his voice was a husky murmur, sending shivers down my spine. "Never have I ever been attracted to a colleague."

We both threw back the last of our drinks. In the silence that followed, Julian looked away, his jaw working.

"Come on, Emily. We need to get out of here or I'm going to do something decidedly *unprofessional.*"

11
EMILY

It had been nearly a week since the dinner with Julian, and he'd canceled on our next dinner only hours before. Luckily I had a best friend with a mission, and after some hastily arranged plans, we were driving to dinner.

A dinner I was going to enjoy and *not* spend going over every possible reason why he had canceled.

"Hey, this is the exit, right?"

Denise peered out of the passenger seat window. "Yes. There's valet parking."

"Fancy."

She gave a peal of nervous laughter. "El Vino is stupidly fancy. Michael told me they have a three-stage interview process for waiters."

"And the food… I've been dreaming of eating here for months."

I'd never been to El Vino—lord knows it was over my budget!—but Denise's insider connection meant we'd be served the chef specials at a discounted price. My friend was happily infatuated, and I got to eat Michelin-star food at a discount. *Win-win.*

A quick glance made it clear that she was still fiddling with her jewelry, quietly staring straight ahead. It was unlike her to be so nervous.

"You look stunning. This guy doesn't know how lucky he is."

She laughed, as if I was being silly, and straightened up. "I'm the lucky one."

"Are you nervous?"

"A bit. It's silly, isn't it? I haven't been nervous with men for so long but here I am, thinking about Michael in that kitchen. We've only been on six dates total. I counted."

I smiled. "Six dates is like a lifetime for you."

"*I know!* That's what makes it feel so serious."

"I can't wait to meet him if he makes you feel like this."

Stepping out of the car, I stretched up to my full height. I might not be supermodel tall, but I'd put on a pair of strappy high heels and a black cocktail dress. I'd listened to peppy music as I got ready and staunchly refused to think about Julian or why he had canceled tonight.

Or how much I wanted to see him again, outside of work.

Denise threaded her arm under mine and we walked inside the dimly lit restaurant. We were met by expensive oak decor and soft background music.

"Denise Lloyd," she announced to the hostess. "I believe we have a reservation?"

The waitress gave us a megawatt smile and quickly led us to a secluded table. "You're very welcome here, ladies," she said. "Let me start you off with a complimentary glass of champagne."

Denise and I turned to one another as soon as she left. "Wow," Denise stage-whispered. "This. Is. Awesome!"

"I should start sleeping with head chefs too if this is the way you're treated!"

She laughed. "This place is really prestigious too, to get to work at."

"For sure." I glanced around at the other guests, all dressed up to the nines. Couples and families dined on white linen-clad tables and from the vaulted ceiling hung a gigantic chandelier.

"It's beautiful, right?"

"It's incredible."

Denise reached across the table for my hand. "And very romantic. Watch out when we get our champagne, because I might have put a ring in the glass."

I pretended to frown. "Now you've ruined the surprise!"

We got the drinks and toasted to her good fortune. I'd seen Denise gush over dates often, but there had been very few men she'd blushed this brightly over.

The food we had was *divine*. The portions were tiny and served on over-the-top plates, but the flavors mingled in exactly the right way. The sea bass was perfection.

I raised my fork in warning to Denise. "You're never breaking up with him. Never, ever."

"Not even if he's terrible to me?"

"No. And if you *do* break up I'm going to take his side."

She chuckled. "I've known you for… eleven years now?"

"Doesn't matter. You can't make lasagna like this."

"I can't blame you. He is pretty fantastic. And speaking of men… Will you please tell me how it went with the bossman last week? I've waited for two entire courses to ask you because I was hoping that *maybe* you'd bring it up yourself."

I took a sip of my red wine. "Well…"

"Well? Silence only means one of two things. Either it went terribly, or you slept with him even though you said you wouldn't."

"Denise!"

"So you did?" Her eyes were round. "Wow. And it's been so long! How was it? Tell me everything!"

"Denise, I didn't *go home with him*. He's my boss!"

She rolled her eyes. "Boss, schmoss. So it was terrible."

"No. It was… really nice. We had a really good time."

"Good," she repeated. "That's what I say to describe my dentist appointment."

"No, it was amazing! He's really charming and funny. I guess I knew that already, but it's different when all that charm is solely focused on you for two hours. And I think he's much smarter than people give him credit for."

"He's the founder of what, twenty-seven different apps? The CEO of a billion dollar company? And you didn't think he was smart?"

I put down my fork and tried to explain. "No, I know. It's just not something I think I considered before. He's so intimidating, physically and personality-wise… I just thought he was rich and did what rich people do. You know. Nothing, really."

"Did you kiss?"

"No. I told you, these dinners were supposed to be as friends."

She raised a skeptical eyebrow. "But it's clear both of you want more."

I thought of the tension between us during the final round of Never Have I Ever, his eyes darkening with interest.

"Yes. It's clear we're attracted to each other."

"When are you meeting him next time?"

I sighed. "It was supposed to be tonight, but he canceled. Said he would make it up to me."

"I bet he will," Denise said with a wink. "In a way that will make *both* of you happy."

"Oh, shush."

"It's a shame he's your boss because he sounds truly great. Not that that particular problem couldn't be solved in one way or another. "

There was a sudden outcry of raised voices, alarmingly loud in the otherwise calm restaurant. Two people were arguing loudly at a table across the room.

Denise whistled under her breath. "Wow. That's some real trouble in paradise."

I couldn't help but agree. The woman was blonde, bedazzled with jewelry and wearing an expensive-looking dress. She was also incredibly upset, hands moving animatedly as she outlined some problem.

Opposite her sat… my boss. Julian was gripping the edge of

the table and tension radiated from stiff shoulders. I couldn't stop staring.

"No way."

"What? Do you know them?"

I shook my head slowly. "That's him. That's Julian. I can't believe it, he blew off our dinner for someone else?"

"What!" Denise leaned forward, squinting toward the table. "Oh, what a day to forget to put in my contacts. He looks attractive, Emily… although very blurry at this distance."

"I can't believe it. What a dick!"

"They're not necessarily on a date. They might be having a business meeting or something."

I shot her a withering gaze. "That woman is dressed up to get looks, not to sign contracts. And they're arguing."

They were still going at it, fighting with the obvious familiarity of two people who know each other well. Julian's profile was strong and the sharp jaw clenched tight. Even at this distance, I could see that his eyes were narrowed. I had never seen him angry before and shivered.

"Look," Denise said. "I'm sure there's an explanation. Maybe he took her here to break up with her. Because he wants to be with you?"

I didn't believe that, but I appreciated her effort. "Maybe. But that would mean that he'd been in a relationship or actively dating while he was trying to, you know…"

"Seduce you?"

"Yes." It hurt to hear it so plainly, but that was the truth. That was exactly what he had been trying to do—some competitive little game. Maybe he played with me on the side while continuing on with the women he *actually* cared for in his life, women who looked like goddesses and wore Cartier bracelets. She was probably his age, maybe closer to forty, and polished to perfection.

"You should go over there."

"And do what? Denise, that's a private conversation." I sunk deeper into the velvet chair and pulled my curtain of hair forward to shield my face. "And he'd better not notice me here."

Denise, ever the kind friend, leaned forward and put a hand on mine. "We can leave if you want."

"No. No, I want to meet Michael, of course. And when will we ever get to eat food like this again?" I tried to grin at her over the table. "Julian Hunt won't keep me from trying whatever delicious dessert a Michelin-star head chef has created."

We spent the rest of the dinner peeking around the corner to try to spot what was happening over at Julian's and Blondie's table. They didn't argue for long and Julian settled the bill with angry movements, his face still locked in rigid lines. I wondered what the woman might have done to make him that angry.

I wondered if I really knew him at all.

They left the restaurant side by side, but not touching, disappearing out into the night.

Denise put down her glass. "Stop it."

"What?"

"I can practically see your mind whirling."

I sighed. "I can't help it! What if they're going home together? Maybe they live together. Maybe they're *married*."

"Emily."

"It didn't say that he was married on his Wikipedia page. But maybe it's just not up to date." I reached to fish out my phone, determined to find answers, when Denise caught my arm.

"Emily! You're spiraling. Think. Does he wear a ring?"

"No."

"Has anyone at the office mentioned a wife or a girlfriend?"

"No," I admitted.

"You might see him at work tomorrow. Ask him. Don't let doubts and fears cloud your judgment. Just literally ask for the truth. See what he says."

Her words made sense. "You've always been so good at this."

"No," Denise said in a level voice. "I've just dated a lot of men. I recognize the patterns."

"Okay. Yeah, I'll do that. I'll just ask him about it tomorrow. I'll be casual and cool about it. A cool girl."

"Maybe she's an angry ex and they just had a wild negotiation about how they're going to divide custody of their sixteen rescue dogs." Somehow, Denise managed to keep a straight face. "I bet she argued to keep all the Chihuahua mixes."

I smiled. "I can actually imagine him getting angry about that."

She tried on a scowl. "No, Pamela, you're *not* taking Steve or Bill! That's where I draw the line!"

I laughed. "Steve and Bill?"

"Come on, he's a techie! What else would he name his hypothetical dogs?"

"You have a point. I bet she named her dogs things like Velvet and Sunset."

"There you go." Denise smiled. "And if he turns out to be a two-timing scumbag? Well, then you were smart to put up boundaries in the first place, and you keep doing what you do best—kick ass at work."

"You're the best friend a girl can have, you know that, right?"

"I know. It's on the card you send me every Galantine's day."

"Only because it never stops being true."

Her eyes shifted to something behind me, widening in surprise. "Oh, Michael's coming! Must be quieter in the kitchen now."

I smiled at her flushed cheeks and glanced over my shoulder. A tall, slim man in a chef's outfit was making his way around the tables, nodding occasionally to guests as he passed.

He just grinned at Denise when he arrived, and she at him.

"Hi."

"Hi there." Denise cleared her throat. "Um, this is Emily. I've told you about her."

I extended my hand. "Hopefully all good. Are you the one we should thank for all this delicious food?"

He grinned. "Yes. I'm Michael. I'm sorry I couldn't come out earlier, but it was really busy. We almost had a full house tonight."

"That's great!" Denise said. "I'm just glad you could slip away for a moment to say hi."

"Did you enjoy the lasagna?"

"Absolutely."

"It was divine," I added. "Sublime. Perfect. I might actually need to get a thesaurus, that's how good it was."

He laughed again and put a hand on Denise's shoulder. They looked good together, like two matching pieces of a puzzle. He was all calm competence in comparison to her lively exuberance.

"I'll come have a seat with you as soon as service is over and we can chat for a bit. It should be after you've had dessert."

"We'll see you soon!" Denise smiled soppily after him as he left.

I grinned at her and waited for her to finally turn back to me. When she did, there was clear warning in her eyes.

"Don't say it."

"What?"

"I know I turn into a lovesick fool around him."

"You do, but I'm very happy that you do."

"Thank you." She reached over and put her hand on mine for what had to be the third time that night. And here I thought I was doing well! "You'll be that happy too one day, Emily, I know it."

I didn't let my smile falter as I looked at her.

Oh yes, I would indeed be happy soon—as soon as I could give Julian a piece of my mind.

12

JULIAN

My former stepmother's announcement had made an already terrible day about ten times worse.
She just *had* to meet. She had *vital* information about Ryan.
The truth was that she was just impossible. Why my father had chosen to marry her after divorcing my mother had always been somewhat of a mystery to me, despite the fact that she had some obviously attractive qualities. She was an excellent cook and she'd always doted on my younger brother.
But you didn't indulge a son who was twenty-one years old and regularly ended up in all kinds of trouble. If it wasn't with law enforcement, it was broken bones and crashed cars. I'd tried to talk to her about Ryan for nearly two years and everything I'd said had fallen on deaf ears.
As long as he knew he could always run to her for more money and a free beach house to party in, nothing was going to change.
Father had left her more than enough in his will to sustain her for the rest of her life, without the need to ask me for money. This, too, was something I had made clear to her on more than one occasion. It wasn't that I couldn't, it was more the principle of the thing. Like how we couldn't talk without a three-hundred-

dollar bottle of champagne at one of Palo Alto's fanciest restaurants.

Yeah. Like I said—*impossible*.

Worst of all was that I'd been forced to cancel my hard-earned dinner with Emily to handle the step-momzilla. Emily had responded pleasantly to the rain check, but I hoped she wouldn't use this as some sort of excuse to spook.

I'd understand it if she did.

This job was a major step for her, which was something I respected. Getting involved with me must look like a surefire way to complicate things. I had to make it clear that it wasn't—I'd never hold anything personal against her professionally.

It helped that I was 99 percent sure she was attracted to me. Hell, she even admitted that she threw the game of pool to ensure I'd win the weekly out-of-office meetings. I'd suspected it at the time, but it still made me feel ten feet tall when she confirmed it.

The problem? I just wanted her. The more time we spent together, the more I had a suspicion that Emily Giordano might be exactly what I'd always been looking for.

She was clever and kind, and more *real* than anyone I'd met in a long time. If I had to wait until she realized that I could be the same for her, I would do just that.

Meanwhile I'd take every opportunity to talk to her. She was only two floors down, a short elevator ride away. On my way in to work the next day, I was thinking it would be so easy to go visit her just to draw out one of her wide smiles. But I knew she wouldn't appreciate that, not at work. I could respect that.

So I settled on texting her from my office.

Julian: Sorry again about yesterday. Hope you didn't miss me too terribly.

But the response was a long time coming, which was weird compared to how rapid-fire she'd been the past week. I found myself glancing at my phone far more often than I would have wanted that morning until she finally answered me.

Emily: I guess you had more important things to do.

I frowned. So she was annoyed that I had to cancel.

Julian: Family emergency, unfortunately.

Emily: Sorry to hear that. Hope nobody was terribly hurt?

God, how easily her mind drifted to the morbid.

Julian: No, nothing so drastic. Are you free tonight? I'd like to make it up to you.

Emily: I can't tonight.

Hmm. Either she'd gotten very cold feet all of a sudden, despite how well we hit it off the week before, or she was pissed off. *Great, Julian.* Somehow, I'd managed to screw this up before it had even begun.

This required a face-to-face conversation, one where I could lay the charm on thick.

Nobody saw me as I took the stairs the two floors down to see her later that afternoon, but I knew I'd be noticed as soon as I hit the marketing department.

Emily cared about her job, so I had to make sure none of the others would suspect what was going on. How? By making the rounds.

Trent was deep into his work, glasses pushed high. He looked up at me in the doorway. "Oh, hey Boss. Do you need anything? I haven't missed that we're having a super important meeting now, have I?"

"You're good," I said. "I just had a few minutes and thought I'd hear how the new launch strategy is going."

"It's phenomenal. Josef and Sasha are working on some graphics that I think you'll love. The original concept was actually Emily's idea."

"It was?"

"Yeah. Great hire. Rachel's not in at the moment, by the way. You just missed her, I think she had some appointment across town."

"Oh." I pretended to look disappointed. "Thank you."

"See you around, Boss."

I strolled out and down the hallway to where I knew Emily's office was.

Her door was ajar and I could hear the faint sound of upbeat pop music coming from inside. I couldn't help myself—I grinned. It seemed this woman would never stop surprising me. A fierce protector of her family, an excellent pool player, a witty conversationalist *and* a sugary pop fan.

I knocked.

The music was instantly shut off. "Come in!"

I leaned against the frame and watched as her face went from pleasant to guarded. *Yep.* I had definitely managed to annoy her.

"Pop music, huh?"

Emily closed a notebook she'd been writing in. "It makes me happy."

"I'm sure it does, although it seems like I don't. Are you annoyed at me, Ace?"

"Whatever would give you that impression?"

I laughed. "The fact that you've looked at me for about five seconds since I arrived. Or that you haven't answered my text about rescheduling dinner."

She looked past me into the hallway and made a quick motion with her hand. "Come in, for God's sake. I don't want anyone to hear you."

Dutifully, I stepped inside and shut the door behind me. "But now you're alone with the boss," I pointed out. "Tongues might wag even more."

She rose and put her hands on her hips. God, but she was luscious. I wanted to map every curve of her body, learn the terrain. Find out how she kissed and how my name sounded on her lips.

"It's a risk I'm willing to take."

I held up placating hands. "I'm sorry for rescheduling so late. Truly."

She flicked her dark hair back. "No worries."

"What do you want me to do? Beg?"

She leaned against her desk and crossed slender arms across her chest. Somehow it only accentuated the curve of her waist and her breasts, making me all the more aware of her beauty.

"You sound desperate, Hunt."

"Let's call me persistent." Because she was a fucking catch, and I wasn't stupid.

Emily raised an eyebrow. "I didn't stay at home yesterday evening, you know. After you blew me off."

"No?"

"No. I went out to dinner with a friend."

Hot jealousy tore through my chest and I had to force down the unreasonable reaction. She was free to do whatever she wanted. The only thing I had was hope and the fact that she might be attracted to me. If I had competition I'd only have to work harder to prove that I was someone she could trust.

"I see," I said smoothly, schooling my face back into impassivity. "Did you have fun?"

"Yes. As a matter of fact, we went to a really nice Italian place."

I gritted my teeth. "The whole white tablecloth, candles and flower deal?"

She leaned forward, her eyes blazing with anger. "*Yes*."

"I'm so glad. Tell me, did you two play Never Have I Ever? Did he make you blush, set your heart racing?"

She ignored my questions. "Let's play another game. Guess who I saw at the restaurant?"

"Who?"

"*You.*" Her voice was an accusation. "Blowing me off last minute to go on a date is rather low behavior, but whatever."

I stared at her. "What?"

"At El Vino? You were sitting in the corner." Emily glanced down at her nails. "You were with a blonde."

I couldn't help it—my face split in a grin. "You're jealous."

She rolled her eyes. "Don't be silly, Julian. We're *friends*."

"Bullshit. You're just as jealous as I am."

"We're *just friends,* you and I."

"All right, sure. So why did it bother you, seeing me with her?"

She huffed. "It's just not decent behavior, that's all. Canceling on a friend like that. I actually think it's rather rude."

I took a step closer. She might not have intended to, but she'd given a lot away. "I don't buy it."

"Julian, honestly, you're impossible." Her green eyes were narrowed as they glared into mine. "I'm not jealous."

"Great. Because I am."

Her eyebrows shot up. "Of my dinner date?"

I ignored her question. "I'll be straight with you. I told you why I had to cancel—a family emergency."

"Yes, but I saw—"

"My stepmother. She insists on going to fancy places whenever we meet to discuss family business. It's annoying, but it's most certainly not anything you should feel threatened by."

Emily glanced up at me through thick lashes, conflict in her eyes. The woman was a stunner. "Your stepmother?"

"Yes. I'm sure you could even look it up online if you don't believe me. Honest."

She laughed suddenly, and an unexpected thrill ran through me at the sound. "Wow."

"Why didn't you come over and say hello?"

"You two seemed to be arguing. And, well…"

"You thought I was taking another woman out to dinner?"

"Yes."

"I have a suggestion, Ace." I cocked an eyebrow and took a step closer, so that we were only inches from touching.

"I'm listening."

"You've just established that you don't want me to date anyone else. No, don't object. Your jealousy did it for you."

Emily pursed her lips. "I was just annoyed."

I couldn't help smiling. "All right, we'll call it *annoyed*. I haven't dated anyone since I met you, and I won't—if you won't."

"You want us to, what, promise not to date anyone? But we're not dating each other either!"

I nodded. "Exactly. We spend time together, and neither of us gets jealous. Win-win."

A slow smile spread across her features. "You were jealous of my date, weren't you?"

"Hell, yeah." I wish I had seen the fucker, so I would have known what kind of guys she usually preferred. "Where were you sitting?"

"Near the back." Emily inched closer and I had to tilt my head down to meet her eyes. I could feel the heat of her body, see the curve of her breasts. It would be so easy to pull her flush against me and savor her softness.

"We don't see other people while we're dating," I murmured. "That stops."

"Indefinitely?"

"Yes. Until we've… figured out whatever this is."

Emily leaned in, almost as if she was swaying. Her lips were open slightly. I couldn't help it—I bent my head and touched my forehead against hers, our mouths so close I could feel the warmth of her exhale.

"Let me tell you a secret," she breathed.

"What?"

"I was out with Denise last night, my best friend since middle school. Not a boy in sight."

I smiled in relief. "You baited me."

"Yes. And somehow, it worked."

I could kiss her like this, give us both what we clearly wanted. Her luscious, warm lips were only an inch away from mine. We didn't break eye contact as Emily wet her lips, almost absently.

Fuck.

My entire body hardened in response to the subconscious invitation. But I couldn't—we couldn't—not here.

I stepped away. "No."

Her hand found my forearm, as if she wanted to keep me close. "Why not?"

"Not in here. It's not a good idea."

Emily's eyes were still molten. "The door is closed."

"Exactly. And if I kiss you here, it won't stop with just a kiss."

Emily rolled her eyes, the desire in her eyes now mixed with a familiar teasing glint. "You're that sure of yourself, Hunt?"

I backed up toward the door even though it physically hurt me to move away from her. "I've never had any bad reviews. Meet me on Sunday. Midday. I have an idea."

"What about tonight?"

I grinned. Now she was the one hungry for me. "I thought you had plans?"

"Yeah, well, plans change."

"They do. Sunday. I'll pick you up."

"Text me," she murmured.

"Oh, I will."

13

EMILY

"*Wear something comfortable.*"

That was all the information Julian gave me for our Sunday date.

I didn't ask for more details, but I *did* tell him to park down the street because I still hadn't told Turner about us. It wasn't like there was anything to share really, at least not yet. And at the moment I had far more pressing issues. What did comfortable clothing mean? Yoga pants and a sports bra? Sneakers and sweats?

I settled on a pair of dark-wash jeans, a white shirt, and a brown leather jacket. Looking in the mirror, shaking out my long hair, I thought I looked chic. Like someone who might even be described as *cool*.

I'd need that—because lord knows I wasn't particularly cool in Julian Hunt's presence. He'd walked into my office on Friday as if he owned it (sure, he *technically* did) and challenged me about my lack of response to his texts. He'd been right to do so.

He'd been right on several accounts, actually. I had been jealous, which meant I was getting far more attached to him than I had expected.

And then he'd given me the best non-kiss of my life. We were literally inches away from touching, and I had felt the warmth from his lips... But then he'd walked away.

Impossible, infuriating and intoxicating man.

Turner was in the living room, sorting through our old collection of movies and DVDs. So much of the house was still a patchwork of stuff from our childhood together with Mom and Dad's old things.

We'd made a vow to sort through things every now and then when we felt strong enough. Lately, Turner had taken to it.

He looked up as I walked past, a stack of VHS tapes before him. "Are you heading to the mall with Denise?"

"Yeah. I'll be home for dinner."

"Good. It's your turn to cook dinner tonight."

"Yes, and I found a new recipe I'm going to try."

I heard him groan as I grabbed my purse and headed toward the front door. "What's wrong with the food we normally make? We know it works!"

"A little experimentation has never hurt anyone!"

"Yes, Emily, it most certainly has!"

I grinned as I closed the door behind me. "Bye!"

A sleek, silver Porsche was waiting for me two blocks down. Julian was leaning against it, casually dressed in chinos and a black leather jacket. He had sunglasses on, arms crossed, looking deadly attractive.

He couldn't possibly be here for me. I was the girl who still knew all the songs to childhood musicals by heart and used to ask teachers for extra homework. Girls like us didn't get guys like him.

Julian looked over and his handsome face split into a smile. "I feel like I'm doing something wrong," he teased. "Picking you up down the street. Did you sneak out of your bedroom window?"

"Yes. I scaled the ivy and crawled through a bush, too. Look. We match."

He glanced from his leather jacket to mine. "So we do. Let's go. I'm taking you to lunch."

"That's why I had to dress comfortably? To eat?"

Julian laughed as he opened the passenger door for me. The interior of the car smelled like new leather and I sank deep into the seat. We would practically be hugging the road in this car, it was so low. This had to be the Porsche he'd been talking about the first time we met.

"No," he replied. "It's for what we're doing *before.*"

"What are we doing before?"

"That, my friend, is a surprise. I have to keep you on your toes."

"Consider me kept." I smiled at him and opened the passenger door. "I can't believe I finally get to ride in the infamous Porsche."

Julian snorted. "*Famous,* if you please. She has a stellar reputation."

He drove with one hand on the steering wheel, eyes glued ahead, the faint scent of his aftershave making it difficult for me to think. Somehow he managed to look competent regardless of what he did—he moved like a man sure of himself and his rightful place in the world.

I wasn't sure any man after him would be able to live up to this.

Before long we were driving through thick forest, greenery, and shrubs. Gorgeous, as always, and not for the first time I was glad to live in a place where nature always was close.

He broke the silence first. "So your brother doesn't know about us, then."

"No," I said. "Though what are we, exactly?"

"You tell me, Ace."

"Friends. Dinner companions." I paused. "Leather jacket aficionados."

Julian's fingers tapped against the steering wheel. "The last one. He doesn't know that we're both aficionados?"

"No. I think it might be safer to avoid telling him something that I don't really understand myself yet."

Julian glanced at me. "And we work together."

"Yes." As much as I tried, I could never forget that fact.

"It's okay. I don't mind being your secret for now."

I leaned back in the seat and watched him. "Am I yours? Your secret, I mean?"

"No. In the office, yes, because I know you want it that way and I respect that. But I can't wait for the day you're more. I'll make sure the whole world knows you're mine."

I rolled my eyes at the exaggeration, trying to hide the way my heart had leaped at his answer. Being around Julian made me feel both brave and beautiful, and more powerful than ever before. "Don't hold your breath, Hunt."

Julian laughed. His right hand rested on his thigh, fingers drumming along to the music as he drove. I contemplated reaching out and threading my fingers through his to see how it felt. Pretending there was an us.

I shook away the crazy impulse. We hadn't even *kissed* yet, for Christ's sake.

He turned off from the highway and up onto a dusty road, off the tarmac. Tall trees crowded the side of the road, wilderness all around us.

"Oh no," I said. "Is this the part where you say that 'you're sorry, but there's just no other way?' And then you barter me to a drug cartel or toss me to the wolves. Don't tell me that you're secretly a billionaire mass murderer, Julian."

"Millionaire," he replied smoothly. "And no, I'm not going to go *American Psycho* on you. Look ahead."

I squinted. There *was* something at the end of the road, just past the trees. Buildings came into view and behind them… an asphalt track.

"*No way*. Is that what I think it is?"

"It is."

"It's a racetrack. Julian, are we racing?"

"You admitted that you threw the pool game. I'm happy you did, but it's only fair that you get what you bet on as well."

"I'm going to get to drive your car? *This car?*"

"Yes. There'll be an instructor, too. We'll race and then grab lunch at their restaurant." He glanced at me sideways, as if gauging my reaction. "Good surprise? Bad surprise?"

"*Amazing* surprise. This is one of those once-in-a-lifetime kind of experiences."

He laughed. "Oh, Emily. That's the kind of mindset we're going to have to change."

———

It didn't take long before we were dressed in a racing tracksuit each with thick padding on the shoulders and stripes down our arms. An instructor led us out to the course, his hand shading his eyes from the sun.

"The track is warm and dry today," he said. "We haven't had a drop of rain for days."

Julian pulled on a pair of leather driving gloves. "That's good. This is Ms. Giordano's first time driving on a racetrack."

"You're in for a treat, then," the instructor said to me with a smile. "We'll start off with a safety demonstration and then take it slow. I'll be in the car with you for both of your turns and we'll explore whatever you feel comfortable with." He put a hand on the roof of Julian's Porsche, smoothing along the polish. "This is a fine 911 Carrera."

"It is, isn't it? I haven't taken her out much lately, so it'll be great to stretch her legs a bit."

"She'll perform just nicely, I think."

Fredrick, the instructor, had us memorize the track and the safety rules. Where to stop, where to brake, the maximum speed we could hit and still make it around safely, and then he and Julian set off.

I stood in the empty stands and watched as he took the course in bursts of speed and slow, controlled turns, taking the curves with expert precision.

It might be my first time on a racetrack, but it didn't look like Julian's first try—not by a long shot.

When he finally pulled up next to me, the car's engine was

practically purring. Julian stepped out with a wide grin. "That," he said, "was *excellent.*"

I smiled at him. "You looked like an absolute pro. I'm sure the car is quaking at the prospect of being driven by me."

"Not at all." He tweaked my nose. "Go out there and give it your all."

"Will you watch me drive?"

Julian grinned. "I wouldn't miss it for the world, Ace."

I raised a finger in warning. "But no critiquing afterward or I'm never going anywhere with you again."

"Critique? Emily, I'm already surprised as hell that you're so enthusiastic about this. I had no idea you were into motorsports. At best, I hoped this would give you a laugh and we'd have a nice lunch." He ran his hand through his disheveled hair and for the first time I realized that, just maybe, he occasionally got a bit nervous too.

"It was a fantastic idea. Now, have a little rest and let me show you how it's really done." I shot him a cocky grin and walked around the car to the driving seat.

Fredrick talked me through the modes of the car, and when I felt comfortable in the seat I gently pulled out of the waiting lot. The car purred under my hands. I'd never been a car person, but it felt like driving silk—the car was just so responsive.

"And now, I want you to let go. Let the car tell you what to do, and listen to when I tell you to brake or speed up. Other than that… The track is yours, Ms. Giordano."

It took me a few rounds to get a hang of the curves and the long stretches of road, to learn the ins and outs of the car. But once I had it?

Speed was addictive. I'd never driven as fast as I did on that track. A wide smile was plastered on my face from start to finish as the car hugged the curves. Fredrick laughed at my exuberance when he finally instructed me to pull back up to the waiting lot.

I unbuckled my seat belt and took a few shaky steps out of the car. Julian was grinning at me.

"Did you *see* that?"

"I sure did."

"This is hands down the best day ever. I can't believe you took me racing, Julian."

He winked at me, hands in his pockets as he stepped close enough that I could smell his aftershave again.

Fredrick cleared his throat. "I'll fill up on fuel and park her by the restaurant for you, sir."

"Thank you, Fredrick." I heard the purr of the car as it pulled away, Julian still focused on me. "You did some excellent turns out there, Ace."

"Oh, did I, Mister Expert?"

"Mhmm." He reached out and hooked his fingers into the belt loops of my jeans, pulling me closer. This close, his handsomeness was no less overwhelming, sharp angles and soft eyes.

His hand cupped my cheek and his thumb slowly traced a line from my cheek to the corner of my lips. "Look at that smile," he murmured.

Perhaps it was the adrenaline or the happiness, but I rose up on my tiptoes and touched my lips to his.

He responded instantly. Reverent hands traced up my sides, cupped the back of my shoulders and tugged me closer. He kissed me with soft, sweet carefulness, like he'd wanted to do this forever and couldn't believe it was happening.

I wrapped my arms around his neck and gave in to the sensations. His hair was silky in my hands, and as I tugged, Julian groaned against my lips.

The softness snapped and the heat between us exploded into fire and flames. Julian's hands pulled at my waist so that my body was flush against his. I could feel the heat of his skin through the thin material of my shirt. Our mouths opened, tongues touching.

He was hard everywhere I was soft and our bodies fit together like they were made for this. Made to twine and support and kiss.

Under his guidance, the kisses grew slower, his tongue

coaxing and gentle. He pressed his lips to mine one final time before lifting his head.

But I wasn't ready to let go yet.

I buried my face in his neck and breathed a kiss at the hollow of his throat, right on the pulse that raced there. Every nerve ending of my body felt frayed, my stomach giddy with butterflies. His arms were tight around me.

"Hell," he murmured against my hair. "I didn't expect… *that*."

I laughed against his skin. "Yeah. Wow."

Julian pushed me back slightly to look at me, his eyes warm. His lips looked swollen and I flushed at the sight.

"You okay?"

"Yes."

"Not going to spook on me?"

"No." I smiled. "Definitely not."

Julian slung an arm around me and tucked me into his side, as if it was the easiest thing in the world, as if we belonged together. Intertwined like that, we headed for the restaurant. "Good," he said. "Because we are *certainly* doing that again."

14

EMILY

After lunch, Julian dropped me off two blocks away from my house, a bemused expression on his face. "I can't get over the feeling that I'm sneaking around with you. But we're both grown, and it's the middle of the day."

"Do you like it?"

His eyes darkened. "Sneaking around?"

"Yeah."

"Sometimes, yes. It can be very thrilling. Like how I'll sneak down into your office tomorrow, just to make sure you—"

I shook my head, smiling. "Julian, not at work, we *can't*."

"It's not fair." He reached across, one of his hands smoothing back my hair. "How can you expect me to work two floors above you and *not* swing by to spend time with you?"

"Because you have work to do. You have to become a proper billionaire, or haven't you heard? You're not there yet."

Julian's crooked smile appeared again. He was so handsome it hurt, my heart stuttering under his gaze.

"I see. My lady has demands."

"*The* lady does, yes. She demands to be left alone at work so she can do her job, for one, which she went to college for and very much enjoys."

Julian's eyes glittered. "Such a modern little lady. A true

inspiration to us all." His eyes shifted down to my lips briefly, and I was suddenly intensely aware of how close we were in the non-moving car.

I swallowed. "She also demands to be let out of this car soon."

"Eager to get rid of me?"

"Please. I've been counting the minutes until I could finally leave."

Julian's laugh was husky. "There you go again. Has your mouth ever gotten you in trouble?"

"Never." *Yes. It got me in this car with you.*

"Did you have a nice time today?"

"Yes, I did." I leaned my head against the soft leather headrest. "I had a fantastic time."

"I'm glad, Ace."

Our eyes caught and held. "I'll see you at work, Julian."

"You will," he said. "It's the large building with my last name on it."

"Asshole."

"You love it."

I smiled at him, my hand on the car door handle. I should go, and yet… this man was lethal.

His eyes were warm. "Kiss me before you leave."

I leaned over the center console and touched my lips lightly to his. My hand curved around his cheek, traced his jaw, the kiss soft and proper.

I traced his bottom lip with my tongue and he groaned in response. "*Emily…*"

"Whoops."

He shook his head, eyes warm. "You'll be the death of me."

I shot him a smile and closed the door behind me. The pavement back home was as familiar as the back of my hand, but I still managed to stumble on a crack in the ground. I hadn't done that since I was eight and bruised my knee.

Damn man with his damn kisses.

Goodbye kisses, too. The ones you give to someone you're planning on kissing again, and again, and again.

The earth underneath me had shifted a little.

These thoughts and more spun around in my head on Monday morning as I headed in to work. All day I was distracted—his presence was everywhere. I saw the Hunt logo on a folder and thought of him. The company's website had a large photo of him, surrounded by a group of software developers, and I caught myself staring at it blankly for longer than I was proud of.

Get it together, Emily.

Rachel popped her head into my office around noon.

"Emily? We're all heading to meeting room C for the meeting on the new branding logos. Are you coming?"

I glanced down at my watch. Shoot. "Yes, of course. I'll be right there." Collecting my papers quickly, I arrived at the conference room in a huff—not that there was any need to hurry. Josef and Sasha were pouring everyone coffee and Trent was still setting up the mirroring from his laptop. Still, I hadn't been this distracted at work for… as long as I could remember.

An hour later and the entire team was frustrated.

"It's not working," Josef declared. "I understand what we're going for here, but something about it just doesn't resonate."

"The color is too light," Sasha pointed out.

I frowned. "I don't think it's light enough," I said. "If we want it to work together with the other Hunt subsidiaries, then we need to streamline them."

"But if we do that, we run the risk of this launch blending in with the rest."

Rachel put her hands on her hips. "I think we need to take in a design consultant on this. Someone who can bring a pair of fresh eyes to the project, come up with some new ideas."

There was an outcry of objections from the various members.

I didn't know if bringing in consultants was a common practice or not at Hunt, but it made sense to me. We'd all been sitting with this for so long that we were practically blind.

My phone vibrated in my pocket. A week ago, I would have waited to check. Now? My heart sped up immediately. I snuck it out and put it alongside my folder.

Julian: I hate to do this after this weekend, but I have to go on an urgent work trip. I'll be gone most of the week.

Despite myself, my stomach sank with disappointment. I wouldn't see him today then, or tomorrow, it seemed.

Emily: This is how it's going to be? You take a girl to the racing course, show her a good time, and then you leave.

Julian: Yes. It's kind of my MO. There's nothing better than a one-race stand.

I had to stop myself from groaning.

Emily: Minus points for that one, Hunt.

Julian: I know. I could feel it as I hit send. Still find me cute?

Emily: Super-duper cute. Like a floppy-eared puppy or a baby otter.

Julian: Very amusing, my sarcastic friend.

Emily: Let's just say that my internal reaction to you has always been "awwww."

Julian: That's only because you haven't seen what I can do. You'll never use the word "floppy" again.

I quickly hid my phone along my leg and looked up. None of my colleagues were even looking at me, deep in discussion about a consultant, but I felt like I was flushing all over.

When I looked back down I saw that I'd gotten another text.

Julian: I can tell by your sudden silence that you have no idea how to respond to that. That's okay. You don't have to. But I hope you're picturing it.

Emily: You're an asshole. I'm in a meeting and now I can't look anyone in the eye.

Julian: Texting on company time? I entirely approve.

Emily: You're texting on company time too, buddy.

Julian: I am this company.

Emily: Fine, hotshot. But absolute power corrupts.
Julian: Good thing I have you to keep me grounded.
Emily: Where will this urgent trip take you?
Julian: New York, then Atlanta. I get back this weekend. Will you save some time for me?
Emily: I'll try. My boss is pretty demanding...
Julian: Fingers crossed.

I slid my phone back into my pocket and re-focused on the meeting. Josef was just finishing up a long tirade about the problems with a potential consulting hire—his opinions came as a surprise to absolutely no one.

My phone was quiet in my pocket, but I felt its weight.

One week.

15

EMILY

Denise clutched at my arm in the darkness. "This reminds me why we stopped going to these places."

I pulled her closer as we narrowly avoided getting hit by a group of girls stumbling on high heels. The music was ear-deafeningly loud, the place packed—one of San Francisco's hottest clubs.

"We're only twenty-five," I told her. "We can't throw in the towel yet."

"I know. Plus, I have to see Michael."

I smiled. Yes, the reason we were here, the one reason we'd decided to go out again to one of these high-end clubs far from home.

The calm and collected Michelin-star head chef had apparently been contracted to provide hors d'oeuvres and catering for the launch of a social media app.

Yeah. If that wasn't the most San Francisco thing you'd ever heard, I didn't know what was.

Anyway, seeing as it would attract quite the illustrious crowd, he had asked Denise if she wanted to go to the event. Which was why he let her bring me, clearly the most illustrious of them all.

"He said our names would be on the VIP list." Denise took

my hand and pulled me through a throng of men who smelled like smoke. A large banner hung behind the DJ with the name of the new app. *Ylang,* it read. I thought it sounded like an essential oil, which only proved how little I knew about tech.

Denise spoke with a club hostess, and with a nod and a smile, we were both let through to the VIP area.

"Space!" Denise said. "There's so much space up here!"

"And can you feel it? The air is so much fresher on the other side."

She laughed and found a table for us. She was right—the VIP section was both roomier and far less crowded than the general area below. There was space to dance, a private bar, and tables filled with food along the walls.

I squinted. "Is that an ice sculpture?"

"Yes. Apparently, the app creator requested it. It's supposed to be shaped like the app's logo."

"Well, it looks like something very different. It looks like—"

"Don't say it," a dark voice warned behind us. "You'll regret it."

Denise and I turned to where a tall, blond man grinned. "I'm sorry, but I just couldn't let you finish that sentence. I know I should have, though. Constructive criticism and all that."

"I'm sorry," I said. "I didn't mean… Um. I'm Emily."

He shook my hand. "I'm Rafe."

"Rafe!" Denise extended her own hand. "You're the creator of *Ylang,* if I'm not mistaken?"

"I am, yes."

"It's a pleasure."

"Likewise. I'm glad to see that you could make it to our little launch party."

"Well, I wouldn't precisely call it *little,*" I said, glancing down to where hostesses were walking through the crowd with sparklers.

Rafe laughed. "You're right. Go big or go home, I suppose?"

"In that case, we're never going home," Denise remarked.

"Have you ladies had anything to drink yet? I'd love to get

you each a glass of champagne. There's an open bar here in this section, and there's great food over by the wall."

"Great food by a great chef," Denise said.

"Of course! You're *that* Denise. Michael mentioned that he was bringing along two guests."

Denise's face flushed beautifully at being recognized and at having her new boyfriend talk about her. I cleared my throat. "Did you work on this app for long?"

He nodded and waved at a waiter to bring us something to drink. "Nearly eighteen months."

"Wow. That's impressive."

Rafe grinned. "Yes, but not quite as—ah, here he is! Glad you could make it, man."

Denise glanced past me, and I heard her small intake of breath. "*No way,*" she murmured. "Em, you won't believe this."

"I wouldn't miss it for the world." The voice was very deep and very familiar. I watched in shock as Julian and Rafe shook hands. He looked… just as I remembered. Tall, with dark, thick and unruly hair.

My throat went dry. It had only been five days but I realized that I'd really missed him—missed seeing the way his eyes danced or hearing whatever preposterous joke he'd make.

There was no one else quite like him.

Julian's attention snapped to me immediately. "Emily?"

"Julian," I said weakly. "I didn't think I'd see you here."

His voice was soft with pleasure. "Neither did I."

Denise reached around me and extended her hand. "I'm Denise, Emily's friend."

"A pleasure. I'm Julian Hunt."

"Let me check where those drinks are," Rafe said. "I'll be right back."

All three of us watched as he made his way to the bar, only to be stopped by a group of men before he could reach it.

"And he was never seen again," Julian said morosely. "The problem with launch parties is that they're never enjoyable for the launchee."

"The launchee?"

"It's a technical term," Julian said with a wave of his hand. "You'll learn the jargon eventually."

"Mhm," I drawled. "Right."

Adrenaline raced through me, my whole body reacting to being close to him. He was wearing a tailored suit, no tie, and the top button was undone. I was *stupidly* attracted to this man, and the week apart had only cemented that fact.

Denise glanced between us and I could see the smile hovering on her lips. "So, Julian," she said in a singsong voice. "What do you do?"

"I work in tech and development as well."

"So original," I commented and took a sip of my drink.

"Not at all. I'm—what do they call it these days? Basic?"

I rolled my eyes at him. There was not a single thing basic about the man, and he knew it. He grinned at me. "I work with Emily here, actually."

"Cool. Hmm." Denise nodded, and then leaned forward, her red hair spilling everywhere. "I'm trying really hard to pretend like I don't already know all of this, but I'm not a very good actress."

Julian's smile split into a wide laugh, his eyes glittering.

I shot her a glare. "Denise!"

"Come on, you knew what you were getting into when you offered to share your PB and J with me on the first day of sixth grade. I can't be held accountable for my behavior. Oh! I think I just spotted Michael! I'll see the two of you in a little while!"

I watched her scamper off in the direction of the food, fleeing from the scene, very abruptly leaving Julian and me alone. I'd have to thank her for it later.

Julian slid into the seat she'd vacated, and I was immediately hit by his cologne, the strong frame of his shoulder and his thigh touching mine.

We looked at each other in silence for a few moments.

"Hi," I whispered.

He smiled. "Hi."

"When did you get back?"

"About four hours ago."

"You look good. New York agreed with you."

"It was the same as always." He shrugged. "Tall buildings and too many people. I missed this place."

"Oh?" I inched closer, eliminated the sliver of space between us. "This club in particular?"

Julian smiled crookedly and gave me a very obvious once-over, eyes trailing down my neck, skimming over the tight black dress I wore, and the small glittery bracelet that circled my right wrist. I felt naked under the heat of his gaze.

"Judging by its current clientele, *yes*."

I swallowed. "How do you know Rafe? Do you belong to the same 'Titans of Industry' club?"

Julian snorted. "Yes. We're on the same mailing list and we go to meetings every month."

"Complain about the estate tax?"

"Always. We compare notes for world domination."

"My money's on you."

His hand reached out, fingers tracing down my bare arm. Goose bumps followed his touch. "And why are you here? Are you looking to hook up with someone?"

"And if I were?"

Julian's eyes darkened. "Then I'm happy I came. I'll be the one in the back, waving a giant homemade sign saying 'pick me, pick me.'"

I burst out laughing. He was being silly, but my insides warmed at the thought. Doubt had crept back during the days he'd been gone. Was I making a stupid decision? Jeopardizing my career for mere attraction? A fling? How long would I have until his attention waned?

"No. I'm here because Denise practically dragged me along. She's dating the Michelin-star chef who's catering the event."

"Michelin-star, huh?"

"Yes."

"That just accompanies his name? Necessary to include in the description?"

I bumped his shoulder with mine. "*Yes*, it is. When your best friend starts dating a hotshot you have to brag a little bit. Don't worry. You'll get there someday."

"Will I?" He raised an eyebrow. "And what might a woman say about me, someday?"

I pretended to consider it. "That's tricky. I mean, billionaire is ruled out—we've already established that. Software developer? Sounds too nerdy. Entrepreneur, I guess."

"That doesn't sound too good."

I shook my head sadly. "I'm not liking your odds, buddy. But hang in there."

He leaned his head back against the seat with a dramatic sigh. "What's a poor man to do? I'll just have to rely on my dazzling good looks, brilliant wit and piles of cash."

I reached out and patted his thigh. It was meant to be a playful gesture, a commiserative touch in the game we were playing, but his hand caught mine. Our fingers threaded, his skin warm and rough against mine.

"Don't," he warned. "Or I'll kiss you right here, right now, and I don't care if your friend sees."

Heat raced through me. I wanted that kiss. I wanted him, this crazy fling and all the crazy consequences that it might lead to.

Would it jeopardize my job? Undoubtedly.

But I hadn't let my guard down in so, so long. And no one had ever made me feel like him. *Ever.*

I stood up and tugged at his hand. "Come on."

"Where are we going?"

I kept my hand in his and steered course for the bar. "We're going to have a drink, and then we're going to dance."

16

EMILY

A very loud and very annoying sound cut through my sleep. The blasting refused to stop, completely without mercy.

I blinked my eyes open.

Daylight. I was in my own bed. There was no one else in it with me.

I closed my eyes again at the blinding headache that followed the establishment of those three little facts. With eyes still closed, I reached out and grabbed my obnoxiously loud phone. How was it still ringing? Didn't phones have mood sensors these days? If not, they should. My mood was loud and clear: make another sound and I'll throw you in the toilet bowl.

It took me two attempts to read the name on the screen.

Denise.

I rolled over and pressed answer, burying my face under the comforter.

"Mgghnnagh," I said.

Her pealing laughter came through the phone. "I take it you're feeling super perky and happy?"

"Ugh, Denise, I swear—"

"I've been up since six. Made pancakes, did the laundry. Even managed to clear out my closet while I was taking a break.

Then I did my taxes for this year, the next year, and the coming decade."

"I hate you."

"I know you do."

"Honestly, you're not sparking any joy for me right now."

She laughed again and the sound cut through my head like a knife. I rolled over and forced my eyes open. The world waited for no one, it seemed. "Did little birds help you dress in the morning too?"

"Funny you should ask, because *yes, yes they did.*"

"I hope they all flew into your window on their way out," I mumbled.

"What was that?"

"Nothing."

"I just wanted to check that you're okay, Em. You were pretty… indisposed when we left the club."

I swallowed at the flood of hazy memories. "God."

"Yes, you could say that," she laughed. "Honestly, you were hilarious."

"*God!* Why did I behave like I was an eighteen-year-old with a stolen ID?"

"It happens. Don't feel bad, Emily."

"I do. How can I show my face at work?"

"No one knows but Julian. You're making this into a bigger deal than it was, honest."

I clasped a hand to my mouth as an awful thought struck me. "I didn't throw up?"

"Nope. Your record is still clean from freshmen year."

"Does Michael hate me? I'm sure he does. If he tells you that I'm a bad influence and you should stop being friends with me, you shouldn't listen."

Denise laughed again. "He doesn't. No one does. We all had a bit to drink."

"All right," I said slowly. "I'm going to ponder my awful existence and think through everything that happened last night. If I need help confirming something I'll text you."

"I'll reply," she said. "But please take an aspirin before you do any pondering."

"No promises."

"Emily."

"Thank you for taking the cab home with me yesterday," I said, remembering.

"Of course. I'm not about to send you off with a guy I just met, regardless of how hot he makes you."

I groaned. "Was it that obvious?"

"Emily, you two made out in the middle of the dance floor."

"Okaythankstalktoyoulaterbye." I hung up and stared at my ceiling for a solid five minutes. If I wanted to be seen as a grown woman, one capable of handling a little office fling with no drama and no consequences, I had effectively blown that image to smithereens.

With my self-respect in tatters, I pulled the sheet up to cover me completely. Hiding from reality to cope with reality, so to speak. Last night had been… there were no words. I decided to do what I'd told Denise I would, and went through the entire evening, step by painful step. Where had it gone wrong?

Julian had shown up.

We'd spoken, and I'd made the decision to go for it. Fortune favors the bold and all that. We'd done tequila shots, and he'd licked the salt from the back of my hand. He'd told me I looked stunning—I could still feel the exhale of his breath on my ear as he whispered it to me. I shivered at the memory.

We'd danced for a bit, ridiculous movements to make the other laugh. Denise and Michael had joined in occasionally, and we'd had another round of shots. This time I'd demanded to lick the salt off of *his* hand.

We'd laughed and danced some more. He was a good dancer, and I'd made sure that we moved closer to each other. Close enough that… we'd apparently made out. Vague recollections of hot lips against mine came back, and I touched my mouth. It seemed impossible.

But no.

I'd challenged him to a racing duel.

I'd said that he smelled good enough to eat.

I'd told him that he was the best kisser of my life… *ugh*. That was a memory I couldn't touch, not even with a ten-foot pole.

A flashback hit me with vivid force. He'd had his arms around my waist, and I'd said that he could come home with me. Or, for honesty's sake, I'd *demanded* it.

Julian had laughed and bent to kiss my lips again.

"Not tonight, Ace. Not like this. But don't you dare think it's because I don't want to."

Well, he clearly had more honor and self-discipline than I did. There was no way I could show my face around him again. If he hadn't minded the eight-year age difference before, he most certainly would now. I'd acted like a teenager. *"That was the best kiss of my life."*

Bleh!

There was a rhythmic knock on my door.

"Emily? It's nearly noon. I made breakfast and left some eggs on low heat for you. But you're going to have to come and eat it soon or I'll turn the heat off."

I groaned again, this time with guilt. Turner. What a great role model for my nineteen-year-old brother I was, coming home drunk in the middle of the night. That hadn't happened since… ever?

Despite the pounding headache, I swung out of bed and pulled on my robe. "Sorry, Turner. I didn't mean to sleep so long. I'll be downstairs in a bit."

"Good."

I hopped in the shower and prayed that the warm water would wash away the shame. It didn't, but my caramel-scented shampoo and conditioner brightened my mood. Bought at a hair salon, the (ridiculously) overpriced set had been a spur of the moment splurge, but not a shower had gone by where it had failed to make me smile. As Denise would say: targeted self-care —get the expensive shampoo and you can survive a shitty car.

I trudged down the stairs fifteen minutes later. My hair was wet and my head still ached, but I felt roughly 1500 percent better. It's scientifically proven that showers have that effect. For real.

Turner sat by the kitchen island with a familiar book and didn't even look up when I entered.

"Are you re-reading that biography again?"

He nodded and shut it gently. "I'm sure there were things I missed the first time."

The smell of bacon and eggs wafted from the stove. He'd put aluminum foil over the pan to keep it warm. My heart swelled.

"You're the best little brother in the world, you know that?"

He snorted. "You're exaggerating."

I grabbed a plate and started scooping up food, pausing to shove a piece of bread into the toaster. "Perhaps. What I mean is: I'm very happy and grateful that you're my brother."

"Oh." A faint blush crept up on his pale cheeks. "I'm happy that you're my sister too."

"Despite the fact that I come home at unseemly hours?"

I took a seat opposite him at the island. I might be playing it for jokes, but I was worried. I had tried to be a role model for so long, but now we were both adults with full-time jobs. The landscape had changed and I didn't know how to adapt.

"You said you were going out with Denise and that it might run late. I wasn't worried."

"Good." I headed to the fridge to hunt down some orange juice. "What are your plans for today?"

"I've finished going through all the VHS and DVDs. Could you look over and see if you agree with my sorting? If you do, I'll drive them over to Goodwill this afternoon."

"Of course, yeah. Thanks for doing all that."

He shrugged. "It needs to be done. I was thinking that we could start on the rooms upstairs next."

Unease churned in my stomach, but I pushed away the fear. He was right. I'd kept the house mostly as it was when we'd lived here as a family, but we were both grown now. One of us would move out soon, and judging by the circled apartments I'd seen in the newspaper I figured it might be Turner.

We couldn't live in the past.

"That's a great idea. I'll help you. Maybe we can start on Mom's hobby room upstairs later."

"Sounds good."

He opened his book again and we fell back into companionable silence. I studied him as I ate. His jaw had grown sharper, and his shoulders slightly wider. When had I missed that? When had he grown up?

I felt my phone vibrate in the pocket of my sweatpants. I dreaded who it might be and took another big sip of OJ.

"Your phone is buzzing," Turner pointed out.

"Yep."

"Aren't you curious?"

No. Just ashamed and wallowing in self-pity.

"A bit."

"Check it," Turner said and returned to his book. I smiled at his unruly mop of hair and his disinterest. Time to bite the bullet... I unlocked my phone.

Julian: I'm guessing you're in somewhat of a delicate state today.

I could feel the heat that flooded my cheeks at his observation.

Emily: The most delicate of states, yes.

Julian: Does it help if I say I am too?

Emily: Sure, but I'm guessing you've already completed your morning run.

Julian: ...

Julian: I plead the fifth.

I sighed and put my phone down on the counter. He was being nice about it, but I'd still made a fool of myself. I'd have to apologize or find some way to backtrack from the sex-crazed, lustful, clearly *too* infatuated woman I'd been last night.

Yeah, I had been in crazy territory last night.

My phone buzzed again.

Julian: Promise me you won't spend the day overthinking.

Hah. Was I that obvious?

Emily: Considering I was probably underthinking yesterday, I better make up for it today.

Julian didn't reply.

No, instead he called me, his name flashing across the screen.

Hell. Could I not answer? Would that be suspicious? My mind raced. In what situation could you text, but not talk on the phone? Someone who was in a library could. Could I say that I was?

"Who's that?" Turner asked, peering over at where my phone was aggressively blaring.

"A friend I met out last night," I replied. Hopping off the stool, I headed for the door to the backyard. "I'll take it out here."

Turner nodded and returned to his book, and I thanked my lucky stars that my brother was not the nosy type.

With a nervous hand, I pressed answer. "Hey."

Julian's tone was teasing. "I was starting to wonder if you were ever going to pick up."

"I was considering not. You know, since my bags are fully packed and the car loaded up. I'm leaving for Canada later today to start a new life."

His laughter reached me through the phone. "It's cold up there this time of year."

"Shoot. I'd forgotten to pack my ski things. Thanks for reminding me."

"You know, I was really surprised to see you there last night."

"I can imagine it was quite a shock," I said and took a seat on one of the lawn chairs. The sun hadn't yet passed the roof of our neighbors' house, and the backyard was a tad chilly.

"Happily surprised," he amended. "I had a good time."

"Despite the fact that I acted like a drunk sorority girl?"

"*Because* of that," he said. "I have a suggestion."

"What?"

"You said you might've saved some time for me this weekend. Let me swing by your place later with a box of donuts. Ensure you're actually okay."

I laughed weakly. The offer of delicious, sugary and fried treats beckoned before me like the gates to heaven. But I felt hollow and my head still ached like a mother-lover, as my grandma would have said.

"Technically, we spent time together yesterday," I pointed out. "That was our once a week."

"Are you turning down food? Ace, now I know you're actually sick."

"Just hungover. I'm going to recuperate and spend some time with my brother, but I'll see you later this week. Perhaps I'll be the one bringing you some donuts."

"I look forward to it."

"Bye, Julian."

"Bye."

17

JULIAN

Perhaps I had pushed too hard. But how could I resist teasing her after what she'd said to me on Saturday?

Hearing her say that she wanted me was perhaps the single biggest ego-boost I'd ever experienced in my life. Lord knows I wanted her, wanted to make her smile and laugh and gasp in my bed. Now, if only I could get her to say it sober…

Given her dedication to her job, I knew there'd be a backlash of some sort. That was where the donuts came in—I would try to bribe her out of her shell with gooey goodness and let her know that she had nothing to worry about. But that had failed.

Thoughts of Emily distracted me from the things I *actually* had to do, like running a company or lecturing my brother. At least I had help with the former, but trying to talk sense into my old-enough-to-know-better brother?

I was entirely on my own.

Ryan sank further into one of the chairs in my office. "Come on, Julian. You're being unreasonable."

I raised an eyebrow. "How am I being unreasonable, exactly? For requiring you to have accomplished something to get your trust fund?"

"Look, it's not what Dad intended when he gave you the reins, and you know it."

It was *exactly* what Dad had intended when he not only put me in charge but wrote a letter detailing how he wanted his affairs taken care of. That he didn't trust Ryan's mother with these decisions or to make the tough calls.

He'd been right on both accounts.

"I understand that you're upset," I tried. "I know what it's like to be twenty and think you know everything. What I'm saying isn't—"

Ryan slumped in the chair and pushed his cap down further. "I get it. My ideas are stupid."

I sighed and prayed for patience. "No, they're just a bit underdeveloped sometimes. If you have something real you want to do, something you've thought through, I'll be happy to hear it. But I don't think opening a diving school off the coast of Costa Rica is going to be your big break, nor should it be paid for by your trust fund."

"It's basically a done deal, Julian. Why don't you believe me?"

I crossed my arms. "I can imagine that it might feel that way. But under no circumstances will I wire transfer 40,000 dollars to your friend 'Jacko.'"

Ryan rose, animosity clear in every line of his body. "Fine. I guess I'll see you around or something."

"Come over for dinner this week."

He shoved his hands in his pockets. "I'm probably heading to Mammoth to ski with some friends."

My heart sank. "All right. Text me when you're back."

He gave a noncommittal nod and headed toward the door of my office. His anger was so palpable that I almost felt like checking my head for horns.

"Ryan, you know I care about you. That's why I'm doing this."

"Yeah, yeah." The door shut behind him.

I sank down in my chair and rubbed my temples. That went as well as I'd been expecting, which was to say *disastrous*.

Ryan and I had never truly been close, something I blamed

about a hundred different people for, including myself. Attempts I made as an adult to rectify that sometimes went very well, and other times… like this.

It was as if he wanted me to be a fun-loving big brother—a part I usually played gladly—but who also indulged him in a way that Dad never had. I knew that my stepmother mainly saw me as a financial asset, and it pained me that some of her perspectives had been passed down to Ryan.

The one good thing on my schedule for the day was a meeting with the press and marketing team. The yearly LA tech industry event was happening this week, and Hunt Industries was scheduled to hold one of the seminars and introduce a few new updates.

But the meeting meant I'd have a chance to see Emily for the first time since she blew me a drunken goodbye kiss on Saturday night, heading into the cab with Denise. I was 99 percent sure that she'd blush with embarrassment when she saw me. Hell, I would bet on it if I could.

The team was already gathered when I arrived at meeting room C. Faint traces of laughter and discussion could be heard through the glass window and I paused just out of sight.

Emily was deep in conversation with Rachel and Trent, her hands moving as she spoke. Her dark hair was loose and long, and now I knew just how silky it felt through my fingers. Sasha slipped them a newspaper article and the entire group broke out into laughter. Emily's eyes glittered with happiness.

She was beautiful, truly, from the inside out. A heart-shaped face framed by her long dark hair, eyes that switched from beguiling to angry to teasing faster than clouds during a storm.

I wanted her in my bed.

I wanted her in my *life*.

As if she read my thoughts, her gaze found mine through the glass and on cue her cheeks flushed a lovely, blush pink.

I couldn't help it—I grinned at her.

Rachel looked up to see what had caught Emily's attention

and, always insolent, rolled her eyes at me. "Will you join us or continue standing outside like a weirdo?"

"Wait a moment," I told them, raising a hand. They all watched me as I pretended to inspect them all, my eyes narrowed. "You passed."

Press and marketing was one of my favorite departments, after the technicians and the software developers. They tended to be quick thinkers, witty conversationalists, and creative. Just like Emily.

As opposed to the, ahem, accounting department or our in-house lawyers. Though thank God they existed, as I shuddered at the thought of having to work in Excel on a daily basis.

"Do you want to start?" Trent asked, but I shook my head.

"No. Go ahead, run your drill."

Emily was two chairs down, too far for me to reach under the table. I glanced her way but her attention was staunchly on Trent.

"All right. Well, this will be the LA Tech and Industry Conference's sixteenth year. It's a massive event, attracting both national and international companies as well as hundreds of investors, web developers, and contractors. I know that not all of you were on the team when the conference came around last year, so I recommend that you use the coming two days to read up. Naturally, the event also draws considerable media and press coverage. We're going to be there for two full days, and by full, I mean *busy.*"

Rachel leaned forward. "And by busy we mean the don't-drink-too-much-water-because-you-won't-have-time-to-use-the-restroom kind of busy."

I cleared my throat. "Our HR rep would frown on that. Please, everyone, I encourage proper hydration."

Trent ignored our interjections. "Most of what we've been working on for these past few months will be displayed. The rebranded interface, the new colors and logo—it will all be there. Hunt Industries will run a monitor and a workshop."

Trent turned to me, expectation in his gaze.

I rose and braced my hands on the table. "This year we're releasing a 2.0 version of the software we developed two years ago but had to pull from market. It's essentially video chat for doctors."

I pulled up an image on the connected projector so they could all see. "It connects doctors with patients in their own homes. Naturally, this isn't meant to replace actual hands-on healthcare, but it allows for people to call and ask about things that don't require a visit to the hospital. Parents might want to ask about a rash on their kid's arm, what to do for a bee sting—that sort of thing. It will save enormous amounts of time and resources for both the patients and the medical staff."

I flicked through the different images, showcasing the interface and the testing rounds. Emily was in the back, watching me with large eyes. While I didn't suffer from stage fright, I was intimately aware of her eyes on me.

"A trial version is available in select areas around the US at the moment, but we want this system to go national. The aim is to get buyers, investors, media—we want everyone to get involved."

Trent nodded. "We have prepared a long line-up. These are going to be busy days, folks, with interviews and articles. I want you to check and double-check your emails continuously these coming days."

I took a seat, and Rachel cleared her throat. "Let's go through the roles. I'll be joining Julian in LA to handle the press section of things—his schedule is packed from morning to evening. Josef, you're following along as well to help with the set-up of the workshop. Trent, Sasha, and Emily will hold down the fort here. Constant communication between us during this time will be crucial."

I frowned. "Just two from the press and marketing team?"

Trent nodded. "We figured that was the best division of labor. Do you disagree?"

"Emily should join as well. She works with press, and this

tends to be our largest event of the year. She'll need to know what to do for next year. Let her shadow you, Rachel."

I could see Emily's piqued interest from the end of the table. The conference would be the best place for her to meet people and learn more about the industry she was new to.

And it would let her see you in action, a small voice whispered in my mind. I couldn't help it. I wanted her to see me as someone she respected, and not just as some rich playboy *almost*-billionaire, as she kept reminding me.

Rachel nodded thoughtfully. "It makes sense. What do you think, Emily?"

Emily's smile was blinding. "I'd love to join you. I'd be doing more or less the same work as here, but being on the ground would give me hands-on experience. I'd be happy to go."

"It's settled then," I said. "Call down to administration and have them book her onto our flight and add another room to the hotel booking."

Trent frowned. "Last I heard, it was full. Administration made reservations for Hunt months back to make sure we got the right number of rooms in the hotel right next to the conference."

"We could share my room," Rachel offered. "If you don't mind?"

Emily shook her head. "Not at all."

"Great. It's settled then. I'll send all of you updated agendas and material, and we'll talk again later."

I caught the look of excitement on Emily's face, nearly identical to the one she'd worn when she realized we were going racing, and my heart did an odd little twist. I didn't know what we were doing, or where we were heading, but I knew I wanted to make her smile like that many, many more times.

18

EMILY

I was in an airplane, in a first-class seat, on my way to LA on a business trip.

Each of those four things on its own—airplane, first-class, LA, business trip—would have been enough to give me the happiness equivalent of a sugar rush.

All four at the same time?

Pinch me.

Traveling like this had never happened when I was in college, and never in my childhood. Our family holidays had been amazing, but they'd mainly been road trips, except for the time we visited my grandma in New Orleans.

When I worked for Pet and Co, I had gone on a business trip to an exhibition on cat food in Sacramento that included an overnight stay at a motel. If I would never have to analyze another ad for cat litter or dog food in my life I'd die a happy woman.

They greet you by name in first class. *Welcome on board, Ms. Giordano. Would you like something to drink?*

If it hadn't been eight o'clock in the morning, I would have asked for champagne.

Okay, fine, if my co-workers hadn't been around I would have asked for champagne, despite the early hour.

Rachel and Josef were working across the aisle from me, their fingers flying over keyboards. It was only an hour-long flight but apparently, things were already getting hot and heavy down at the conference.

I took a steadying breath. I'd done all that I could do. I'd practically worked until midnight every day for the past week to ensure I knew everything I might need for these events. If someone asked me to describe the SEO plan for the new healthcare system, I could recite it forwards, backwards and sideways.

HTML, CSS, UX, UI, API, and SDK.

It was like practicing for the SATs all over again, but I felt shakily confident in my newfound computing knowledge. If everything else failed, I'd hold up my press badge as a weapon, shouting *I create ads, not apps!*

It would have to do.

I'd packed my suitcase with three of my best business-casual outfits, perfect for the kind of expensive-but-slouchy look that seemed so popular in the tech world. Josef always wore button-downs and chinos, for example, and Rachel regularly sported silk blouses in neon colors and casual prints.

My stomach was a mess of excited nerves. My first real work trip. I was going to *kick ass*. I was going to get a solid hour of work done on the plane and then skip along to the first-class bathroom to spritz on perfume and run a brush through my hair. I'd arrive in full control and smelling of florals.

At least I'd planned to—but then a certain someone chose the seat next to me and ensured I couldn't think of anything but him. Either it was a cosmic joke, or it was the maneuvering of a very influential, very charming, very insistent CEO.

Julian propped up a small laptop on the tray table but didn't open it. There were a million things I felt like saying to him, but none in front of our co-workers across the aisle—who might or might not be listening.

Julian's hand tapped against the chrome of his closed laptop. "Are you excited, Emily?"

"Yes. Thank you again for suggesting that I should go on this trip."

His eyes flitted to where Josef and Rachel worked across the aisle before they returned to me. "Don't mention it. It'll be a good learning experience."

"I think so, too."

This was the first proper conversation we'd had since the phone call on Sunday, apart from the necessary work talk. I needed to make up for what happened over the weekend—make sure he knew I wasn't just a young employee who couldn't handle her alcohol.

I wanted to be as cool as the women he usually dated.

But my mind refused to come up with witty things to say. It had gone silent, unable to focus on anything apart from the way our legs touched and how close his hand was.

Julian glanced across the aisle again and his jaw clenched in frustration. With a meaningful glance at me, he pulled out his phone. My confusion was short; he offered it to me after a few seconds of typing. He'd opened a new page on Notes.

I should have requested seats far away from them.

I couldn't help the smile that spread across my features. My fingers brushed against his as I took the phone from him.

Why? What would you have done if we were alone?

Julian's smile was sly as he typed his reply. *Ordered us both something to drink and challenged you to another game of Never Have I Ever. I've never played it airborne before.*

This time, his fingers lingered slightly over mine as he handed me his phone.

I grinned and typed my response. *Please don't mention anything pertaining to alcohol around me ever again, please and thank you. Also, it's not even nine o'clock in the morning.*

He was openly smiling now. *Don't start. You were cute.*

You're an enabler, I typed back. *Shame on you.*

If by 'enabling' you mean complimenting a beautiful woman I'm interested in, then sure, I'll take it. I can enable you all night.

The blush spread across my cheeks like wildfire and I pulled my hair forward to cover my expression. Our co-workers had only to look across the aisle to see us. Beside me, Julian coughed to hide his laughter. Damn man with his damn words.

I should say no out of principle, I wrote back. *Anything complimentary on my part and your head might explode.*

Good call. We are on an airplane, after all.

We weren't even talking about anything real at this point, but the smile that hovered on my lips refused to disappear. *I take my civic duty very seriously.*

Julian snorted. *Dropping you off around the block from your house, passing notes in class... why do I feel like a high schooler around you?*

My heart beat erratically in my chest as I read his words. That made two of us. *I'm still waiting for you to ask me to prom. You can't just assume, you know.*

Julian didn't share my hard-won restraint—his mega-watt smile was wide. *Perhaps I want to make it special. When you least expect it, Ace. Consider yourself warned.*

I rolled my eyes at him and settled back in my seat. Our legs were touching from the thigh all the way down to the calf, now. As I watched, Julian deleted our whole conversation and jotted down a much longer message.

I want you to know that I'm not going to hold you to anything you said on Saturday evening. I want you sober and sane when you finally admit that we're perfect together.

I looked up at him, his eyes glittering with humor and sincerity. "Okay," I murmured.

His hand traced a line across his leg, nearing where mine was resting. "Just okay?"

"No. It's great. I'm—"

"Julian, do you know— Oh, sorry. Were you going through the agenda?" Rachel leaned across the aisle, her expression focused.

"Yes," Julian responded smoothly. "But I think we have it under control. What's up?"

I exhaled shakily and opened my own laptop. A narrow escape, sure, but I knew I was in deep, deep trouble.

I was developing feelings for Julian freaking Hunt.

19

EMILY

Imagine if Disneyland had been designed by the editorial staff of *Forbes,* and sponsored by the founder of a massive social media company.

Can you picture it?

Neither could I until I was standing wide-eyed inside the LA Tech and Industry Conference. It was a mixture of people, gadgets, and oddly enough—an inflatable bouncy castle. At one stand, a man was projected into a scarily realistic hologram ten feet away. Drones whirred above us.

"Soak it in," Rachel said to my right. "This is nerd paradise. Keep a steady hand on your phone, or someone might take it."

"There are pickpockets here?"

"No, I mean someone will offer to reprogram your software and give it back to you with fourteen new apps, all in the beta stage. Just hold on to it."

I patted my phone through the pocket of my grey blazer. *I'll protect you, little one.* "Thanks."

Rachel handed me a badge with my name and the logo of Hunt Industries on it. "This is your lifeline. It gets you in everywhere you need to go."

Josef put down the heavy bag with camera equipment next to us and quirked an eyebrow. "She's right. I've been told there's even a black market for them, for people who didn't manage to get access to this place."

"What a great business idea."

"I know, right?! You could probably get a couple of hundred bucks for it."

"And your severance check," Rachel said dryly. She was eyeing a map of the hall and the connecting buildings. "We're setting up shop in studio eighteen. Come on, you two. Let's head over there before we have to meet Julian for his first interview."

"The man is a machine," Josef grumbled, bending to pick up the camera bag again. I could only agree. I'd seen Julian's schedule for the conference, and if I'd been anxious about my own, it was absolutely nothing compared to his. For a solid hour today, he had ten-minute interviews scheduled back-to-back with various tech magazines. During these two days, he was the face of the brand, and the world was watching.

By lunch, my feet ached.

By afternoon, my head had joined the chorus too. I had shaken so many hands, each person I met more smiley than the next, that I probably ought to douse my hands in sanitizer.

"You work for Hunt Industries? That's amazing!" was the standard response.

Somehow, the name seemed to unlock something—a gleam in their eyes. Sure, I'd known how big Hunt was when I took the job, but it was something else entirely to see people's perception of me change with the statement. Julian's reputation certainly preceded him. I was handed twelve resumes—I counted them— all of which I politely slipped into my purse and said I'd pass on to HR.

Rachel and I were texting every five minutes.

Are you setting up for the interview with B.H. Wells?

Yes, questions read through and approved. Are you almost done with the press conference?

Yes, heading your way now. Should be in studio nine in a minute.

I had laughingly suggested that we should have brought walkie-talkies, but it was the truth.

Astonishingly, Julian looked just as put-together and devilishly handsome as he had on the flight in the early morning hours. He'd changed from his chinos and blazer into a fitted dark suit, *sans* tie, and his hair was neatly combed back. He seemed to be wearing all of his titles at once—bad boy billionaire, playboy philanthropist, Ivy League graduate, CEO and a world player on the tech scene. The faint trace of a smile never left his lips, as if he was ready to break out into *it's-nice-to-see-you-again* at any given moment.

And why hadn't he run for president yet? Who knew? I didn't doubt that he'd win that too if he put his magnificent mind to it.

Rachel or I spent a not insignificant portion of the day just escorting him back and forth between interviews. We were his armor—the bulletproof vest.

Someone came up to talk to him—*Sorry, Mr. Hunt doesn't have time right now.*

The interview ran over time—*We're going to have to cut it there. Mr. Hunt has a busy schedule.*

We played bad cop so he could flash an apologetic smile and skip out without offending anyone. Yeah, he could've run for president.

I remarked as much when we were waiting backstage for a panel he was participating in. *How tech is both a disruptive and creative force.* It would be livestreamed, and Julian would be joined by several other creators and moguls. His name was listed first on the prospectus.

"Politics? No, I'd be a terrible politician."

I shook my head and peeked around the curtain. The assembled crowd was massive. "That's a shame. You'd gain a lot of support." *All* women eligible to vote, no doubt.

Julian pulled me back, an arm around my waist. "How does it look out there?"

"Good. A lot of people."

He quirked an eyebrow. "It's a good thing I don't have stage fright."

I would rather have walked naked into a beehive than do what he was about to do, but I kept that to myself. "And you're all set? Have everything you need?"

Julian ignored my questions altogether. His lips curled into that crooked smile that meant he was about to say something outrageous.

"How many times have you been asked out today?"

"What?"

"This place has a nine-to-one distribution of men to women. Half of them have most likely never seen a beautiful woman up close before. And a woman like you?" He ran a strand of my hair between two fingers, eyes warm. "You could walk out of here leading the pack."

I swallowed. "Three times."

"I'm not surprised."

There was no reason to elaborate, nothing to be defensive about, but my voice was breathy when I added: "I turned them all down."

Julian's eyes darkened. His hand reached down and clasped the badge hanging around my neck. "I like that my name is on this."

"I couldn't get them to drop it."

His eyes flashed back up to mine, humor dancing in them. The collar of his shirt was slightly askew, and I reached up on my tiptoes to fix it. I stiffened the collar and flattened the fabric over his wide, strong shoulders.

"There," I murmured. "*Now* you're ready."

We were close enough that I felt the warmth of his exhale. "I was born ready."

"Mhm?"

"Mmm." He bent to close the distance between us, lips about to close on mine, but a deafening sound rang out from the speakers. We both jerked back.

"Sorry! Just some mic feedback," the moderator called out. "We're almost ready to begin—all of our panelists are waiting backstage. Sorry to have kept you waiting, folks."

"Showtime," I told Julian, curling my hands into fists. A dimly lit space with my stunningly attractive and expert-kisser boss? *Deadly.*

Julian grinned and took my hand in his, pressing a kiss to the soft skin at my wrist. "Wish me luck, Ace?"

"Break a leg," I whispered.

"Our first panelist is none other than the young tech genius from San Francisco who gave us *Audio-Feed.* He's here this year to introduce two new products his company is releasing, and we couldn't be more excited to hear about them. Julian Hunt, everybody!"

Julian gave me a wink before disappearing out on stage. He walked confidently and gave the crowd a single, strong wave before shaking hands with the moderator.

I sank down on the chair provided for me backstage and tried to catch my breath. He was a force, and I wasn't sure if I was strong enough to survive him. My phone screen lit up with a new message from Rachel.

Is he on stage? Everything OK?

I took a deep breath and typed back a quick response. *Yes, he's fine.*

Damn fine.

Dinner that evening was a simple affair—the four of us grabbed pizza in a small restaurant opposite the conference hall, wall to wall with our hotel. It was nearly ten in the evening, but I wolfed down slice after slice as if I was carbo-loading for a marathon.

Which I was, in a way. We still had another day of the conference to go.

Rachel picked a piece of pepperoni from her pizza and glanced over at Julian. "You've never joined us for post-conference victory pizza before, Boss."

He raised a finger at her. "Only because you've never invited me."

Both Rachel and Josef laughed at that. "*Right.* As if that was what was missing. *An invitation.*"

He rolled his eyes and reached for another piece of the barbecue chicken. The others might have dropped it, but I was curious. "What do you usually do? Don't tell me you've hit the gym or something previous years. No one can have that much energy, not even you."

Julian looked over at me with glittering eyes, as if daring me to let him prove *just* how much energy he had. I looked away quickly.

"Oh no," Rachel said. "He usually has dinner with some of the other big names, discussing world domination. Three tech titans walk into a bar…"

"Or you go on some steamy date. It was an actress when we were here two years ago, right? I can't remember the name now." Josef frowned. "It made the headlines. Great publicity for the company, Boss."

"Josef," Julian chided.

"She was in a space movie that year, I think. Right?"

Julian took a bite of his pizza and avoided my gaze. "I'm a man of discretion."

Rachel was grinning. "Josef, Julian's personal life might be a goldmine for us, but we don't *tell* him that."

"Is that so?" I leaned back in my chair. "No famous dates this time around?"

Julian played with the rim of his glass and shook his head slightly. His gaze felt like a caress, warm and secretive, holding a secret only we knew. "No, not this year. I'm actually seeing someone."

"Oh la la," Rachel said. "I can imagine she'd object to you taking Hollywood out on the town."

Julian's gaze slid to mine again. "She might. Not that I'd want to, anyway. I've always been a one-woman kind of man."

"Is this a serious thing?" Josef asked.

"It's in the early stages so far," Julian said. "But I have high hopes."

My heart was beating so loudly I was amazed that nobody called me on it. I wouldn't be surprised if Rachel turned to me at any second with a shocked gasp, declaring that she knew I was the woman in question. *J'accuse!*

I met Julian's gaze. He looked exactly like I felt. Calm on the surface, smoldering below.

"But it's going well so far?"

He gave me a small smile. "I think so, yes. Even if I don't always know what she's thinking."

The mood had changed between us, and I was sure I wasn't the only one who'd noticed. I reached for the last slice of pepperoni and cleared my throat. "Just invent an app for telepathy."

The others laughed and the conversation continued away from dating and Julian and *me*. Under the table, his knee touched mine gently. I glanced up to see him give me a questioning look. *Are you okay?*

I smiled at him. *I've never been better,* I thought.

Hunt's new health app was launched with roaring success the next day. It was the latest in a trend that seemed to be sweeping the tech world, with a revolutionary interface and a platform capable of reaching thousands of healthcare providers within months.

Julian was practically aglow on stage when he introduced it. Calm and controlled, in a fitted gray suit, he projected confidence. But underneath it, I could tell that excitement was thrumming through him. This was his passion. He genuinely believed in his work, in his creations—in what he had to offer the world.

I watched him from the back of the room, just as transfixed as the rest of the audience. It had become clear to me that I didn't just like Julian.

I was head over heels.

Later that evening, the full day done, giddiness hung in the air. The launch had been phenomenal. I could hear the Hunt technicians joking with each other as they packed down our workshop gear, laughter and exhaustion in their voices. I knew how they felt. I was starting to realize that these huge launches and events had a lot in common with sporting events. Once the adrenaline was spent, all you had left was a worn-out sort of happiness.

Rachel grinned at me. "Finally, huh?"

"Yes, finally," I agreed. "My stomach is practically eating itself."

She laughed. "So is mine. You've done some really great work these days, by the way. I was glad to have you by my side."

"It's been fun! We've had some great teamwork."

"We have. Thank God it's over though. I think I could use about two weeks' vacation."

"Me too."

Rachel zipped up her jacket. "I'm heading to my sister's for the evening. She lives here in LA, so I'll spend some time with family and sleep at hers. Congratulations, Emily. You get the hotel room all to yourself tonight."

"Oh," I said weakly.

"That's a good thing, no?"

"Yes! Yes, I mean, of course I don't mind. I hope you have a great evening. See you at the airport tomorrow morning then?"

"Yes, bright and early." She rolled her eyes. "*Too* early."

I watched her grab her bag and give me a cheery wave as she hurried out of the conference hall. So I'd be alone in my room tonight, with Julian Hunt himself just two doors down.

My mind went straight for the gutter. I tried to stop it; I gave directions, I called out, I coaxed. But there was no use. The facts were the facts—there was nothing in the way of the two of us spending time together tonight. Nerves were already going haywire in my stomach and I forced myself to take a deep breath.

I hoped we would spend the night together. I'd been fighting my attraction for him from the beginning, but it was a useless battle and I'd made a strategic retreat. When a man like that is delivered into your life, you don't waste him, and I didn't plan to.

Only… it had been a while since the last time I'd had sex. Between working and taking care of the house and Turner, meeting men hadn't been on my to-do list for the last few years. And while living vicariously through Denise had given me many laughs, it hadn't really prepared me for this moment.

My eyes tracked Julian on the other side of the room. He was helping the technicians carry a large beam and had taken off his fitted blazer. He said something, and I saw the others grin as they carried it across to an electric truck. He really could talk to anyone, I thought. I doubted any of the other CEOs who had attended the conference stayed to help packing down afterward.

Julian bent, muscular thighs straining against his suit pants as they carried the heavy beam. Absently, he pushed his shirt-sleeves up higher to reveal strong forearms. I wondered how they'd feel around my bare waist. I wondered how I'd managed to stay away from him for so long.

I wondered if he wanted me as much as I wanted him.

As if hearing my thoughts, Julian turned. A smile broke across his features as he saw me and strode over. "Are you watching me, huh?"

"Mhm," I said. "Rachel is going to be at her sister's tonight. She just headed out."

"All right, good to know."

"As in, she's *staying* the night there," I clarified. I was probably the most uncool woman in the history of dating at the moment, but it felt really important that he got this point.

Julian's eyes slid to mine. "I see. Well, we should get dinner, in any case."

"Sure. We're all done here now, anyway."

He glanced down at his watch. "It'll just be the two of us, actually. Josef is grabbing a drink with some programmers from another company."

"Fraternization, but okay."

He chuckled and leaned in close, his voice soft against my ear. "Just us, it seems. I hope you're all right with spending some time with me alone again."

My stomach did Cirque-du-Soleil-worthy somersaults. "I'm okay with that."

We headed toward the exit, his suit jacket slung over one shoulder. How could he still smell amazing after a full day of running around?

"You have two options."

"I do?" *My room or yours?*

"There's a restaurant in the lobby of the hotel. That's the simple option. *Or,* I could make some calls and try to find a reservation for a nice place somewhere else. It's the lady's choice."

"Oh, I see," I said with an exaggerated nod. "This is a date, and you need to get some paparazzi photos taken. Well, I'm committed to anonymity."

Julian laughed. "Both Rachel and Josef like to run their mouths sometimes. No, I just want to spend time with you."

"Let's go to the hotel restaurant. It looked good enough, and it's already pretty late."

He nodded and held the door open for me. "Sounds great to me. I have a feeling I'll be paying more attention to the beautiful woman opposite me than my food anyway."

20

EMILY

The hostess made sex-eyes at Julian when we arrived. A part of me was annoyed at her, but the other part was in full agreement. *You and me both, sister.*

"We have the perfect table for you, sir." She shot him a blinding smile as we followed her to a table in the back.

"I'll get you both a menu in a second. Meanwhile, would you care to start with something to drink? A glass of wine, perhaps?"

Julian's eyes were on me. "What would you like, Emily?"

"A glass of white wine, thank you. And some still water."

"I'll have a glass of red," Julian said.

"Coming right up!"

"Wow," I said when she retreated. "Does that happen everywhere you go?"

"Does what happen everywhere?"

I rolled my eyes at him. "Never mind."

Our menus arrived and we ordered in quick succession. The table we'd gotten was secluded, half-hidden from the other guests' view.

Our conversation flowed as naturally as it had the previous times we'd spent together. He was easy to talk to, a skilled conversationalist, and highly receptive to whatever stupid joke I was making.

Julian cut his steak with expert precision and I admired the strength of his hands, the five-o'clock shadow along his jaw. My body felt alive with energy.

Tonight. He'd hinted enough times that he wanted me.

I felt woefully inexperienced suddenly. How did you initiate something more intimate after this? Should I slip him my room key before dessert with a sly wink? Was a coy smile enough?

The last time I slept with a man, it had been with a former co-worker following a particularly wet Christmas party. It had been memorable only in how exceedingly *unmemorable* it was.

Julian probably had high standards. I took another peek up at the hard cut of his jaw, the way the light played across the wide splay of his shoulders. Two years ago, on this day, he'd dated an honest-to-God actress. Like, someone whose job description included looking beautiful.

What if he used names for positions? Some sort of advanced sex jargon? "Let's do the overhand twisted pretzel, Emily." There was no way I could fake knowing how to do that. I'd end up breaking a leg, or worse, embarrassing myself in front of him.

Julian put down his knife and fork and was looking at me with an amused smile. "You've gone quiet over there, Ace."

I shook my head stronger than the question required. "No, I'm just thinking."

"About what?"

"About... Oh! This." I grabbed my purse. "I spoke with a press agent today about a great opportunity for you and I completely forgot."

"It's been a busy few days."

"Yes, but this seemed exciting..." I searched through the veritable ocean of business cards I'd amassed.

Julian laughed at me.

"I know, I know. It's like they've bred and multiplied in here when I wasn't looking."

"That's a conference rookie move if I've ever seen one. Us seasoned professionals learn to say no, or toss them the first opportunity we get."

"But they might come in handy later"

He snorted. "Emily, you don't need to keep all those, trust me. Unless you're looking to switch jobs?"

I looked up. "Oh, they're not for me. Well, mostly not. I tried to take as much information as I could for Turner."

Julian blinked at me before his gaze warmed. "You really help him, don't you?"

"Well, of course. This is his chosen field, what he wants to work with. As long as he's on this path I might as well try to pave as much of it as I can."

He leaned back, eyes thoughtful. "Remind me to ask for your advice on my brother someday."

"Ryan?"

"Mhm." He raised his fork in caution, a piece of sirloin pierced on it. "Not tonight, though. Tonight we're having fun."

It felt like he had a direct hotline to my heart and my stomach and… slightly lower than that. I gulped down my wine. "Fun, huh."

"Yes. And before you try, this doesn't count as one of my allotted weekly dinners."

"Oh, it doesn't?"

His eyebrow quirked. "No. This is circumstantial. Work, dinner is needed, and we made the best out of the situation. But it doesn't count."

"Oh."

"Which means we're going somewhere the coming week. I have a place in mind."

"Where?"

He leaned back and grinned. "You know what? I think I'm going to let that be a surprise."

I rolled my eyes to hide just how excited that made me. "Fine. Be that way. See if I care."

His grin widened. "Well. So?"

"So…" I trailed off, unsure of what he was expecting. Was this the point where we went upstairs to his hotel room? I hadn't finished my pasta. It was really good pasta. But then again… My eyes raked up his chest, the strength in his arms. Pasta had nothing on him. I'd go gluten-free for life if that was the required sacrifice.

Julian nodded to my purse. "*So*, what did you want to show me?"

"Right! Let me look… here it is." I pulled out a silver-plated business card. "I was approached by one of the producers of those online lectures, on ideas that are worth spreading. They're planning an event in San Francisco eight months from now and they're really interested in having you as one of the keynote speakers."

I slid the business card over to him. I'd already photographed it, front and back, and starred it on my phone.

"Wouldn't that be so cool?"

"A talk?"

"Yes. You'd be amazing."

"You think?"

I frowned at his lack of enthusiasm. "Julian, of course. You were excellent on that panel yesterday and you're a great public speaker."

He seemed to ponder the idea, glancing out over the mostly empty restaurant. "I suppose I could think about it. But those speakers usually have something to say, some wisdom to impart."

"You're passionate about your business and about the positive impact technology can have. You have loads of wisdom to share! I can't think of a single reason why not."

His lips curled into a small smile and his eyes were warm when they met mine. "You really think that highly of me?"

"Yes, I do. The world deserves to hear what you have to say."

His hand rested on the table between us, and I reached for it instinctively. My intention was a quick squeeze, but he flipped it over and took mine in a tight grip.

"You didn't always think this highly of me." He avoided my gaze, eyes on our clasped hands. His thumb rubbed small circles in my palm.

"No, I guess I didn't."

"When did it change?"

"My view of you?"

Julian nodded, and I couldn't help smiling. "Want me to pad your ego a bit?"

His hand tightened on mine. "Indulge me, Ace."

"Gradually, I suppose. Over those once-a-week dates. The racetrack. Watching you at work… you were truly great at this conference."

His eyebrows shot high. "So watching me work was a turn-on?"

"Hugely. Talk to me about bytes and vectors, *please.*"

Julian laughed. "If only I'd known that from the start! I would have talked about nothing else. I would have been in your office all day and bored you to death."

His hand was warm on mine, and our knees touched under the table. We'd finished eating, and our glasses were long since empty.

Be brave, Emily.

"Let's go upstairs," I told him. "I want to spend more time with you."

His eyes were dark and calm, but I felt the energy radiating off him. It always had, as if he vibrated at a slightly higher frequency than everyone else. "All right. Let me just settle the bill."

"We're splitting it."

Julian laughed, actually *laughed.* "We most certainly won't. Besides, this is a work trip. If it makes you feel better, consider this a part of a per diem."

We were silent as he paid, the still overly attentive waitress fluttering her lashes. This time I took a tiny step closer to him and slipped my hand under his arm.

Julian rewarded me with a soft smile at my open display of affection, a smile I was growing increasingly fond of. It felt secret. Something he didn't show to the stage or the crowds of adoring fans.

We walked in silence toward the elevators. I felt electric, the air between us humming with things unsaid and promises unfulfilled. The voice in my head refused to stop ranting.

He smells fantastic.

How do I initiate this?

Why hasn't he initiated it?

It would be so extremely awkward if he turned me down, I realized as the elevators closed behind us. *Again.* How could I show up to work after that?

But why would he? I knew he was attracted to me, even if he'd always been respectful about it.

Julian's hand skimmed across my waist as he reached to press the elevator button. "You have to actually tell these things where you want to go." His voice was husky, sending goose bumps across my skin.

"Whoops," I murmured.

The corridor on our floor stretched out before us, wide and empty. I knew we'd reach my room before his—I'd already spied the number on our booking sheet. Yeah. I'm just stalkerish like that.

We walked in silence to my door.

"This is me," I said and waved to room 802. "Home sweet home."

Julian smiled. "I had a really nice time tonight. Thanks for dinner."

I nodded.

808, that was his room number. Turner once told me that eight was a lucky number in China, that people paid premium money for phone numbers with lots of eights in them. I'd never been superstitious, but I suddenly clung to the fact. His hotel room was lucky. *What could go wrong, Emily?*

Julian opened his mouth to speak, but I cut him off. "Do you have a minibar?"

He nodded slowly. "I do."

"How about a round of Never Have I Ever at yours?" I leaned against my hotel door. "I'm not tired quite yet."

Julian's swallow was audible. "Good idea. I'm in 808."

"I'll be there in a few minutes. Just let me freshen up."

His gaze didn't leave me as I opened the door and slipped inside. *Hunger.* That was what I had seen in them. It made me brave, made me giddy with nervous anticipation and triumph.

Alert the press—somehow, this was going according to plan. I pushed my hair back and took a good look in the bathroom mirror. I was wearing the same makeup I'd applied at seven AM that morning, my formerly pristine blouse wrinkled every which way, and my hair was, to put it in mild terms, a mess.

Okay, Emily. *Think.*

I stripped down, tied my long hair up and hopped in the shower. I scrubbed away grime and quickly shaved my legs. I brushed my teeth. I moisturized everywhere and ran a brush through my hair. When finished, I saw a somewhat wild-eyed but put-together woman in the mirror. Dark hair hung shiny down my shoulders, and the soft cashmere sweater I'd put on hugged my chest. Sure, I wasn't a model or an actress, but I looked pretty good. I felt sexy and clean.

Deep breaths.

The door to my hotel room shut with an audible, ominous click, and I walked down the corridor to his room with my shoulders back, rehearsing the plan. Have a drink first. Have sex second. Easy enough.

The numbers on his hotel door stood out with large, gold-plated numbers. "Wish me luck, guys," I murmured to the eights and knocked.

21

EMILY

Julian opened his hotel door almost immediately. For a long moment, all we did was look at one another.

"Hey," he said softly.

"Hi."

He'd taken off his suit jacket, white shirtsleeves rolled up. His hair looked like he'd been running his hands through it. Slowly, his eyes raked down my newly changed attire, my throat going dry.

"Um, are you going to let me in, or…?"

Julian winked. "My bad."

His room was larger than mine and Rachel's, though only by a little. A massive king-sized bed dominated the center and I forced my eyes not to linger on it, or my mind to psych myself out at the thought of what might come next.

By the large windows was a small seating area. A cart from room service stood next to it, complete with an icy wine cooler. I ran a hand over it, small water drops chilling my fingers. "What's this?"

Julian grinned and watched me peruse the different drink options on display. "You said you wanted to avoid alcohol for all eternity, and I'm nothing if not supportive. So I ordered an assortment of non-alcoholic drinks for us."

There were ice-cold bottles of Coke, Pepsi, Fanta, fresh-pressed orange juice, Shirley Temples and what looked like virgin daiquiris. I grabbed one of them, a red and sloshy drink with a tiny umbrella.

"Yeah," he said, nodding as if I had spoken. "That was the drink I figured you'd choose."

"I'm that predictable, huh?"

"Sometimes."

I bit my lip and kept my gaze on his. With calculated movements, I left the seating area and took a seat on his bed. A hand behind me, I leaned back and watched him. *Not so predictable now, Hunt.*

His gaze had darkened as he followed my movements. With a quick move, he opened a can of soda. "What did you want to play again?"

"Never Have I Ever," I said. Sitting here, with him staring at me like that, I couldn't think of why I'd been nervous. He made me feel more powerful than anyone ever had.

Julian smiled crookedly. "Ladies first."

"Never have I ever injured myself when trying to impress a girl or a guy."

Julian took a sip of his Coke with a long-suffering look, and I motioned with my hand, making the universal sign for *and?*

He sighed. "Fine. I attempted a skateboard trick in front of a girl I had a crush on when I was eleven. Ended up breaking my wrist. My *right* wrist."

"Wow. That must have been very painful."

"I spent the next five weeks getting out of every school assignment because I couldn't write with my left. Not legibly, at least."

"Did you at least get the girl?"

"No. She ended up going to the school disco with my best friend."

"Poor baby," I murmured.

"I've since made a full recovery," he informed me. "Both my heart and wrists are intact."

"Glad to hear it. Your turn."

"Never have I ever fallen in love at first sight," he declared, and didn't drink.

I sighed and took a sip of the frosty, sweet drink.

Julian's eyebrows rose. "Wow. Really, Ace? I figured you'd be more of a get-to-know-the-guy kind of girl. One to take it slow."

I patted the space next to me on the bed. "Come here and I'll tell you."

The bed sank as he took a seat next to me, and I scooted up further, sitting cross-legged against the headboard. "It was with my first crush, Dustin. He was in the year above me in school and when I saw him at a roller-skating party, I was lost. I knew I *had* to be with him, at all costs." I shrugged. "Young and foolish."

Julian was smiling that soft, secretive smile, the one that made my chest hurt. "That's cute, but could you really qualify that as *love?*"

I wagged my finger at him. "You wouldn't dare say that to fifteen-year-old me. I wrote his name on every page of my notebook and thought I knew *exactly* what love was. Dustin and I would grow old together."

"I'm glad you didn't."

"Me too," I said. "He later dropped out of high school and got a girl pregnant when he was seventeen."

"Ouch."

"Yeah." I swiped a hand across my forehead dramatically. "Dodged a bullet there."

"On to better and bigger things."

I couldn't help myself. "Bigger?"

Julian's eyes turned flat with surprise and desire. He put his drink down and turned to me fully. I was struck again by how large he was, how much physical space it felt like he occupied. The bed felt small with him sitting on it. "I want to play another game."

"You do?"

"Truth or dare. If we're going to play these games, we might as well go full high school."

"All right. But I warn you—if you dare me to run through the lobby half-naked, shouting something obscene, I won't. I'm a rule-breaker like that."

Julian's lip curled into a crooked smile. "Trust me, I would never dare you to undress in front of people."

I took a long sip of my drink to pad my suddenly parched throat. "Alrighty then."

"Truth or dare?"

"Truth," I said.

"When was the last time you were in love?"

"Wow. When you said truth, you really meant, like, *truth.*"

"You'll be able to return the favor soon enough."

"It was with my last boyfriend. It ended years ago." It wasn't a difficult question. James was the only one I'd really been in love with, although I supposed it had been a form of puppy love. We'd dated from the age of nineteen to twenty-two, but I was such a different person by the end that I'd forgotten why we had ever liked one another.

Julian opened his mouth but I stopped him. "No, it's one question per turn."

"Fine, fine. I'll play nice."

"Good." I traced the rim of the daiquiri glass. "Last time you were in love?"

"Very original."

"I felt inspired."

Julian glanced out of the window to the dark city beyond. "It's honestly been a while. My last relationship, too, I suppose. It ended a couple of years ago."

I nodded. "So we've established that."

"Truth or dare?"

"Truth. Hey, I don't feel like moving from this room. Can't we just declare that we only do truth?"

He gave me a crooked grin. "Or we just say that all potential dares must be limited to this room."

Heat swept through me at his gaze, at his words. "Mhm," I said. "Clever addition."

"I've been known to have smart ideas on occasion. Tell me honestly, then. What was your first impression of me? Right off the bat, when we met at that club."

I looked down at my drink, choosing my words wisely. "Honestly? I thought you were an asshole."

He laughed. "Yes, you made that clear."

"But I was attracted to you from the first second."

Julian's eyes darkened again, gaze heavy. "Something we have in common, it seems."

"So it would seem."

"I choose truth," he said, voice low now.

"Have you ever had sex in a hotel room?"

His eyebrows shot to the ceiling, and I could swear that he leaned in closer. "I have," he replied. "Have you?"

I shook my head and took a sip of my drink. "No, I never have."

He laughed, a low and husky sound that sent goose bumps down my spine. "I think we're starting to mix up our games."

"We can create new ones." I scooted closer to him on the bed. "Do whatever we like."

His hand found my ankle, bare skin below the hem of my pants. His thumb smoothed over my skin, sending shivers up my body. Such a small, innocent touch, and yet…

He suddenly glanced down and then back up at me. Very carefully, he leaned closer and took a deep breath.

"Julian, what are you doing?"

"Ace, did you shower before coming over here? I smell soap. And your leg is… *very* smooth. Did you shave too?"

"Maybe. Yes."

Julian's hand paused on my leg, his eyes closing. "Oh, Emily. I need you to know that I didn't ask you to accompany us because of…" his words drift off, and he swallows hard. "I had no expectations. I genuinely thought it would be a good learning experience, that you'd enjoy it."

His thick hair, usually wavy and pushed back, curled around his temples. On impulse, I reached out and ran my fingers through it.

"I know that. I still want you."

With a sigh, he reached up and gently removed my hand. "This is not how I wanted it to happen."

His rejection was soft, but it was rejection nonetheless.

It hit me like a freight train—how I must look to him, dressed up and showered and delivered to his hotel room. My stupid, silly seductress persona. I moved away from him.

But I moved too fast.

My glass tipped slightly in my hand and the bright red drink sloshed over the edge. It spilled down my thumb and along my wrist, staining the edge of my shirt.

"Shit."

"Are you okay?"

"Mhm." I was up and off the bed in a heartbeat, heading to the bathroom like an Olympic sprinter. My cheeks were flaming—I could feel the heat rushing up to my face, my eyes tearing up. *Step 2, proposition him* was complete.

Too bad it was a complete failure.

I turned on the faucet and tried to wash away the sticky, sugary liquid. I didn't look in the mirror. I knew I'd see someone with blotchy skin and hurt eyes and I might do something stupid, like cry, because of my own foolishness. He was completely within his rights to turn me down. Nothing to be upset about.

I heard footsteps, and then silence, the only sound that of the rushing water.

"Emily, are you all right?"

I looked over to see him leaning against the bathroom door, with his strong jawline and handsome face all concerned.

"I'm fine. Don't worry about it."

"Emily, I need you to know that—"

"It's all right, Julian." I didn't look at him as I toweled off.

"The only reason I don't think—"

"Honestly. I understand that you're not the one to—"

He crossed the space between us in two quick strides and spun me around, trapped me within the circle of his arms. "Damn it, Ace, will you listen to me?"

I was lost to the green of his eyes, filled with emotions I couldn't name. All I did was nod.

"I planned on doing everything by the book with you. I want to date you. I want to make sure you feel good, feel secure. I'm not in a rush, Ace." His fingers on my waist moved, stroked along my ribs, and I found myself rising up on my toes to get closer to him. "Seducing you on a work trip wasn't a part of my plan."

"And you object to a change of plan?" I asked. Julian's hands tightened around me, his lips only inches away now. I knew how they felt and I knew how he tasted. It was all I could think of.

"I'm afraid of the consequences."

"Because we work together?"

His smile was tight. "No. I'm afraid you might bolt after."

"What if I promise I won't?" My hands found their way up along his chest, traced his shoulders.

"I'd want to believe you," he murmured. "Not sure I can."

I fit myself against him, my breasts against his chest and my hips aligned with his, and touched my lips to the corner of his. "Believe me."

Julian groaned in defeat against my mouth. "You're lethal," he murmured.

And then he kissed me.

It wasn't like the racetrack or even that night at the club—there was nothing sweet or reverent about these touches. Both of us too eager and too heated. We had wanted this for too long.

Julian's lips traced my jaw and my neck. I burned everywhere he touched, as if fire trailed his hand and his lips. A strong hand pulled the neckline of my sweater to the side and I had to grasp his shoulders as he followed the length of my collarbone with kisses.

More. I needed more.

I grabbed the hem of my sweater and pulled it up, wanting it off. Julian gave a husky laugh at my eagerness and large hands helped me tug it off.

He fell silent immediately. I shook my hair out and watched as his gaze and hands skimmed my sides, up to trace the curve of one bra-clad breast.

"Ace," he murmured. "You kill me."

I tugged at the buttons of his shirt, just as eager to get to his skin as he was to mine. "Fair is fair."

Julian helped me with the buttons and I could finally pull his shirt off. If I'd ever thought it was the form-fitted suits that made his chest look so broad, I was proven spectacularly wrong.

He was cut like a swimmer, wide and strong goodness tapering down to a taut waist. Abs and muscles and a smattering of dark, dark hair across his chest.

My hands were on him the second the shirt dropped— exploring the planes of his stomach, the stretch of his shoulders and the warmth of his skin.

I wanted all of him, all of the layers between us gone.

"Wait." I reached back, my hands finding the zipper of my skirt. Julian watched me as I slowly let it drop and fall into a puddle on the floor, leaving me in only my underwear.

His chest rose and fell in deep, agonized breaths as his gaze swept over my body. "Ace…"

Whatever he was going to say disappeared in motion and want. Julian grasped my waist and lifted me up, placing me on the edge of the cool marble sink. The cold made me gasp.

Julian smiled against my lips. "Whoops."

"I forgive you," I murmured, my lips at his neck.

"Thank you." His hand seared a path down my abdomen and onto my thigh. "You're so beautiful. Absolutely stunning. I've thought that since the first moment I saw you."

I didn't recognize myself. I should be nervous—I should be second-guessing myself right about now. The whole situation was surreal, me sitting in a brightly lit bathroom with the most handsome man who'd ever walked the earth.

But I didn't even hesitate as I reached back and unsnapped my bra.

The straps slid down my arms and I tossed them away. Julian gave a slow, strangled sound. "Holy hell, Ace…"

Maybe that's why I wasn't nervous. Julian's gaze made it clear that he wasn't somewhere else or thinking about somebody else. I'd spell-bound him just as deeply as he'd captivated me.

His hands were big and rough and everywhere—they were teasing my nipples, pulling me close, and tugging at my hair. The fire that had always been between us was an inferno now. We were close to each other, skin against skin, but I wanted to be closer still. I wanted to feel his body against mine—inside me.

"You're still dressed," I said against his lips. "Not fair."

Julian gave a weak laugh and stepped back just enough to let me push his suit pants down his hips. They were quickly discarded, revealing the impressive bulge in his boxers. My throat went dry. Of course, he had to be extraordinary in *all* areas.

His hands tugged me forward on the counter, grabbed my knees and I wrapped my legs around him. We fit perfectly at this height.

Julian swept my hair back and trailed his lips and tongue up my neck. I could feel the heat of his breath, the pounding of his heart. "Let's go to the bedroom."

I was not moving from that spot. I couldn't—I needed him, and I needed him now.

I ran my hand down his stomach and shook my head. He was hard and wedged close, but I managed to stroke the length of him through the fabric of his boxers. Julian growled and rested his head against my shoulder.

"Fuck," he said. "All right. But you first."

Strong hands grabbed a hold of my panties and *tugged*. Obediently, I raised my hips and he slid them down my legs.

Nerves came back in a rush as I was completely bared to him. But the sudden sense of insecurity was soon over—Julian's hands were there immediately.

Long fingers stroked up my thighs and a warm hand cupped me entirely. One of his fingers parted my slit and found my center, and I couldn't help but moan. I looked up at the ceiling and gave in to him, to his hand and his fingers. I couldn't watch what he was doing to me. It was too much—the illusion would shatter, and I'd revert back to the self-conscious woman I was instead of the vixen I was channeling tonight.

Julian kissed me as his fingers continued their torturous exploration. With exquisite slowness, he slid a finger inside. I gasped.

"You're wet." His voice was incredulous. "You're so wet for me already."

I wanted to laugh. *Of course* I was. Julian was the single most attractive man I'd ever met. He would be able to raise me from the dead with one of his crooked smiles.

I reached down and stroked his cock through his underwear, and he rewarded me with a sharp exhale. His hips bucked once, involuntarily, into my hand.

"And you're hard as a rock."

Julian wrapped his arms around me and all of a sudden I was off the counter—I was in the air, being held close to his strong body.

"That's it. Bedroom, Ace."

"No. Here."

Our eyes met, and his went nearly black with desire when he realized just how much of a tinderbox I was. One match and I'd ignite.

His hands released me and I slid to the ground. Our bodies were touching from head to toe. Strong fingers gripped my hips and dug into the skin of my ass. "You sure?"

I wasn't acting on thought anymore—only instinct and desire. I turned around and bent over, resting my arms against the cool marble. "I need to feel you inside me."

I could see him in the mirror, could see the exact moment his careful restraint stretched and snapped. With quick movements, he pulled off his boxers.

My mouth went dry at the sight of his ready cock, proud and swollen.

"Condoms." His voice was a growl. "I'll get one. Stay."

I was left bent over in the bathroom with my pounding heart. I'd always anticipated that being intimate with Julian would feel good, and that giving in would be like this, which was partly why I had made the decision to do so. But this was something else—and he hadn't even entered me yet.

Julian returned with a shiny piece of foil, and in a practiced move, he tore the packet open and rolled on the condom. From there, he didn't do what I had been expecting, though. Sure hands wrapped around my waist and pulled me up, pressing me flush against his body—much bigger than mine. Facing away from him, I could feel the hot length of his cock against my ass.

"Look," he said in my ear, voice husky. "Look at yourself."

I did—I saw us in the mirror. Me, entirely nude, and him, so big behind me. His eyes were filled with admiration and desire as we looked at one another.

A strong hand wound itself into my hair and forced it back ever so slightly against his shoulder. We both watched as his hand slowly trailed down my neck. "Do you see? Do you see how beautiful you are?"

I gave a breathless nod.

"See how your breasts curve perfectly here." His hand cupped my right breast, let me feel the weight of it. "How your waist dips in here, and how your hips flare out like this… and here… this is what I like the most."

Julian's hand covered the triangle between my legs perfectly. His fingers found my wetness again, and I would have been embarrassed by it if he hadn't groaned at the sensation and whispered in my ear how much he loved it. *"You're ready for me."*

Sure fingers circled my swollen clit. Watching everything in the full-length mirror was beyond erotic, a situation more intense than any I'd ever experienced before. Julian's mouth was relentless against my neck, his fingers circling.

"I want to hear you moan," he said, slipping a finger inside me and pressing the heel of his hand down on my clit. I couldn't help it—I did moan. His teasing had put me on the brink, and I knew I was close…so close to coming.

I grabbed his wrist. "I want to come with you inside."

His cock, trapped between our bodies, twitched in agreement. I wanted it, I wanted him—I needed to make him feel as crazed with desire as me.

Julian groaned, his hand abandoning my pussy to tease a nipple. "You're killing me," he murmured. "Do you know that? The power you have over me?"

Didn't he know it was the other way around? Since the day he walked into my life, he had owned me completely. There was no one else.

A strong knee nudged my legs apart. "Spread for me, Ace. Up onto your tiptoes."

He bent his knees slightly to make us more aligned and then I felt the head of his cock, strong and sure, nearing my wetness. Julian slid it along my slit once, twice, coating himself and driving me mad.

His voice was a growl. "Look."

I watched in the mirror as he pushed in and sheathed himself to the hilt. He was everywhere—behind me, around me, inside me. It was too much and still not enough.

"You okay, Ace?"

I gave a nod, words lost to me, and watched as he began to move behind me. Slow thrusts gave way to deep, quick strokes, and soon he was setting a pace that had me gasping.

Strong fingers dug into my hips and I keeled over, hands grasping the marble and holding on for dear life. This was raw and real, and I'd never been so aroused in my life. I knew I was going to come hard like this, from him and his movements.

So this is how it's like to be fucked by a god, I thought, the ridiculous statement making me smile. It wasn't fair. Sex shouldn't be allowed to be this good.

Julian pulled me back up against his body. Strong arms wrapped around my waist entirely as he continued to move inside me. He claimed me. "I want to see you. I want *you* to see you."

His hand was relentless, finding my clit again and rubbing circles as he continued pounding into me. Pleasure swept through my body in waves, rising and cresting and wavering dangerously high. It was too much.

I was so entirely, entirely lost.

"Come for me, Ace," I heard him growl. "Come for me."

And I did.

My moans echoed off the bathroom walls as I shattered around him. Pleasure raced through my pelvis, my limbs, turning my legs to Jell-O. If he hadn't been holding me up, I would have fallen over, helpless against the current.

I couldn't stop it even if I had tried.

My pleasure ignited his and I watched in the mirror as Julian's eyes narrowed, his face taut. I'd never seen him so unleashed before—so entirely in his element.

I had wondered a lot about who the real Julian was. I had admired the businessman who spoke in front of crowds of thousands, the playful boss who nevertheless enjoyed complete respect from his employees. The older brother, the stern financial head of his family. The charming and good-looking millionaire philanthropist.

But seeing him come undone in the mirror and his handsome face lined with pleasure, I believed that I'd found my favorite version yet.

It was a version I didn't want to share with anyone.

He groaned deep and husky as he came, hands clasping me tightly against him and the frantic beat of his heart against my back. Inside me, I could feel the rhythmic pulses of his cock as he emptied himself.

We were one, consumed by emotion and desire I'd never felt before. For a long while—minutes, hours, years—neither of us could speak. The intensity hung in the air and still raced through my veins. My mind was trying and failing to play catchup.

His husky chuckle in my ear made me smile. "That was intense."

"Very."

With a ginger movement, he slipped out of me and stepped back. I frowned at the sudden lack of his warmth, but he was gone only long enough to dispose of the condom. Julian grabbed me and lifted me up so that we were once again body to body and skin to skin.

His voice was thick with satisfaction. "Am I allowed to take you to the bed now?"

"Yes." I rested my head against his shoulder, reveling in his strength and the pleasure that still radiated through my body. We'd just had what could only be described as the best sex of my life, and I knew I wanted him again. And again.

And again.

Julian set me down next to his bed and pulled back the covers. We slid in, the sheets soft against my skin. Julian dimmed the lights. He reached for me immediately and cradled my body with the curve of his larger one. A hand traced circles along my hip, the other smoothing my hair back.

"Just give me fifteen minutes," he murmured. "And then I can go again."

I gave a sleepy laugh. "Wow, Julian. I think I'll need a week to recover. That was… wow."

His laughter was a soft breath against my temple. "Take as much time as you need, Ace," he murmured. "I'll be here."

Wrapped in Julian's arms, it didn't take long before sleep claimed me just as thoroughly as he had.

22

JULIAN

My dreams bled into reality that night.

Emily had fallen asleep in my arms, in my hotel bed, her warm skin resting against mine. It would take a stronger man than me to resist following her into oblivion.

At some point during the night, I felt her trying to slide out of bed, sitting on the edge. I'd acted on instinct—wrapped an arm around her smooth waist and pulled her right back into bed with me. She'd laughed and squirmed, which only meant I held her tighter.

"And where do you think you're going?"

"My room?" Emily had said it like a question, and I answered firmly by sliding my leg between hers. She smelled warm and feminine, and I took a deep, sleepy breath.

"Don't you dare. You're sleeping right here."

She'd twisted in my arms, turned so she could press those soft lips against my neck.

"So bossy."

I had only been half-awake, but I managed a faint laugh. "That's my job, Ace."

We woke up to the garish sound of the hotel wakeup call. A disgustingly chipper receptionist let me know the car for the airport would be downstairs in thirty minutes.

"Mhm," I said. "Thanks. Bye now."

"Remind me again who booked these flights, and why on earth it had to be so early?" Emily slid out from under my arm and sat up at the side of the bed, gingerly stretching from side to side. The sheet pooled around her hips, and I saw the smooth expanse of her back, the faint curve of a breast. Her dark hair was a beautiful mess.

When she didn't get a response—I'd temporarily lost the ability to speak—she peeked over her shoulder.

"You're not falling asleep on me again, are you?"

"No." I bent a knee to hide my erection. Morning or not, the sight of her nude body illuminated by the faint light of dawn would stir even the most tired of men.

"We have to get going."

"Not yet, we don't." I reached for her, but Emily rose and danced away with a grin.

"We'll be late."

"I don't care." She might be out of reach, but I now had a full view of her beautiful, naked body. Curved in all the right places, soft to the touch, surprisingly responsive. I knew what she tasted like—and I wanted a second round.

Emily saw the desire on my face and her cheeks grew red.

I grinned. "You're not getting shy on me now, Ace?"

She rolled her eyes and started rummaging around for her clothes. A sweater was put back on, jeans quickly tugged up along shapely legs. "Only because I know exactly what you want to do now."

"Am I that obvious?"

Emily gave a snorting laugh. "Yes. But we don't have time." She paused by the hotel door. "Take a shower. I'll meet you in the lobby."

She looked so cute with messy hair and well-kissed lips, and my chest tightened at the sight. But before I could say anything else she slipped out of my hotel room and it shut smoothly behind her.

I lay back down and gazed at the crown molding in the ceiling, the intricate and detailed twists. The scent of her still clung to the pillow beside me and the sheets smelled of us. It had been so long since I'd taken a woman in my arms and felt what Emily made me feel. *Alive. Wanted. Seen.*

The woman was nothing if not unexpected. I'd been prepared to go slow, to take things day by day, to convince her that being with me was a good idea. That *we* were a good idea. But she'd taken things into her own hands, *literally,* and given me the best sex of my life.

Hell, I'd never found a woman so wet and ready for me *before* I'd even touched her. None had felt as right in my arms, as if they belonged there.

Images of her refused to leave me as I packed my few toiletries and hung my suit back into the garment bag. Emily was in my head through every step, even as I took a scalding shower. Somehow, even though she'd *just* left me, I missed her.

I could barely look in the bathroom mirror without getting hard, thinking about what we'd done the night before. Taking her from behind like that, having her twist and grind and moan… blood rushed south at the thought.

Never before had a woman wanted me so. And her hungry kisses, the fit of her tight, warm depths… It was enough to make a man half-crazed with worship. We'd fit like we were made for it. She'd taken all of my length and more, pushed back against me like mine was the best cock she'd ever had. My vain heart hoped it was.

Lord knew she was the sexiest woman I'd ever seen.

I turned the water in the shower to cold.

Thirty minutes later I stood in the empty lobby with Josef, glancing at my watch. Emily should be down by now, and she usually loathed being late. My mind conjured up images of her in her hotel room, overthinking what we'd just done—or worse —regretting it.

Josef yawned next to me.

"Out late?"

He nodded. "Those programmers, man. They really know how to cut loose."

"When you'd get back in?"

"I don't think I should be telling you that, Boss."

I forced myself to look relaxed. "I don't mind."

"Yeah, although I—"

I didn't hear him. Emily came hurrying through the lobby. Her hair was in a high ponytail that swished along her back and she was wearing a massive smile.

"Sorry, sorry! I didn't mean to keep you waiting."

The smile that spread across my face was one part joy, two parts relief.

Josef huffed. "You're two minutes late, Em. We're not about to stone you for it."

She bumped his shoulder. "How did your fraternization campaign go yesterday?"

He laughed and gave her shoulders a light squeeze. I knew they were friends, knew Josef was like that with everyone, but my insides still squeezed with jealousy. I knew I couldn't touch her like that in public. She'd never let me, not yet.

"The car should be here. Let's go."

They both fell into step behind me as we headed out. The same soapy, floral scent followed her as last night, and my stomach clenched.

Emily teased Josef mercilessly in the car on the way to LAX about his wild night out, while I spent most of the ride cursing his existence. It wasn't the poor man's fault, of course, but the rules Emily had set dictated that no one knew about us. An hour earlier she had been sleeping in my arms, and now she was in the backseat, a wall of professionalism and secrecy raised between us.

I spent the ride reading emails, and when we met up with Rachel at the airport, I knew that my tone was curt. My plan had been to seduce her slowly… cook her breakfast. Treat her the way she deserved, but curiously enough, it seemed like she didn't expect anything from me.

All four of us spent the time before the plane took off working and I had no shot at getting a few words in with her. The need to know what she felt about last night, about me, felt like a weight on my shoulders.

Boarding opened and we headed on first with the rest of the first-class passengers.

"I'm in aisle six," Emily said. "Rachel, where are you?"

"Six too. We all are. I'm in seat A."

"Oh, I'm C."

"Could we switch seats?" Rachel asked her. "Julian and I could spend the flight going over the coming week's media announcements."

We most *certainly* did not need to do that.

"No, we'll push that to later," I said. "I'll debrief Emily about her views on the conference."

Rachel raised an eyebrow but said nothing. Emily and I took our seats across the aisle from the others and I watched as her hands fastened the seat belt. Now I knew what those hands felt like, wrapped around me or pressed against my chest.

She was so close, but so far away. I couldn't make a joke about yesterday. I couldn't ask how she felt or make sure we were on the same page.

The plane took off, the familiar feeling of weightlessness overcoming me. Our eyes met.

"You okay?"

Her gaze softened. "Yes," she murmured. "I'm great."

"I'm glad to hear it."

I leaned closer, just enough so that I could speak without the risk of anyone hearing us. "Cross your legs."

Her eyes glittered with amusement, but she did as I said. I angled her open laptop slightly so that her crossed legs and screen shielded us from view.

I took her hand, held it out of sight from the others. Her skin was warm and smooth against mine. "Let's debrief in a bit," I said, leaning back and closing my eyes. "I didn't get a wink of sleep last night."

I heard Emily's soft laughter, felt the squeeze of her fingers.

"Funny. Neither did I."

23

EMILY

I waited for the best possible moment before I shared the news with Denise. All other subjects were covered first—my business trip, her recent dinner with Michael's mother and sister, the latest episode of the reality show we both watched. I was lulling her into a false sense of security.

"The conference sounds *terrible,*" she commented and popped another macaron into her mouth. "But I'm glad you had fun."

I reached for a pink, strawberry-flavored one. "Sure, the industry isn't exactly my scene, but I love the press work. Where did Michael get these?"

"He has a baker friend downtown who he hires occasionally for events and stuff. These are great, right?"

"The best. I wonder why I've never seen that place."

"It's kinda hidden behind a laundromat. A shame, really."

I watched her take a bite of a lemon macaron, her face shifting into pleasure, and decided to drop the bomb. "There's actually something I need to tell you about the conference."

"Mhgmn?"

"I slept with Julian." I closed the box of macarons. "And I think we've both had enough of these for today."

Denise's eyes turned into saucers. "Em! You've been here for nearly an hour and you tell me now?"

"Whoops?"

"No. No, no, no. This is exactly like that time you waited two full days to tell me you'd kissed Sam Feller in middle school, and how did I react then?"

"Not well."

"Tell me everything." She grabbed the box of macarons and clutched it tight to her chest. "And I'm going to have the rest of these and share none with you as punishment."

I leaned back against her fluffy couch and grinned. "Well, what do you want to know?"

"You're wearing that huge grin, so I already know it was good. Who initiated it?"

"It was mutual. It happened in his hotel room, though."

"Classic business trip hook-up. That's so *hot*," Denise whispered with a dreamy look—I knew she was picturing an array of steamy TV scenes.

I laughed. "There were no long, angsty stares or desks dramatically swept clean." And there hadn't been… just heated dinner conversation and marble sinks.

"How was it?"

"I don't know how to describe it. It was great." The fire between us had burned so hotly, and there had been none of that first-time fumbling or nerves. How did you explain something like that?

Denise sighed. "Come on, Em. I've told you nearly everything about Michael. And how many of my sexual exploits have I shared over the years? You owe me one good story."

"Hey now, you've shared far more details than I have ever asked for."

"I considered it my civic duty to educate you." She waved a dismissive hand. "Now *tell me*."

Heat crept up my cheeks at the memory of the feelings he had elicited. "It was the best sex of my life."

Denise clapped her hands in excitement. "Really?"

"Yes, really."

"Oh, I'm so happy for you! That's exactly what you deserve. Thank God you decided to actually go for it!"

"And the best part is that I think he wants to do it again. That we'll have an actual affair."

"I'm not sure it's called an affair when both people are single?"

I rolled my eyes. "Fine. A sexual relationship? Hooking up?"

"Nothing more? You don't want to get serious with him?"

The thought had crossed my mind.

But the idea of Julian Hunt as a boyfriend... it was daunting. I couldn't see us going to the movies, settling down with him on the couch, bringing him into the house I shared with my brother... it felt odd.

There was no way he'd fit into my life—he was too big and I was too anonymous. And he would undoubtedly want someone who could share his spotlight.

"No. Julian Hunt isn't the kind of man you have a serious relationship with. Besides, he propositioned me in the office canteen that first time, Denise. What kind of man does that if he wants a truly serious relationship?"

"An infatuated one."

I laughed. "No, this is just casual, trust me. But I don't mind. I'm going to ride this wave as far as it'll take me."

Denise moved over and settled next to me on the couch. "Okay, but I want more details."

"I've already told you loads!"

"No, you said it was the best sex of your life. That is entirely devoid of detail."

I sighed. "What do you want to know?"

"How long did it last? What was his body like? Did he go down on you? How big was he? Did you come? How did he—"

"Ugh! Stop!" I grabbed a pillow and covered my face with it. "I'm not going to talk about it."

Denise laughed. "Well, what was so good about it then? Why did it qualify as—"

"Oh! I think that's my phone!"

"You're so full of shit!"

"No, I'm not! Can't you hear it?" I grabbed my purse, the familiar ringtone becoming more pronounced as I searched for it. "See?"

Denise narrowed her eyes at me. "Saved by the bell, Em. But I won't let you off the hook that easy."

I finally found my phone, the screen lit up by a familiar name.

Julian Hunt.

"Oh no. It's him."

Denise gave me a huge thumbs up, her eyes wild, and I hurried to answer.

"Hello?"

A familiar voice greeted me. "Ace."

"Hi, Julian."

"Did you get home safe from the airport?"

"Yes." I played with the strap to my bag and tried to keep the smile off my face. "I did. Did you?"

"Yes."

"Good."

He cleared his throat, voice deeper when he spoke again. "I haven't been able to stop thinking about you."

My grin widened. "I might have thought about you occasionally as well."

Julian's husky laughter sent butterflies through me, reminding me of his touch in that hotel room. "Let me take you out this weekend."

"Take me out?"

"Yes. Food, some talk. I need to make sure you don't have any regrets."

I bit my lip. "I think I can *show* you that I don't have any regrets."

My statement was met with surprised silence on the other end. Unfortunately, that wasn't the case behind me—Denise gave a loud guffaw at my words. I turned and waved for her to pipe down.

"What was that?"

"I'm at a friend's place. Denise, you remember?"

"Of course. How could I forget?"

"When do you want to meet?"

"Tomorrow," he said. "Let me pick you up again."

"All right. And…"

"I'll wait a block away."

"Thank you. I'll see you tomorrow, then?"

"You will." His voice sounded like he was smiling. "Goodnight, Ace."

"Goodnight."

We hung up and for a second, I just clutched my phone to my chest.

Tomorrow. He really did want to continue whatever-this-was for a while longer. The excitement of it all made me grin.

"That sounded *really* good. Like, amazing."

"You didn't even hear his responses!"

"I didn't need to in order to know he's into you."

"Denise!"

"He is." She raised an eyebrow. "And so are you."

I sighed. "I am. I'm such a goner, aren't I?"

Denise grinned and offered me another macaron. "Yes. Welcome to the club, Em."

24

EMILY

The following two weeks were filled with more sex than I had had in a lifetime. Was it possible to overdose on orgasms and smiles? If it was, I would never consider rehab. Put it on my tombstone—"death by Julian Hunt." Let it be known that I'd died happily.

We texted like we were teenagers, often and nearly always about something silly. The man clearly had more time on his hands than I thought megalomaniac CEOs possessed.

When I pointed it out, he texted back that he was canceling meetings and regularly brushing off clients to give me the shortest response time possible. Okay, so he was clearly exaggerating, but his answer still did weird things to my stomach.

Despite my objections, our standing weekly appointment held. "We already meet up for this," I'd murmured into his ear, my hand already trailing down the hard planes of his chest, finding the buckle of his belt. "Why do we need designated time in public as well? That's time we could spend… doing this."

"Because I want to spend time with you fully clothed, too, Ace." Julian's words had been decisive, but his hands, roaming inside my wrap dress, told a different story.

I had slipped off the dress, stood in only my underwear, and given him my best *come hither* look. "But I look so good unclothed."

Julian's groan of desire was the only response I got. He had made quick work of my bra and panties before spreading me wide and bringing me to the brink with his tongue and fingers.

Never before had I been so confident in bed, so bold with my statements. Julian always made me feel like the sexiest woman alive. Somehow, he wanted me just as much as I wanted him, and I reveled in it.

For our non-date dates, I was always careful that we chose places away from work with low odds of bumping into anyone we knew. Julian rolled his eyes when I led him to lunch one day, blocks and blocks away from the office.

"Is this when you reveal that you're a serial killer?" he teased, turning my own words back at me. "Luring me back to a shady studio and I'm never to be heard from again?"

"Maybe. I'd say my last goodbyes if I were you, Hunt."

We made it to the Italian restaurant I'd been looking for, a slightly garish place with plastic vinyl booths and enormous portion sizes. Julian laughed at my choice of venue but gladly folded himself into the small space and ordered lasagna.

He didn't fit in; he never did, really, anywhere. There was just too much life contained in him. People watched him wherever we went—their eyes trailing his movements and gestures.

I watched him as we ate, the steadiness of his hands, the breadth of his shoulders, and the unlikely softness behind his eyes when he smiled at me sometimes. How could this man be mine to enjoy? How could he be real? He still felt like a figment of my imagination sometimes, just like the things we did together.

Too good to be true.

"Ace," Julian said, putting more parmesan on his plate. "You're watching me."

"No."

He bit his lip to hide a smile. "I don't mind. I know I'm very handsome."

"And very modest."

"That's why you like me."

I couldn't help the smile that spread across my face. I really did like him. More than I should—more than a fling with your boss warranted.

"Tell me more about your childhood," I said before heaping another spoonful of spaghetti into my mouth.

Julian leaned back in the booth. He looked entirely relaxed, his smile affectionate. "Are you sure you got enough pasta for lunch, beautiful? I'm not sure it will—"

I grabbed a napkin from the dispenser and tossed it in his direction. It fluttered uselessly down onto the table between us and he broke out into genuine laughter.

"Ooh. Scary, Ace."

"I asked you a question, you know."

"I know." His hand settled next to mine on the table and he gently traced the line of my finger. It wasn't technically against the rules of things we shouldn't do in public, but judging by the way the butterflies in my stomach sprung to life, I knew it wasn't exactly innocent.

"I had a great childhood. My mom was doting, the type who packed me lunch bags every day. She divorced my dad when I was about thirteen, but they continued to have dinner once a week. I think they fell out of love more than anything."

"No crazy fights?"

"None."

"How about your dad?"

"Aren't you the curious one today?"

"We don't talk a lot about you."

"Only because you're infinitely more interesting."

I frowned at him. "That's decidedly not true, Mr. Fortune 500. There are tons of things I want to know."

"Like what? What time I get up in the morning? If I stretch before or after a workout? What the secret to success is? The pin code to my credit card?"

Julian's tone was teasing, but the questions were eerily

familiar to many of the ones I've read in interviews with him. No doubt the world was determined to figure out what his secret was.

Hard work, I could have told them all, having seen how hard he pushed himself. How his eyes lit up when he spoke about technology's ability to push boundaries and create a better world.

"No," I said softly. "Did you practice an instrument when you were a kid? Did you grow up with pets? What movies make you cry? What's your favorite holiday?"

Julian looked at me for a long while, a crooked smile on his face. It looked more real than any he'd ever given me before. Mentally, I added this version of him to my roster, to the version of him I got when we were alone. It was the version I liked the very best.

"You're a rare jewel, you know that?"

I felt a blush creep up and looked back down at my pasta. "And you're avoiding the question. Again."

He chuckled. "All right then, whip-cracker. My dad wasn't at home a lot, but we had a great relationship and he was very supportive of my interest in programming. He passed a couple of years back. Ryan took it harder than I did, I think, mainly because he was still so young."

"I'm sorry."

"Thank you." His finger traced mine again. "I played the flute as a child."

"The flute?"

"Yes. Horrible instrument. I was never any good, just red in the face from all the blowing." He held up a finger at me, staving off my smile. "Don't say it. I heard how that sounded as I was saying it."

I bit my tongue. "I won't."

"We had a dog named Nancy, a German Shepherd. I don't generally cry at movies, but—"

"Don't tell me you're afraid of showing vulnerability."

"I'm not!"

177

I shook my head sadly. "I thought you were more secure in your masculinity than that, Julian."

"Ace, I've—"

"No. I'm disappointed."

He laughed. "You're impossible. *Yes.* I have gotten teary-eyed at movies, but I can't remember when I last did. But I'll have you know that I did, in fact, get a bit misty-eyed when I saw *The Notebook.*"

The pride he took in this little revelation made me laugh. "Okay, you're just making this up!"

"I'm not! Why is that so hard to believe?"

"It's just a bit cliché."

"Are you seriously telling me you can watch that movie with a dry eye?"

I gave a sheepish shrug. "I might."

"And you're the one giving me a hard time? I'm thinking you might be a psychopath now. I should call for help. Where's the waiter?"

I kicked at his leg under the table. "I'm not sure why that movie didn't get me. But I definitely cry to others."

"Tell me."

"*The Lion King. Black Beauty.*"

"So basically anything that's animated and acted out with animals. I'm not sure that's much better."

"I guess." I grinned. "But I did cry at *Titanic,* and there's not an animal in sight!"

He snorted. "That movie just made me mad. So much mismanagement, from start to finish. The captain was an idiot. Also, that door was *absolutely* big enough to fit both of them."

"I know! Why do you think I was crying?"

Julian grinned at me, his eyes soft again in the way that made my stomach tighten. Dangerous, dangerous ground. I knew I should be guarding my heart, but he made it more difficult with each passing day.

"My favorite holiday was when my dad and I went camping."

"Camping?"

"Yes. Why do you look so surprised?"

"I'm not sure... you just don't strike me as the camping type."

He laughed. "I'm not sure if I should be offended or flattered by that."

"Um... flattered? I've never gone camping."

He put his fork down. "You can't be serious."

"My family never did the whole outdoorsy thing. My parents were dentists!"

"That's it." He shook his head. "I'm going to take you camping one day."

The idea felt absurd. "Really? You're going to take me camping?"

"I have to introduce you to nature, clearly." He glanced down at his smartwatch. "We're meeting with the outside consultant in twenty minutes. Let's pay and head back."

We settled the bill and headed back out into the dry summer air. My dress was work-appropriate, with a three-quarter sleeve and ending just above my knees, but it was considerably cooler than Julian's gray suit. But if he was too hot, he sure didn't complain.

As we turned the corner to the office, he leaned down to whisper in my ear. I'd grown very familiar with the scent of his aftershave by now, but it still managed to leave me a bit breathless. "What would you do if I put my arm around you right now?"

I glanced around, made sure no one saw, and then gave him a sugary sweet smile. "I'd key your Porsche the next time we go somewhere."

Julian's laughter made me smile.

The meeting we were heading to was with an outside hire, a consultant hired to bring new ideas to the table—the decision that had been so controversial in the press team. Rachel had found the graphic designer, and in her classic Rachel way, she hadn't informed me or the others about who he was. *But he's great,* she'd hurried to add. *Stellar track record.*

Julian would supervise the meeting—partly because he was interested in the creation of the new logo—and partly, he'd told me, because he wanted to be in as many work meetings with me as possible. *I love watching you when you have to act all professional with me,* he'd told me a few days earlier… right before he had tugged my panties down with his teeth.

Julian pressed the button for the eleventh floor and took my hand in his as the doors to the elevator closed. "This ought to be interesting."

"It's going to be absolute chaos." I reached up and pressed a kiss to the sharp line of his jaw. "I have no doubt you'll enjoy every moment."

Julian's smile was sly as he tugged me closer. "You know me so well already."

The elevator gave a loud, cheery sound and slid to a stop. I took a step away from him.

"Oh, so cuddling with your boss in the elevator is considered too intimate?" He frowned. "I'll have to make some changes."

I couldn't help grinning. "Just behave, Hunt."

"Yes, ma'am." Julian followed me through the wide corridor toward the meeting room. Animated discussion drifted toward us, with raised voices and awkward laughs.

Five heads turned and I instantly regretted that we hadn't staggered our arrivals. This might seem suspicious.

But they all just smiled. Rachel put a hand on the shoulder of a fair-haired man. A very, very familiar man. Recognition flooded through me, along with acute shame.

"Mr. Davis, it's my pleasure to introduce you to Julian Hunt."

But Mr. Davis only looked at me, a smile growing on his face. No, no, no. This couldn't be happening, and not *here* of all places.

"Emily?"

"Ben," I said weakly. "It's been a long time."

He rose gracefully and rounded the table. "I didn't know you now worked at Hunt Industries."

"I do, yes." I extended a hand—*act professional, Ben*—but he gave me a hug. I patted him awkwardly on the back once and shot a sideways glance at Julian. He was staring at the back of Ben's head, disapproval written on every line of his body.

I extricated myself. "Ben, this is Julian Hunt. He is the founder and CEO of Hunt Industries and will join us today."

Ben extended a hand. "Mr. Hunt, it's a pleasure to meet you."

Julian raised an eyebrow and shook Ben's hand with slow, heavy strokes. "Likewise, I'm sure."

"Have you had Em working for you long?"

I couldn't help it—I physically cringed. Ben was digging his own grave deeper with every passing moment and doing his very best to pull me down with him.

Not to mention the fact that six people in this room were listening to every word spoken, and with every word, the situation became more and more unprofessional.

"Ms. Giordano has been working as a press secretary at this company for nearly two months now." Julian's voice was ice. "She is excellent at her job."

"I'm sure she is."

I cleared my throat. "Shall we have a seat, gentlemen?"

"Let's." Julian pulled out a chair for me—something he had never done before—and while he didn't touch me, I imagined I could feel the proprietary hand he wanted to put around my waist all the same. I took a seat next to Rachel and opened my work tablet.

"Let's begin."

Everyone ignored me.

Trent leaned forward. "Have you two worked together before?"

Ben nodded. "Yes. I occasionally did work for Pet and Co, where Emily was the main point of liaison. So we've collaborated on graphic design work in the past and have established good lines of communication."

"That's terrific to hear," Rachel said. "That means we have

some familiarity going forward. I'm sure Emily can vouch for your work?"

I gave a nod. "Yes, he's an excellent graphic designer."

Ben pulled out a folder. "I've started brainstorming a few ideas since we last spoke, but how about you first walk me through your product plan again?"

Julian was mostly quiet throughout the meeting. It was a silence I was used to—I'd seen him adopt the same stance in panels and interviews. Not a ripple of emotion showed on his face, and for all intents and purposes, he looked like the consummate professional. The broad-shouldered tech mogul, the legend.

I knew he would ask me about Ben's familiarity later.

And the worst part was… I'd have to answer.

25

JULIAN

It was Mr. Davis—*Ben*—who suggested that the team should go out for dinner that evening to continue discussing the launch. It was a bit forward, yes, but not unheard of. With anyone else, I wouldn't have batted an eye.

But he'd asked it with a slick smile aimed toward Emily, and with far too much meaning in his eyes. Josef accepted immediately, but to my surprise, so had Rachel. When Emily gave a shallow nod as well... my decision was made.

"I'll have my assistant give Rent a call and set up a table for us," I said. "It'll be on Hunt."

Ben's eyebrows rose. "That would be an honor, Mr. Hunt. I appreciate you taking the time."

"This launch is important to me. Someone will text you the details."

"All right. That sounds good." Trent cleared his throat, throwing me a look. "I think we're done here for now, then."

I could feel the eyes of my employees—they were as surprised by this as Ben. Few were the times I met outside hires, not to mention accompany them out like this. I didn't technically have the time, but I would postpone my evening meeting. Emily's gaze was the heaviest.

Ben caught her after the meeting, and the last thing I heard was his eager voice before the door shut. I wanted to save her from that. Barge in and declare that I had need of her for some task or another. But I knew she didn't want my protectiveness, didn't want me to claim her in public.

Wouldn't let me call her mine.

An unwelcome but loud part of me feared it was because of who I was. That she didn't see a future with someone like me, with someone who had to fly on business trips nearly every week and whose name was mentioned in newspapers. Being with me—actually *being mine*—would come with strings.

It wasn't something I had dwelled on for a long time. Most women I had dated in the past had been thrilled with the prospect and had practiced poses in the mirror for their close-ups. It wasn't very attractive behavior.

On one occasion, a woman had mentioned, just out of the blue, that she admired how a famous billionaire's wife was handling her husband's fortune and philanthropy foundation. *She's a role model of mine,* the woman had said and looked down at her salad with calculated demureness.

I'd asked for the check then and there.

These women had been so pervasive, it hadn't been until Emily that I'd really reflected on the fact that some women might not want that life. Instead, they might actually distance themselves from me because of it.

And Emily hadn't given me much indication that she found me interesting beyond the merely physical. Hell, I had to fight to keep the weekly dinners on the books because they were the few times we met fully clothed—when I could talk to her and take care of her and try to make her fall for me.

But there were things men like Ben could give her that I couldn't, in terms of normalcy. And God knew Emily could get someone else in a heartbeat if she chose to—the woman was a complete stunner. A swish of that dark curtain of hair, a slow wink of her green eyes... She could have her pick of the litter.

I just had to continue making her want to pick me.

Rent was one of the trendiest restaurants in the city. It served overpriced food on oversized plates, with far too little in each dish. But judging by Ben's appreciative smile when we entered, he enjoyed being courted to fancy places.

"I'll be with you in a moment, Mr. Hunt," a smartly dressed young man said as he darted out from the hostess stand. I undid the top button of my shirt and wished I was anywhere else than here.

My house, for example, with takeaway pizza and Emily's legs in my lap, her laughter in my ears.

At the moment, she stood next to Ben as they chatted. She'd slipped into a black sheath dress that hugged every aspect of her figure. Her hair hung shiny down her back, reminding me of how it felt wound through my fingers or looked spread as a curtain around her when she rode me.

Focus, Julian.

Ben gave her a wide, toothy grin and reached over to put his hand on her bare shoulder. Basically sexual harassment, if I had anything to say about it. But judging from Emily's animated gestures and responses, she didn't feel harassed at all.

Rachel bumped her elbow into mine. "You're acting weird."

"No, I'm not."

"Okay, let's say for argument's sake that you're not. Since when do you join us for dinners with random contractors? Your time is valuable."

"It's like I said: this product launch is important to me. I want to ensure it goes well."

"Uh-huh."

Rachel and I went way back, but she was starting to get on my nerves. "Honestly, Rachel, you're reading too much into this."

"Am I? Or maybe I've just been working for you for the past six years." She shrugged. "I just want to see you—"

She was interrupted by the waiter. "This way! Your table is in the back."

We followed him through the dimly lit restaurant. Emily sidled up to me and the familiar scent of her perfume hit me. God, I wanted her.

"Julian?"

"Ace."

"I feel like I should tell you something."

"I'm listening."

Her eyes flicked to where our party was weaving through the tables before she found my eyes again. There was concern there, and that more than anything made my stomach tighten with anticipation.

"Ben and I had a one-night stand once. It never meant anything, not for me."

My jaw clenched; it was automatic. *Fuck*. The smarmy bastard.

"I see."

Her hand curled around my arm, but her voice was decisive. "Julian, it was a long time ago. I just wanted you to know."

"Of course. Don't worry about it."

"You're sure?"

"Yes. Thanks for telling me, Ace."

She gave me a small smile, one of intimacy and hope, and it made my jealousy melt a bit. God, but she was beautiful. So entirely good. It took all the effort I had to not grasp her hand in that moment—I had never wanted anything more. To make sure that everyone knew we were together.

Instead, I nodded toward the table.

"Come on. Let's go get this dinner over with."

"Let's."

My jaw clenched when I saw that Ben had saved a space for her. His smile was still too slick, too sure of himself. Not for a moment could I see what Emily had once seen in him, but then again, I was decidedly biased against him.

"Did we lose you guys?"

"We had something to discuss." I took a seat on Emily's left. "Have you had a chance to look at the menu?"

Rachel and Josef had, and made their choices very clear. Ben was a vocal participant, but neither Emily nor I spoke. She was engrossed by the menu like the foodie she was, her teeth worrying her lower lip. I had to stop myself from smiling at her obvious internal debate.

"What would you recommend?"

She shot me a warm, sideways glance. "Get the ceviche. You'll enjoy it."

I closed my menu. "Done."

But that was the full extent of our one-on-one conversation at the table that night. It turned out—unsurprisingly, to me—that Ben was quite the talker. He managed to charm both Rachel and Josef with his stories from university and press anecdotes.

I was silent, watching him as he entertained.

"Have you heard of *Jax*?"

"No," Rachel said. "What's that?"

"It's a revolutionary new hair product. A mixture of hair gel and hair wax. The idea is that it will completely eliminate the need for either by being one, combined product. I'm working on that too, at the moment. It has huge investor capital behind it."

I had to drink some of my wine to keep from laughing out loud.

Emily cleared her throat, her voice measured. "I didn't know there was a difference between gel and wax?"

"Oh, but there is!" Ben launched into a nearly ten-minute discussion, during which I saw Emily's mouth twitch several times. She was struggling not to laugh and it instantly made me feel a hundred times better. I had already decided that he was a fool, but I liked that she thought so too.

The only part I hated was when he slung an arm carelessly around the back of her chair.

"You should have seen this girl back at Pet and Co," he told all of us, voice conspiratorial. "She was a star."

Rachel nodded over her wine. "I can imagine. She's been an asset to us at Hunt."

"She singlehandedly ran that company's entire promotional team. Did she tell you about their terrible management? Have you, Emily?"

She shot him an irritated glance. "I don't really like talking about my previous employers like that. I learned a lot at Pet and Co."

"Of course, of course you did," Ben backtracked. "I didn't mean to—"

I cut him off. "Emily is a highly valued employee here at Hunt. Her ideas for several of our upcoming product launches have been nothing short of impressive. I think I speak for all of us when I say we don't doubt she was just as effective in her previous jobs."

Ben nodded at me. "Right you are, Julian. Well said."

I had to resist the urge to roll my eyes. The only thing that made it better was a familiar hand, hidden under the table, squeezing my knee in thanks. I knew Emily shared my irritation.

Dinner didn't last much longer after that. We all turned down dessert, and while Josef and Ben wanted to grab another drink, the rest of us made it clear that it was time to call it.

"A smoke to cap off the night?"

"I'll come with you," Josef said, and the two of them went out for a cigarette.

Rachel excused herself, too. "I'll be right back. Ladies' room."

Emily and I watched her retreat. "And then there were two…" she murmured.

I sighed and reached for the bill, pulling out the corporate card. "So this was an interesting evening."

"You're jealous."

"No, I'm not."

Emily's lips quirked into a smile. "Yes, you are."

I frowned and looked out across the restaurant, but she refused to give up. "Admit it, Julian!"

"Fine," I said. "I'm jealous. It's not a good look, I know."

Emily bit her lip and lowered her dark, thick lashes. "Actually, I kind of like you like this."

I let my hand inch closer to hers on the table. "Do I have anything to be jealous of?"

"I don't know. He *is* kind of considered a catch in the media world. Plus, he has a great new idea for hair wax. Sorry, *Jax*."

"Don't ever repeat that idea to me, thank you."

Her smile was wide. "But Julian, it's two products in one! Clearly you recognize a great business opportunity when you see one."

"Let me get my checkbook," I said dryly.

Emily glanced around, and then her fingers touched mine. "He's a fool, and I only want you. I'm sorry you had to go through this."

Her green eyes were flicked with concern, and I wanted so much to kiss her. Instead, I covered her hand with mine entirely. "You're so beautiful, Ace. Inside and out."

She glanced down at our hands. "You can't say things like that."

"Why not? It's the truth. And I'm sorry for being jealous."

"Don't be. I think— Oh." Emily pulled her hand out of mine as Rachel returned.

"Is everything settled here?"

"Yes. Let's head out."

Rachel raised an eyebrow. "So, he's a bit of a handful, isn't he? But I think he's fun."

"Just make sure he does what we're paying him to do."

"Don't worry, I will. I'll go grab our coats and tell the guys it's time to go."

As soon as the door closed behind her, I caught Emily around the waist. She twisted in my grasp. "Julian!"

"They're gone," I murmured against her cheek. "I couldn't resist."

Emily glanced at the door, but it stayed resolutely shut. "Someone might come back."

"Let them."

She let out a breathless chuckle and twisted again, but this time to bring us closer together. Heat swept across my body as her perfect breasts were suddenly pressed against my chest. She smelled like floral perfume and sweetness and I wanted her.

"Come over to mine tonight. Spend the night."

"It's a weeknight," she said weakly. "I can't."

"Tomorrow night then. It's a Friday. I'll cook, we'll watch a movie… and I'll eat you for dessert."

Her mouth went round with surprise and I grinned at her expression. I bent and pressed my lips to the soft skin below her ear, where her pulse fluttered erratically. I had quickly realized that it made her knees weak—and I exploited it any way I could.

"Give me more of your time. Trust me, Ace."

"Okay," she breathed. "I'd love to."

I pressed a kiss to her lips before releasing her. "I look forward to it."

She looked both flushed and disoriented, and I loved that I had that effect on her. That I could make her feel even a fraction of the dizzying effect she had on me.

"Um. Yeah," she murmured.

"Very eloquent, Ace."

She stuck out her tongue at me and I laughed.

"Very scary," I taunted and opened the door for her. She shot me a final, heated look before stepping out into the cool night and reuniting us with the others.

26

EMILY

Julian's house was very, very impressive.

It was large but tasteful—an old structure that had been transformed with modern architecture in mind. Large windows, sleek furniture, and books everywhere. Nestled in the green hills above Palo Alto, it was a secluded oasis of amazing views and wide spaces. The type of house I had never once visited before.

I teased him and asked if he had decorated it himself. Julian had rubbed the back of his neck. "Well, no," he said finally. "I hired an interior designer when I bought it. It was faster."

"But this…" I stopped at a glossy book detailing the history of computers, decoratively placed on a coffee table. "Surely you bought this."

He had laughed and come up behind me, wrapping his arms around my waist. "Will you deduct points if I say no?"

"No, I'll say that whatever you paid that designer probably wasn't enough."

He pressed a kiss to my neck and tugged me along toward the kitchen. He patted a kitchen stool for me to jump up on before heading to the kitchen counter. He'd already laid out vegetables on a platter, a cutting board and knife ready. There was something so intimate about cooking together, being together like this. Without work clothes on, without people around. Just two people enjoying each other's company.

I grinned at him as I washed the tomatoes—I couldn't help it, seeing Julian Hunt measuring up pasta…

"What?"

"Nothing. Just that you look hot, doing that."

He shook his head with a groan. "I can't tell if you're mocking me or not, but it's working."

"I'm not, I swear."

"Tell me you can stay the night." He put the pot down on the stove, heading toward me. I knew exactly how he'd try to convince me. "I want you in my bed."

I looked down at my tomatoes and pretended to hesitate. "Oh, I'm not sure if I can…"

"You're allowed to have your own life." He wrapped his strong arms around me, and pressed hot lips against my neck. "Your brother is grown."

I put my own hand over his. "Oh, okay then."

"Really?"

"I might have already told him I'd be at Denise's tonight."

Julian's kiss nearly knocked me off my feet.

We'd spent time in hotel rooms, in restaurants around the city, half-hidden in his car. But spending time in his house—in his bed—that evening felt more intimate than anything we'd done before.

"Ace, it's Saturday," Julian argued, flipping off the covers. "We can stay in bed for as long as we want."

I laughed and tugged at his arm, still wrapped around me. "But we already *have*. Julian, you can't possibly go again without food. I know I can't."

"But I've already eaten." He grinned and rolled over, pressing kisses to my naked shoulder. My body was still in bliss from the *two* orgasms he'd already given me. I'd been afraid of not living up to his expectations, but Julian seemed insatiable.

And so was I. One look at those eyes, at the deep V on his stomach… Yeah, he made me into a sex-crazed teenager again. Actually, scratch *again*. This was the first time I'd ever been this head-over-heels infatuated.

His kisses traveled up my collarbone. "I can't help it. I've never been with anyone like you."

I laughed and tugged at his hair, the rough strands sliding through my fingers. "What does *that* mean?"

He lifted himself up on an elbow. "That it's never been this good with anyone else. That even when I've just had you, I want you again."

My face must have registered the surprise I felt because Julian grinned and ducked his head. "Tell me how it is for you," he murmured against my skin.

I continued to run my fingers through his hair. "I've never been with anyone like you either. And sex with you is definitely the best I've ever had."

His answering grin was filled with pure, masculine pride, all vulnerability suddenly wiped away. "I *knew* it!"

"But that's hardly surprising. I have more limited experience than you do."

"I'm not that much older. I'm not exactly looking to retire anytime soon, Ace."

"Yeah, but—" I stopped. I didn't know exactly how much I wanted to reveal, but Julian picked up on my hesitation with laser focus. He lifted himself off me completely.

"But…?"

I threw an arm over my face, shielding my eyes from the morning light, and confessed. "Itmighthavebeenawhilebeforeyou."

"What? Ace, talk to me."

I sighed. "It might have been a while before you."

"Really?" He tugged at my arm, prying it away from my face. "How long?"

"Two years."

He looked floored. "I thought you said you had one-night

stands, back when we played that drinking game. I thought Ben was one?"

"I took one sip of the drink, because I've had a one-night stand—once. Ben is the only one. And before that I was in a relationship, remember? I told you about that."

Julian pulled me closer. "So I'm the third man you've ever slept with?"

"Yeah, I guess."

He made an amused sound. "You guess?"

"I *know*," I corrected and pulled the comforter over me. "Gosh, how embarrassing."

"Why would it be?" He dug me out, tucked me against his body again. "I love that you enjoy sleeping with me—you have no idea how much. And while it wouldn't matter if there were more men before me, I'm selfishly glad you've not had more experience."

I snorted. "Because I have less to compare you with?"

Julian's hand smoothed across my stomach, traced the curve of my hip. "Because I don't like the idea of sharing you, even with your memories. I know. It makes me sound terrible."

I thought of the photos I'd seen of him and all the tanned, perfectly plucked women he kept on his arm. Jealousy was a trait I recognized well.

He swept my hair away and kissed the nape of my neck. It was a sweet, gentle touch. "The hotel bathroom was a mistake," he said softly.

"What?!"

"You deserved music, roses—the works. Hell, a bed, even. That's what I had planned, you know, and then you... Well, I should have waited."

I flipped him over and pinned him to the bed, straddling him. "No. *No.* That was exactly what I wanted, remember? Are you telling me that you didn't enjoy it?"

Julian sighed, his hands on my hips. "You know I did."

"Right. And so did I." I bent and kissed him, pouring all my determination and want into the touch. "I'm not a delicate little thing, and I'm not in over my head. I love being with you. I want to keep being with you. Now, I'm going to go downstairs and make us some coffee, and start preparing breakfast. I'll make you some too if you promise you won't mope about?"

He sighed and smoothed his hands down my naked thighs. "All right, all right. Let me just take a shower first."

"Good." I kissed him one last time and then bounced off the fluffy bed. "And I'm stealing one of your shirts!"

"Take them all!" he called as he headed into the bathroom. I chose one of his large button-downs and folded the shirtsleeves the way I'd seen him do so many times. In his wardrobe mirror, I looked flushed and happy, my cheeks glowing with life. My hair was a tousled mess, but I recognized a hopeless cause when I saw one. The shirt covered my butt and a bit of thigh, but other than that my legs were on full display. Perfect for a bit of teasing later.

I whistled as I turned on his espresso machine and dug out eggs from the fridge. *Omelets.* I had just begun chopping up chives and tomatoes when I heard a key turn in the front door.

I froze. What the hell?

Julian was still upstairs and I could hear the water running. Calling out would alert whoever was entering.

Still carrying the knife, I inched toward the hallway. I should have brought my phone down with me.

My heart was a hammer in my chest.

I paused when I heard the distinctly masculine sound of someone clearing their throat.

"Bro, are you home? Why aren't you answering your phone?"

Suddenly I was face to face with the infamous Ryan Hunt. A smaller, far less adult version of Julian—his hair longer and clothes baggier. His eyes widened when he saw what I was wearing and the knife in my hand.

"Ah," he said—a whole world encompassed in that small word. "So *that's* why he's not answering."

For a wild second I thought he was referring to the knife, that

I'd done away with Julian, before rational thought filtered back in. My heart still pounded.

"Um, yeah," I said. "Yes. Sorry. He's upstairs. Why don't you come in and wait for him?"

"Nah, I don't think he'll want company," Ryan ran a hand through his hair and started heading for the front door again. I remembered Julian's remarks about his brother and frowned.

"No, please stay. I know he'll be happy to see you. Do you want an omelet?" He looked torn, so I decided to really press. "I can make it with whatever you want. Ham, cheese, onions, tomatoes… Just let me know."

His resolve broke, and he tugged off his jacket. "Ham and cheese then, thanks."

We spoke a little as I finished up a couple of omelets. When asked what he does for a living, I learned that Ryan was doing "a bit of this and that," and I didn't pry. He lived fifteen minutes away and occasionally he would go running with Julian in the mornings.

"Though we haven't for a while," he said, and his voice didn't have that guarded tone I'd heard when he whipped open the door earlier. It had been a tone I recognized from my own younger years—back when you treated the world as if it might bite you every step of the way.

Julian appeared in the doorway to the kitchen. His hair wet and dark, but his expression was darker still.

Please don't snap at him, I thought.

Ryan straightened. "Hi, Jules."

"Hi." Julian stepped over to me and leaned against the fridge. "I wasn't expecting you today."

"I came over on a whim," Ryan said. I could see his knee bouncing under the center island.

I decided to save him. "And I insisted that he'd stay for some breakfast. You like ham, don't you, Julian?"

He turned his gaze to me, eyes on mine before they traveled down my bare legs. "Yes, I do."

With a Mary Poppins' worthy display of calm domesticity, I

plated two omelets and put them on the counter. "Why don't you guys start? I've made coffee as well and there's orange juice in the fridge. I'm going to take a shower."

Ryan mumbled a thank-you and grabbed one of the plates. Julian's hand trailed along my waist as I passed, uncertainty and gratefulness in his gaze.

"Thanks," he murmured.

I nodded and headed up the staircase. Whatever they needed to talk about, I figured it might be good if they talked alone. So I made sure my shower lasted *forever,* scrubbing my scalp and lathering myself with his 99-cent body wash. It seemed that men, regardless of how much money they made, never really learned to appreciate the difference. I'd have to get him some fancy stuff one day.

Much later, properly dressed and hair plaited, I waited by the staircase, trying to hear what was going on. Was the coast clear? Could I go downstairs? I didn't know how much time they needed together, but I also didn't want them to have to come looking for me. *Did we lose you up here?*

Voices drifted upwards and I paused on the staircase, feeling like a snoop and also unable to stop myself.

"Nah, I dropped him. He wasn't a good friend, in the end."

I heard Julian's snort. "That's good. It takes time to figure out who's in your life for short-term interests and who's there to stay."

"Yeah."

"I meant to tell you—I got front-seat tickets to the playoffs next week."

"You did?"

"Let's go, like old times."

"I'm down. Just text me the details."

"I will. Pass me the juice?"

"Sure."

There was a delicate silence, and I figured it was probably safe to come down, but just as I began to move I froze again.

"So. The chick you have upstairs."

"*Emily.*"

"Yeah, Emily. Am I crazy, or do you seem a bit taken with her?"

Julian was quiet for a moment as I waited with bated breath. "Yes," he said finally. "She actually works at Hunt Industries."

Ryan laughed. "Dude, I can't believe you. You've got more game than I give you credit for. Your own employees?"

"It's not like that. Don't be crude."

"Hold up, are you two serious? She makes a mean omelet, and she's gorgeous, so you could do a *lot* worse. Hey, don't look at me like that. You know it's the truth."

"It's early days yet." His voice was clipped. "We're changing the subject now. You know she might come down any second, Ryan."

"All right, all right. But it's been a long time since I've seen you look like that at anyone."

I heard Julian's annoyed exhale. The conversation drifted to sports, and after waiting a little bit longer I wandered downstairs.

It turned out that Julian had made an omelet for me with mushrooms. It was piping hot when he put it in front of me. I joined their bantering, talking about nothing in particular.

I'd been worried about intruding but it seemed like both of them were happy for my presence, as it made sure no personal issues were mentioned. I was like the adult referee at a primary school soccer game. *One point to the orange team!* It was a shame I hadn't brought a Tupperware container filled with perfectly sliced orange wedges, too.

Ryan stood and shoved his hands in his pockets. "Thanks for breakfast," he told me. "I'll head out."

Julian walked his brother out to the entrance hall. "All right, man. I'll text you about the game."

"Sounds good."

"Do you need money for gas?"

Ryan rolled his eyes, but it was good-naturedly. "No, I have enough, thanks though. Emily, it was nice meeting you."

"You too."

The door closed behind him and the house was silent once more.

I jumped up onto the kitchen counter and watched Julian as he quietly walked back into the kitchen. He didn't say anything, just looked at me for a long time.

"It's okay that I invited him to stay for breakfast, right? You're not mad?"

Julian closed the space between us, nudging my knees apart so he could stand between them. Warm arms wrapped around my waist. "No. Why would I be mad?"

I ran a hand through his still damp hair. "You looked... surprised. Cautious."

He sighed and I felt the warm exhale against my neck. "We don't have the best relationship, and it's been strained lately."

"Is that so?"

"Yes." Julian closed his eyes in pleasure as I tugged at the hair at the nape of his neck, my fingers gently digging into tensed muscles. "Never stop doing that."

I grinned. "I'll have to use my hand sometime, you know."

His lips curled into that small, crooked smile. "No. I forbid it. Stay here forever."

I shifted closer, wrapped my legs around him. "Maybe this should be your next invention. A robotic head-scratcher."

Julian snorted. "No. I know the limits of technology, and no one could replace you."

I tugged him closer and rested my head against his shoulder, closing my eyes against the sudden swell of emotion inside. He'd told his brother that it was early days yet, and that was technically true, but still...

I'd told myself to be wary from the start, to accept this for what it was: a fling. Okay, so it was guaranteed to be the most memorable fling of my life—and definitely the best sex—but something with a clear end in sight. Men like him, who lived in places like this, and who spoke in front of crowds like that, didn't end up with me.

He smelled like soap and man and clean clothes, and when his hands tightened around my waist I nearly had to swallow my sudden tears of despair. I had grown too attached. I wanted *more*.

I googled pictures of him last week for fun, but all I'd seen were the various models he'd been pictured with in the past, one high-definition photo after another barreling me deeper into despair.

Despite my precautions, Julian Hunt had captured my heart. It would inevitably break.

"Hey," he murmured. "What happened?"

I burrowed my face closer to his neck and reveled in the strength of his body pressed against mine. It had become familiar to me so fast—the hard shapes of his chest, the curve of his biceps, the happiest of happy trails. "Nothing. Just thinking of how I don't want you to invent a robot to replace me either."

Julian laughed softly. "Good. I promise I won't. And hey, you were great with Ryan. Maybe it's because you have a younger brother too."

"Maybe," I said. "Or I'm just the troubled-youth-whisperer."

"Either way, would you want to meet him again? I have a feeling… maybe you'll be able to reach him where I can't. I think you'd be good for him." Julian shook his head, the movement jostling me. "But maybe it's a silly idea. You don't have to—"

"Of course I want to."

"You do?"

"Yes. He's important to you."

Julian's eyes darkened as they gazed into mine, and then I was lifted up and off the kitchen counter. I wrapped my arms around his neck, clutching at him as he moved.

"Where are we going?"

"I had plans to suggest a quiet walk around the area, something cute and date appropriate. But no." Julian carried me into the living room and unceremoniously dropped us down onto his wide couch, not loosening his grip on me. "I think I'll just keep you captive here instead."

I settled against the pillows, looking down at where he rested against my chest. Julian narrowed his eyes at me and demonstratively lifted my hand back up to the nape of his neck.

I grinned and continued stroking through his hair. "There are dirty dishes in the sink," I murmured, teasing. "Great big coffee books about tech history to read."

He didn't even bother opening his eyes. "Fuck the dishes. Fuck the books."

"You're insatiable."

Julian sighed in pleasure as I continued to stroke his hair. Dark, long lashes against high cheekbones. The straight, strong nose, lightly dusted with a tan. His hair was thick and dark, and somehow naturally fell in an elegant wave. His strong body was a warm and pleasant weight on top of me. I never wanted to move from this spot.

I continued to watch him and run my fingers through his hair, thinking that these were the moments I'd treasure when everything inevitably went south.

27

JULIAN

The invitation was glossy to the touch, the name printed in bold capital letters. *Innovation Awards.* The event was massive. I'd attended it for the last four years, but this time was different.

I was one of the nominees in the category Greatest Outreach and Social Awareness Program. It was all because of the health app, as well as the new solutions to the hospital interface systems we'd developed.

The dating apps, the games—all of that was minor league shit. What I wanted to do was to find creative, tech-based solutions to real-life problems. And the industry had decided to honor that. From the moment I'd received the email about the nomination, I'd entertained the idea that I might win.

How could I not?

I'd been competitive since birth, and it wasn't impossible. Hunt Industries was one of the fastest growing players in the business. And if I was lucky enough to win, there was only one person I wanted with me.

Emily.

But that would mean coming out as a couple. It meant that everyone in the company would know. It meant change. While I was more than willing to say fuck you to anyone who had anything negative to say, I'd learned the hard way that she would have to come to me.

But things seemed to be going my way.

She'd won Ryan over the past weekend, big time. He'd actually asked me later if he could ask her some questions about press and social media marketing, and I'd struggled to hide my surprise.

Emily had very quickly become the most important thing in my life. I wasn't quite sure how to show her that yet, or how to hint at it without making her freak out. When Ryan had started talking about my feelings toward her, with her just upstairs, my heart had been beating fast with nerves. If she had come down and heard that—heard him saying just how in love I looked—I feared that she might have bolted.

Slow and steady, Julian…

As if I'd summoned her with my thoughts, Emily appeared at the threshold of my home office. Her hair fell in thick waves around her smiling face, her sundress clinging to her body. She was just as beautiful as she had been when I first saw her, in that dark club—but when she smiled at me?

It took my breath away.

"I'll order some food before I have to head out. What do you want?"

"Pizza."

"Again? Can't we do sushi?"

I grinned. It had become a habit of ours—she'd come over, we'd sleep together, and eat takeout before she left—despite my attempts to get her to stay over again.

"Get whatever you want, Ace. We can order from two places."

"That's such a waste." She frowned down at her phone. "We'd have to pay two delivery fees."

I laughed and rose, crossing the room to grab her around the waist. I hoisted her up easily.

"Julian!"

"You're ridiculous." I carried her down the hallway. "Get whatever you want. It's my app and account, anyway."

Emily's laughter was soft and sweet in my ear. "You really know how to be romantic."

I gathered her closer and sank down onto the large couch in my living room. "I can be romantic."

"Mhm, sure."

"You're the one who won't let me, you know."

Emily bit her lip and watched me with amusement. "Is that so?"

"Yeah. Not being seen in public, no dinners with candlelight, no flowers..." I trailed off and pressed kisses to her soft skin. "What's a man to do with those restrictions? The only thing I have to offer is a wide selection of takeout options."

Emily chuckled and rolled her hips against me. I couldn't help groaning at the sensation as she ground right across the growing hardness in my pants.

"How about we skip takeout," she murmured, "and go straight to dessert?"

"You're very persuasive."

I felt her smile against my lips before she kissed me. There was something about her touches that always managed to completely undo me. She was sexy as hell, don't get me wrong, and she knew how to please a man. But she also touched me with tenderness and just a hint of nervousness. As if this meant more to her than her words let on.

As if *I* meant more to her than her words let on.

So I tugged her closer and kissed her back, willing my own kisses to tell her all the things I longed to do. To coax her into accepting this thing between us—into accepting the idea of becoming more.

28

EMILY

I was deep into my work, phone momentarily forgotten, and obsessing over a new print layout. We'd settled on a logo but there were still things to be decided with the slogans, the color schemes, and more importantly—the new website overhaul.

The door to my office was slightly open, a habit I had yet to shake. I glanced up only to see Julian slip inside with a devilish grin. He gently shut the door behind him, a cup of coffee in his hand.

"No knocking, Hunt?"

He was dressed in a navy suit that offset his green eyes and his hair was in perfect order—making me long to muss it up.

"I think we're beyond knocking."

"Did anyone see you?"

"No. I snuck through my own building, hiding behind filing cabinets and servers, all to make it here unseen."

"My very own spy."

He turned sideways, a serious expression on his face as he cocked an imaginary gun. "Hunt. Julian Hunt."

I rose from my seat. "Dork."

"What can I say? Once a nerd, always a nerd."

I gave him a very clear once-over. There was absolutely nothing about his tall, strong frame and masculine jaw that said *nerd.* He looked like he regularly ran on the beach and spent the mornings before work hiking. It didn't hurt that I knew he had the abs of an underwear model, toned to perfection.

"Don't look at me like that," he said darkly. "I only have a certain amount of self-restraint, and you're testing it right now."

"Stop looking that handsome and maybe I'll stop."

"Ah, but then you'd leave me," he declared and put a hand over his heart. "And I wouldn't be able to take that."

I laughed and hoped he didn't notice the blush that spread on my cheeks. As if *I* would ever leave him. "Are you free tomorrow afternoon? I have two hours before yoga with Denise. I could swing by yours…"

Julian gave a husky laugh and put both hands on my waist, pulled me closer. "A two-hour flyby? Why, Ace, it'll be difficult, but I think I'll be able to finish in that time."

I ran my hands up his powerful chest. "More like twenty minutes," I teased.

"Thirty," he breathed. "Times two."

He leaned in closer and gently nipped at my lower lip, his fingers digging into my skin.

I groaned against his mouth. It had been three days since we'd last touched like this. "We can't. Not in the office."

Julian didn't loosen his grip, just moved to kiss along my jaw. When his mouth touched the sensitive spot on my neck, my knees actually went a bit weak.

I swallowed. "Julian."

"Mmm?"

I pulled at his shoulders. "No one in the office can know."

He kissed the top of my collarbone before leaning back with a resigned expression. "As much as I enjoy sneaking about, how much longer until we can tell the others?"

I blinked at him in disbelief before I burst out laughing. "Julian, *never.* Just imagine how awkward it'll be!"

"Why? They'll get over it. If you're concerned about HR, I'll make sure to talk to them first. Your job will never be in jeopardy because of this."

"Thanks, but Julian... come on. Imagine how it'll be when we're no longer doing this." I gave his wide shoulders a little squeeze for emphasis. "It'll likely be weird enough between the two of us, not to mention if the others knew!"

Julian's eyes went wide, frozen—I couldn't read the emotion in them. It was as if a wall had suddenly slammed up between us.

I rose on my tiptoes and rubbed my nose playfully against his. "Don't worry. I'm sure we'll be adults about the whole situation. I'm not concerned."

His hands tightened slightly around my waist before he let me go entirely. "Good. I guess I'm not concerned either, then."

"Great," I said, a bit confused. "So... we won't tell them. Agreed?"

"Yes, agreed." He kissed me on the forehead once before he headed toward my office door, shoulders squared. "I'll see you later, Emily."

"Yeah. I'll be at the four o'clock staff meeting."

He nodded once and slipped out my office, the same way he'd come in, not bothering to glance back. I sank into my office chair with a sigh.

The conversation refused to leave me, try as I might to push it away. Was this when he began tiring of me? When I refused to flaunt our whatever-we-were in front of our coworkers? I should be allowed to make that choice.

Hell, I had a lot more to lose than him. The CEO and founder of Hunt Industries wouldn't be called into the HR office, wouldn't be given sly looks in the hallways by people wondering if every success I had came from my prowess in the bedroom. He wouldn't have to endure the snickers of coworkers or see the potential loss of respect in their eyes. I'd heard Rachel and Josef that night when they joked about Julian's dates—I'd heard them loud and clear. I wanted to earn my promotions and earn the respect of my peers. This job meant the world to me.

I hoped I could make him see that.

The next day, Rachel burst into my office, Sasha and Josef in tow.

"Guess what?

"What?"

"We just closed some of the final details on the upcoming pitches on the package software launch. That deserves some celebration."

I couldn't help grinning. "You're always in the mood for celebration."

"Factual." Josef nodded.

"We're heading to the pool pub after work to grab a celebratory beer before we all head home," Rachel said. "Come with us?"

I glanced down at the mountain of paperwork before me. "Well, I'd love—"

"Pleaaaaaase," Sasha pouted. "Work hard, play hard, you know. That's practically the unofficial motto of Hunt."

I laughed and looked back up at them. "All right, I'll be there!"

For the remainder of the day, my phone refused to stop staring at me. It might have been lying inconspicuously on the desk, the screen black, but I knew it was basically daring me. *Use me*, it beckoned. *You know you want to.*

What could I say in my defense? I was weak.

Despite not having heard from Julian since we spoke yesterday, I texted him about the drinks. We'd have to act professional around our colleagues, but I wanted to see him, especially after the odd conversation.

I had now seen up close just how much he worked. Days, evenings, weekends... an hour or two of fun with his employees might be good for him. And I wanted to be around him, even if it was only as friends and co-workers.

Julian didn't respond.

Not as the hours passed, not as I met up with the others and we headed to the bar. Trent nabbed us the same high table as last time. The others ordered a round of beer and began dissecting the successful product launch as I tried to surreptitiously check my phone every five minutes.

Nothing. Complete and utter radio silence.

Sasha slid into the seat next to me. "Okay, you need to put that *away*. No more working. Do you think I haven't seen you across the table?"

I dropped my phone back into my bag, probably looking as guilty as I felt. "You're right. Live in the moment, and all that."

"Exactly. People go on these digital cleanses and stuff, which I'm sure we all need. Not that anyone in this town would be able to listen, though."

Rachel leaned in. "Sasha, are you telling Emily of our plan?"

"No, I hadn't gotten to that part yet. Let a woman work, jeez."

Rachel laughed, but I made a show of looking between them with mock terror. "Oh no. Is this the part where you tell me I've worked at Hunt long enough to be initiated? Is it all actually a facade for some weird doomsday cult?"

Sasha nodded. "Yes, tonight we're sacrificing lambs under the full moon."

I shivered. "I knew this job paid too much. There really is no such thing as a free lunch."

Rachel laughed. "Weirdos. No, we have a different plan—a good plan. You're single, right?"

Oh. Damn.

If I said no, they'd ask who I was dating. Lying wasn't my strong suit.

Hoping they would drop it if I said yes, I gave an Oscar-worthy shrug. "I'm not really dating anyone at the moment."

"That's terrific!" Sasha grinned. "Here, give me your phone."

"Not until you tell me why."

Rachel leaned back with a winning smile. "Oh, only because Hunt has invested in a dating app that recently hit the market, and we're about to create a profile for you."

I groaned. "This is a terrible idea. I'm not going to meet anyone through this."

Sasha stopped me with an earnest gaze. "If you honestly don't want us to, we won't. But you can't tell me it won't be just a little bit of fun. Let's swipe a little, make a game out of it."

I bit my lip, but my inner people-pleaser won. "Okay, fine."

There was no chance in hell that I was going on a date, but I'd had enough fun playing around on Denise's accounts not to know the potential for amusement. And technically, it was *research*—it was a Hunt app.

One beer and many laughs later, the guys had sidled off to play darts. I was deep into my second one and glancing at my watch when I heard Rachel's loud exclamation.

"Bossman! Didn't know you were coming."

Julian approached us. My stomach clenched, like it always did when I saw him. He had a beer in hand, still in a suit but without a tie.

He didn't look at me.

Why hadn't he texted me back to tell me he was coming?

"Come join us," Sasha said. "We're playing a game."

I slid deeper into the booth to give him space. He took a seat without so much as looking my way, but the scent of his aftershave hit me like a physical weight.

I glanced at our co-workers, who didn't seem to be paying us much attention. I moved a tiny bit closer to Julian and was rewarded with a flick of his dark green gaze. It was like opaque glass, beautiful and impossible to see through.

"The silent treatment, huh?"

He took a sip of his beer before he answered. "I just had to gather my thoughts, Em."

Em. Not Ace, not the nickname he had called me since the beginning. My stomach was tight, but not with excitement this time—with nerves.

"Okay," I said. "Let me know when you're done."

He took another sip but didn't respond. From my peripheral view, I saw what Sasha was doing—looking at upgrading my dating account to some form of superior plan, which would involve money—and rolled my eyes.

"Sasha, *no way.*"

But both she and Rachel just laughed, bent over my phone, dark and blonde hair blending together. They had amused themselves for at least half an hour over that thing.

Julian frowned. "What are you two doing?"

"We've created a profile for Emily on *Burn,*" Sasha said. "Rachel and I are being the ultimate wing-women."

"And by that, she means that they're using my likeness and description as a game," I quipped. "How many guys have you passed through by now? A hundred?"

Rachel elbowed me. "More like a thousand. But you've already had, like, twenty matches."

I felt Julian stiffen beside me. "Really? I didn't know you were single, Emily."

"It's just a game," I said. "They wanted to test out the new Hunt Industries app, and they were in need of a guinea pig."

Rachel nodded. "Emily was most generous. We're planning on rewarding her by setting up multiple dates with gorgeous, eligible men."

I tried to play her words off with a laugh, but my cheeks burned. I didn't want any dates. The only man I wanted was sitting right next to me, growing stiffer and colder by the second, and somehow I had managed to screw this whole thing up. A smarter woman than me would have seen this situation a mile away.

"I'm not going on any *Burn* dates." My tone was decisive. "They could be serial killers, or worse, still live with their mom. No thank you. I'll stick to dating the old-fashioned way."

Sasha stuck my phone out to me, where *Burn's* sleek interface framed the admittedly well-taken photo of a man my age. Before I could look at it, Julian snatched my phone.

He looked through the man's photos. "Quentin. Likes to garden, works in telecommunications. Oh. He's even written his height and favorite color here. Solid guy, clearly knows what women are looking for. A shame he hasn't given us his horoscope as well."

Sasha laughed and took the phone back. "Isn't he a darling? You have to talk to him, Emily."

I sighed and looked up at the ceiling, trying to think of a way out of this. Could I faint? Fake an emergency phone call?

"Show me another one," Julian demanded. "Someone she's matched with." Both Rachel and Sasha seemed delighted at his interest, but I heard the menace he was masking under layers of charm. Julian was pissed.

"Here."

He was silent as he looked through the profile of a sweet-looking guy with glasses. "Here's your nerd, Emily. I know how much you like them. Says here that he'll cook you homemade pasta bolognese. *Looking for the woman of my dreams.* Oh, and he's added a photo of himself with a dog. Clearly boyfriend material, although you'll probably be so bored by your first-year anniversary that you'll beg him to try any position other than missionary."

Sasha and Rachel collapsed into a howl of laughter, and I blushed furiously red. Julian met my gaze with a hard one of his own.

Anger blazed behind the cool exterior.

Whatever game this had started out as, I hated it now. These men didn't deserve to be matched with someone who had no intention of dating them. And they definitely didn't deserve being ridiculed like this.

I grabbed my phone back. "I'm not doing this anymore."

"Oh, Emily," Sasha said. "Don't listen to the boss. I'm sure some of those men are great guys."

"I'm absolutely sure they are." I rose from my seat. "Please let me out, Julian."

He rose stiffly. "Where are you going?"

"To get some air," I tugged out my jacket from below our mountain of coats, "and check up on my brother. See you in a bit."

I made a beeline for the exit, fully aware of the fact that Julian would likely follow me. I knew our co-workers would see it. And for the first time, I didn't care.

No sooner had the door closed behind me than I heard it open again. I didn't even need to glance back to know who it was, but I did it anyway.

Julian's eyes smoldered.

"What's the matter with you?" I asked. "That little game in there was harmless. I had no intention of ever meeting with anyone."

"You told them you were single," Julian said, biting off the label as if it was ugly, as if he hated saying it.

"Yes, because I don't want anyone at work to know about us. We spoke about this yesterday and you said you understood."

He crossed his arms and I saw how his jaw worked. "Do you know what you also said yesterday?"

"What?"

"When this thing is over between us. That's what you said. I've thought about it since, but I don't think it was a slip of the tongue."

I swallowed, suddenly overwhelmed with this whole conversation. "That was poor phrasing. I'm sorry for saying it like that... Julian, I guess I just thought it was obvious."

"What was obvious? Spell it out for me."

"That we're having fun and getting to know one another. We're great in bed together. But, you know, one day you'll want something different." I shrugged. "We don't exactly win prizes in compatibility."

"And clearly you have no intention of us ever getting serious if you're out here looking on online dating sites."

"Julian, you're acting jealous. *Over an app.* Your app, I might add."

"No shit I am! Yesterday you admit that you've already put an expiration date on us, and tonight you're out looking for my replacement. *I'm sorry* if I'm not super thrilled about being told I'm a placeholder."

213

"That's not what you are," I said, feeling it all slip out of my hands. "You're the best man I've ever… I've ever been with. You know we have great chemistry." In a desperate attempt to make sense, I reached out, ran my hands down his chest. He pulled away from me.

"So what am I, then? A sexual adventure? A palate cleanser before you settle down with Quentin, or Jim, or Miguel? Someone you could *actually* tell your co-workers and family about?"

I was silent, mainly because he'd hit the nail on the head so perfectly. I had been treating this as a temporary thing, an affair, something too good to be true. I'd not given our future a single thought.

"Your brother still doesn't know," he said. "Does he?"

I shook my head mutely. "No. I didn't want to…"

"Introduce me to him as your temporary lover. I can get that." Julian shook his head and stepped away from me. There was so much emotion on his face that I felt my own heart ache. This was going wrong, all wrong, and I couldn't find the words to stop it.

"That's not what I meant—this isn't what I want. Julian, I…" But nothing came.

He shook his head again, and this time his voice was resigned. "I know what I want, Emily. Let me know when you've decided. But I'm done being your dirty little secret."

He walked across the parking lot toward his car, shoulders hunched slightly as if he was protecting himself from a blow or walking against heavy wind. I pressed a hand to my aching chest.

I'd always anticipated that he would walk away from me one day. And somehow, I had never considered that my own words and actions would be the reason.

29

EMILY

My phone lay silent and judging beside me.

"Stop looking at me," I told it and turned it facedown, but it kept spreading its negativity. Or maybe that was me.

I'd brainstormed a hundred different texts I could write to Julian, ranging from the cheeky to the plainly desperate. My last attempt had read *"I'm sorry. Please forgive me and take me back. I'll do pretty much anything."*

But I hadn't sent anything, and I hadn't called. There'd been complete silence between us for the past two days. He'd conveniently been out of the office on Friday, and I'd spent my Saturday with Denise—although she was very nearly unbearable. She was so loved up with Michael that I was surprised she wasn't bursting at the seams with happiness.

It wasn't fair either that she ended up more or less agreeing with Julian. By the end of our yoga class, she had me a guilty, sweaty mess.

"You downloaded a dating app?" she hissed at me during downward dog. "And you told him you had already planned your breakup?"

"Whoops," I mouthed, staring at her upside down. "I tried playing it casual."

"And come down into cobra… like so. When you're ready, rise into the warrior position." The yoga teacher did a sinewy move that only circus performers could follow. I struggled into the uncomfortable split-like pose and glanced over at Denise.

She shook her head at me. "The man has feelings, Em. And you hurt him."

"I know. I screwed up."

"You did. I've never seen you this happy with anyone before. Get your head out of your ass or I'll do it for you, and go make it up to him."

"Silence is paramount," the yoga teacher hissed from the front, shooting Denise a look that didn't say *namaste* as much as *shut the hell up.* "It allows us to connect with our intuition."

We shifted into a lotus position, stretching out in front of us in a way that sent pain up my back. Was it normal to be this stiff at the tender age of twenty-five?

I felt Denise poke me with her toe but I kept my eyes firmly shut.

"I'm listening to my inner voice," I murmured to her.

"Good," she grumbled back. "Glad to hear my words have reached you."

They had.

That was the problem—now I had to decide whether I was brave enough to swallow my pride and admit I was wrong. Admit that I wanted something unknown, to throw myself out there. Being with Julian was like nothing I had ever experienced before. It would be the greatest adventure of my life.

When I arrived home that evening, Turner was rummaging through our pantry. Bottle after bottle of laundry detergent and old cleaning solutions were unceremoniously deposited in a black trash bag. I leaned against the doorway, still sweaty and sad, and watched him work.

He finally turned. "Oh. Hey. Didn't hear you come in."

"I should have made more noise."

"No." He shook his head. "You didn't scare me. Did you know we have a detergent that expired in 2007?"

"Nope. I don't think Nan or I ever really ever went through that cupboard. I've just sort of been filling the front shelves with what we need and using that."

"Well, all of it should go."

I smiled and glanced down at the package of dried sponges he was holding. "Does it spark joy?"

He snorted and tossed the expired rags into the bag. "I'll never understand that. Either something is useful, or it's not. There is no in-between."

I took a seat on the sofa and watched him work. "Well, sometimes things are sentimental in value."

"I suppose," he said and tied the black trash bag shut. This was such a massive thing for us, cleaning out the old house. For so many years I had tried to keep everything as it had been right when Mom and Dad passed. To keep the routines, to ensure that as little as possible changed for Turner. We'd stuck to the schedule religiously, never straying, and it had become as much a source of comfort for me as for him.

But looking at him now, I realized that my little brother had become a young man. With his shoulders back, he looked handsome, quiet and strong.

When had that happened?

"Hey," I said. "When did you grow taller than me?"

"When I was sixteen and you were twenty-one. Why?"

I didn't answer, just watched him work quietly, unable to contain the emotions raging inside of me. It all felt like too much.

Turner glanced over at me when I didn't respond.

His eyes widened. "Em? You're crying?"

I nodded, feeling like I'd dropped the ball entirely. I was supposed to be strong and happy, to keep working toward goals and to be the supportive big sister. Yet I was failing completely.

Turner sank down next to me on the couch. "Why? Are you hurt?"

I watched him scan me, looking for signs of pain, and shook my head. "No. This is emotional."

He nodded once and leaned back, visibly relieved by my

statement. "Okay. Good. Do you... do you want to talk about it?"

I took a deep breath and pulled my legs up beneath me. I tugged at a loose thread on our beige couch and wondered where on earth I should start.

"Are you happy at work? At Hunt?"

He nodded. "Yes. I enjoy it. Why? Did something happen at work?"

"No," I said shakily. "I've noticed that you've been circling apartments in the newspaper. Do you want to move out?"

Turner's face split into a sudden, unexpected smile as his gaze flicked between me and the bookshelves behind me. "No. I don't need my own place. I've been trying to hint to you that you could move out if you wanted to."

"Turner!" I hit his leg playfully, and his grin grew wider. "It's not like you to be so sneaky!"

"I know. But I thought you might be sad if I brought it up directly, so I tried to plant the idea in your mind."

"You've watched *Inception* too many times."

"That's not possible," he replied immediately. "It is a masterpiece."

I smiled and watched him, wiping away the remnants of my tears. "Why do you think I should move out?"

His gaze flicked away from me entirely and settled on the view to the patio, his hand playing with his watch like he always did when he was nervous.

"You had to give up a lot of things when Mom and Dad died, for me. But you need to live your own life now too. You've taken care of me for long enough. Not that I want you to stop, but... we can't live in the past. I'm good."

New tears threatened to choke me up. Turner was so rarely willing to share his internal, emotional life with me, that any bits and pieces he revealed I held close to my heart.

"Turner," I said, unable to continue.

"I have a job. You have a job. I think it would be good for you to have your own place. The settlement left us both with enough money to branch out, plus I want more space for a server I plan on building."

I swallowed, hard. It was so typical of him to suggest this so matter-of-fact, like it wasn't a big deal. Like we wouldn't be splitting apart for the first time since he'd been born.

"I'd still want to eat dinner together a few times weekly," I said immediately. "And you have to continue replying to all my texts."

"Even the ones that don't make any sense?"

"Especially those." I nodded. "Yes."

The small smile was back on his face. "All right. Deal. And you're not mad at me?"

"Mad? Turner, you're the best little brother a girl can have. No, of course I'm not mad."

"Good." A faint blush crept up on his cheeks and he rocked forward a bit. I knew he disliked emotional conversations, found them trying, but I had to keep going while I had the courage.

"But you might be mad with me. I have to tell you something. It's not something I should have kept from you."

His eyes flicked to mine for a brief moment. "Tell me."

"I've been seeing Julian for the last couple of weeks."

Turner gave a slow nod. "At work, yes."

"Romantically. And I didn't tell you at first because I wasn't sure what it was between us. If it was serious or not."

"All right… okay. Did you read the HR policy handbook we were given when we started? Because while there is no mention of non-fraternization, there is talk of inappropriate relationships on page eighteen. The phrasing isn't very clear."

In spite of myself, I almost smiled. "I have. There is nothing explicitly forbidding it."

"Good. Is this your first relationship since James?"

I nodded.

"I'm glad."

"You are?" It felt as if a weight had lifted from my shoulders.

I'd had no idea how he would respond when I eventually told him, and my scenarios had ranged from the outraged to the disappointed. *He's your boss, Emily.*

Turner shrugged. "Yes. Julian Hunt is clever. You could do worse. I've seen some of his coding work, and the other engineers seem to worship at his feet." He frowned suddenly, a thought striking him. "You don't, do you? He's not infallible, Emily. Nobody is."

"No. No, I don't. Although in all honesty, I might have ruined it all. We had a big fight a few nights ago."

Turner rose from the couch and gave me a gentle squeeze on the shoulder. Without another word, he began sorting through the shelves again. "Was he in the wrong?"

I sighed and admitted the truth. "No, I think I was."

Turner frowned at a bottle of window cleaner. "Do you want him in your life? Does he spark joy?"

I thought of Julian's crooked smile and amused gaze, the way his body curved around mine. The soft sigh he made in his sleep when I nestled closer against him. The pain in his eyes when I admitted that I hadn't expected us to last.

"Yes," I said. "He really, really does."

"Then it's easy. Say you're sorry."

I looked over at him, his easy confidence and airy manner. My brother, who had always had a foot in a higher plane with his mind racing a mile a minute. I'd been so proud of him as a child. *My little brother can solve one of those colored cubes,* I remembered bragging in class. *He's six.* Todd in my third-grade class had once called Turner *weird* and I had shoved him during recess. Best detention I ever had.

"What if he doesn't accept my apology?"

Turner looked over at me as if the idea hadn't even struck him. "Well," he said slowly, "then he doesn't really care about you. You always forgive the people you care about."

I snuck up behind him and wrapped my arms around his waist, breathing in the familiar peppermint smell of the gum he always chewed. A little awkwardly, Turner's hand came up to pat my arm.

"Thanks."

"Anytime," he said. "Anytime."

30

EMILY

My hand danced with nervous energy across the steering wheel as I stared at Julian's front gate. A stalker. That's what I had become, a creepy lurker with a box of cookies on the passenger seat and a wildly beating heart.

We hadn't spoken for three days. No texts, no calls. Judging by the expression in his eyes on Friday, I hadn't really expected him to reach out, but every day we didn't talk still hurt.

So quickly, he'd become a fixture in my life. Someone who saw me for me, someone who made me laugh and who I could share my innermost thoughts with. Only when I saw the disappointment in his eyes did I realize how much I had come to value his opinion of me—how much his high regard meant.

So I'd showed up, heart in my hand, to apologize. I'd circled the block twice before I parked the car. Inside, my nerves were playing bongo drums, making me queasy.

What if he'd already moved on? I would knock on the door and he'd ask *who are you*, like a scene from one of those bad soap operas where characters kept getting amnesia.

An even worse thought struck me. What if he was in there right this second, making jokes with some other woman as she flipped omelets for their morning-after breakfast? I hoped she burned them. I hoped she stuffed them full of cilantro. He hated cilantro.

Denise had texted me a perky *good luck!* and asked me to call her after to let her know how it went. That had been thirty minutes ago, and I refused to text and tell her I was too chicken. And if I sat here any longer, I'd likely have the neighborhood watch arrest me for loitering.

Grabbing the package of cookies, I repeated my brother's calm instructions to myself. *It's easy. Just say you're sorry.*

I got out of the car with more resolve than I felt and smoothed a hand over the navy blue sundress I'd put on. It ended in a row of ruffles and the bodice was covered in little white polka dots. With my matching suede boots, I felt cute and summery. *Dressed to impress.*

The walk up to his giant oak door felt unreasonably far. I'd always appreciated the fact that he lived in a normal residential area, albeit Palo Alto's absolute finest, despite his wealth. There were no fingerprinted gates or retina scanners to prevent drop-ins.

I took another deep breath and I rang his doorbell, clutching the box of cookies tightly. Bringing them felt silly all of a sudden, a childish gesture, and I glanced around wildly for somewhere to discard them. My heart was beating like a jackhammer.

But then the door opened, and there he stood.

Julian regarded me coolly with a phone pressed to his ear. "No, I'd like you to email the documents," he said to someone on the other line. "If we can move fast on this deal, we should."

"Hi," I mouthed and gave a little wave.

Julian narrowed his eyes and stepped aside, allowing me to enter. All right then. Not exactly a warm welcome, but perhaps I didn't deserve one.

He was wearing his normal slacks and worn loafers, but the casual shirt he'd thrown on stretched taut across wide shoulders and thick biceps. The urge to touch him was instant. Three days without feeling his arms around me or his lips at my temple—I was burning.

He walked through the large foyer, on through the living room and out onto the patio. I followed awkwardly. The familiar wrought-iron chairs and table greeted me. There was a giant bottle of ice water next to his open laptop.

Not an omelet-making bimbo in sight.

"Yes, I'll sign, but only if that concludes the matter. This can't come back to haunt us at a later date."

I sank down into the chair opposite Julian and studied him as he listened to the person on the other end. His face was as strong and handsome as ever, but there were faint circles under his eyes and his jaw was clenched tight. He looked every inch the CEO, and a very pissed one at that.

I put the box of cookies on the table and crossed my legs, making sure my hem rode up a bit. It was a dirty trick, but I had to ensure he listened to me. Reminding him of how good we'd been together in every way possible wouldn't hurt.

Julian nodded at whatever his conversation partner said. "That's reasonable. Make sure it's iron-clad, but handle everyone involved well. This will bear Hunt's name."

There was a brief pause and I glanced down at where his fingers danced across his knee. Perhaps he was nervous, too, or at least anxious to get this over with. It made me feel a tiny bit more confident, but then he barked a harsh *talk to you later* and put his phone down on the table with more force than a thousand-dollar smartphone would have preferred.

I shot him a smile.

Julian didn't return it. He only leaned back in his chair and crossed his arms, making it crystal clear that I was going to be doing the talking.

"Hi," I said softly. "I'm sorry I didn't call ahead."

"I was home."

"I brought you some cookies. I know they're not homemade, but I really can't bake. Like, at all. Honestly, I'm doing you a favor here by not exposing you to my non-existent skills."

Julian barely afforded the pretty white packet a glance, his eyes entirely focused on me. "Why didn't you try to contact me?"

"Right after we... argued?"

He nodded.

"I figured you needed space, that you wouldn't want to hear from me right away." I glanced down at the crease of his T-shirt, the neatly sewn hem. "I was scared of what you'd say when I did."

"Of what I'd say?"

"Yeah."

"I'm more interested in hearing what you think."

I took a deep breath and met his gaze, willing it to grow soft and familiar again. "I've thought a lot about what I said to you last week, both at the bar and the day before. That I expected us to end."

Julian glanced away, a muscle in his jaw flexing. "You had already planned for it."

"I'd resigned myself to it being just a fling. You were right about what you said: I'd never really given the idea of us a real chance."

"Why?"

Understanding my own emotions and actions was difficult enough sometimes, not to mention explaining them to him. But I had had three days to think this through.

"Because you're too good to be true. Because I can't fathom why you'd see a future with me. Because... I didn't think you were a relationship kind of guy. Because we work together. Because for the past five years, Turner has been my main worry and whoever dates me, gets Turner too." I glanced back at him. "I was so focused on what I potentially had to lose that I didn't think about what I stood to gain."

He nodded and looked at the box of cookies on the table absent-mindedly, deep in thought.

"White chocolate chip macadamia," I murmured. "I brought out the big guns."

He didn't smile, but his eyes softened when he looked back

at me. "You didn't think I was a relationship kind of guy," he quoted. "Was it something I did? I tried to show you that I wanted more than just sex."

"No! No, absolutely not. I really need you to know that." I reached out and grabbed his hand. "The reason I didn't commit to the idea was never because I didn't want more with you. I guess I was just... protecting my heart?"

My throat grew dry as I met his deep, steady gaze. This was an adult conversation about an adult relationship with a man who knew what he wanted and the way he wanted it. It scared the hell out of me just as much as it excited me.

"I'm sorry for hurting you. I never meant to."

Julian exhaled and looked down at our clasped hands. "I can understand that, I think. Besides, it's not like I've been blameless. I have something to apologize for too."

"You do?" Unease churned in my stomach, and the image of the bimbo reappeared immediately. I shoved her unwelcome image away. Julian would never.

He sighed. "I knew you wanted to keep what we had private from our coworkers. I said I respected that, and I believed I did, but my actions sometimes said otherwise. I'm sorry I didn't do a better job of listening to your signals." His hand squeezed my fingers.

My chest ached suddenly with tenderness. I wanted to reach out and smooth away the crease of worry between his thick brows, trace the line of his jaw until he relaxed.

"No, Julian, you were great. You *are* great. I'm sorry I didn't properly explain why it mattered so much to me. I never wanted you to feel like I didn't value what we had."

"Had?"

"Have," I corrected. "If you'll still have me."

"If," he murmured darkly. "As if I'd ever turn you away, Ace."

Julian opened his arms for me, and I shifted forward, smiling as I settled onto his lap. Our bodies fit together comfortably, finding their way through the awkwardness. He smelled of aftershave and Julian, the way that only he smelled. I pressed my hand against his chest, right where his heart beat steadily against my palm.

"I missed you," I murmured into the warmth of his neck.

Julian's arms pulled me tighter against him. "I missed you too. I feared you wouldn't talk to me again."

I pulled back. "You thought I'd ghost you?"

His hand tugged on a silky strand of my hair, not meeting my eyes. "I had faith that you wouldn't. But I'd seen your anger that night, and I know you value your independence. I couldn't be sure you would choose to come back to me."

Softly, I leaned forward and pressed my lips to his. I poured everything we weren't ready to say yet into that kiss—my respect, my desire, my love—all for him. Julian kissed me gently, reverently, his hands stroking my sides until I had to pull away.

His mouth quirked up into his familiar crooked smile, the one he used when he was fully himself and in a playful mood.

"I have two conditions."

"Okay. Name them."

"I want you to delete *Burn* from your phone."

Shame colored my cheeks, but for this I had already made amends. "Already done. I deleted it immediately, the very same night. I've already matched with you and I don't need anyone else."

His thumb traced my side, smoothing little circles on my ribs and sending goose bumps along my skin.

"The second condition?"

"That you spend at least an hour every day doing this." Julian lifted my hand up to the nape of his neck, his eyes shuttering when my fingers curled into his thick hair.

I laughed. "You're like a very large, very masculine cat."

"I think that's just called a lion," he replied. "Thanks."

"I don't think I can manage an hour of this every day. I have to go to work, you see. My boss is very demanding."

Julian shook his head. "I've already cleared it with HR. It's a new company-wide policy."

I smiled and watched the dark of his lashes against his tanned skin and reveled in the strength of his arms around me, the thickness of muscles in the thighs beneath me and the hair that curled at his temples.

Julian Hunt was a legend, but he was also a man, and he was *mine.*

"I have a condition, too," I said, my fingers still stroking his neck. It was corded with muscle under my touch.

"Tell me."

"I told Turner about us yesterday."

Julian stilled. "Did you really?"

"Yes. He was happy about it."

"He was?"

"Yeah." I smiled at his dazed expression and leaned in closer, pressing my lips to his. "Will you come to dinner at our house tonight?"

Forgive me. Love me. Never leave me.

Julian smiled against my lips, a sweet, intimate smile that spread warmth through my body. We were starting something much deeper, something real—something I knew would change me forever. I wanted it all.

"I'd love to," he murmured. "Does this mean I don't have to park a block away?"

I laughed, loving the way his eyes danced with happiness. "You're cordially invited to use the driveway."

31

JULIAN

The feel of Emily in my arms and her relieved smile stayed with me long after she had left. She was all I thought of as I showered and dressed, and as I made the short drive over to her place for dinner.

I had said that she would have to come to me when I walked away on Friday, but I knew it had been a lie. I would do anything to get her back.

How could I not? Emily was everything I wanted, everything I hadn't known I needed. But I'd made a deal with myself—I had to let it go three full days. I had to give her the chance to come to me first. If we were going to last, and if I would get the chance to call her mine, she had to come willingly.

And she had.

My body still felt the weight of her in my lap and against my chest. Touching her again after these days apart felt like heaven. Her scent, her hands on my skin, those perfectly plump little lips… If I kept up reminiscing, I would have to readjust myself in my seat.

I glanced at the digital clock on my dashboard. 06:58 PM. Perfect. Punctuality was important in their household, and I wanted to knock on the door at exactly seven.

Was I overdoing it? Maybe. But I knew what a massive step this was for Emily, so if I could simplify it for her, I would.

I pulled up at her house. There were candles lit in one of the windows, but otherwise it was entirely calm, front lawn mowed and their car neatly parked beside mine on the driveway.

The house was cute and ordinary and didn't match its extraordinary inhabitants at all. Emily was strong, funny, determined. She said things that surprised me on the regular. Turner… well, he was a prodigy. There was no other word to describe what he could do with the zeroes and ones, and I could say that without a shred of jealousy.

I put the car in park and grabbed the large bouquet of flowers I'd picked up on the way. The Porsche suddenly felt garish, ostentatious, parked outside on this residential street. I should have taken the Jeep.

Focus, Julian. I was thirty-three years old, experienced and successful, and I was *nervous* for this.

While I'd been joking with all the comparisons to high school, that was exactly what I felt like—a teenage boy going to meet his girl's parents for the first time.

I rang the doorbell. There were a few sounds of a scuffle, and then the door opened. Emily's cheeks were rosy and flushed, and she had an apron tied around her waist.

"Hi," she breathed.

A slow grin spread across my face. "Hey, Ace."

"I can't believe you're actually here."

"Neither can I."

She pushed the door wide. "Come on in."

I followed her into a small hallway, filled with shoes. The house smelled like fresh bread.

"I thought you didn't know how to bake?"

Emily shot me a smile. "Turner's the one doing the baking tonight"

"A man of many talents."

She bit her lip as she looked over at me, still paused in the hallway, her dark hair swirling around her face.

"Stop that," I said darkly.

"Stop what?"

"Looking at me like that."

Emily gave a low laugh and the sound shot through my body like adrenaline. Taunting me, reminding me… I caught her around the waist and pulled her up flush against me.

"Julian!"

I pressed a kiss to her cheek. "It's been four days since I last had you in my arms, properly. That's four days too many."

Emily melted in my arms, her eyes filling with desire. I could feel the soft swell of her breasts against me and need pulsed through my lower body. If she continued looking at me like that…

I caught her lips with mine, and as we kissed, the world felt right again.

She finally pulled away with a chuckle. "Come on, let's go to the kitchen."

"Must we?"

"My brother," she said with a raised brow. Her hands slid down my chest before she caught my hand in hers. I was tugged through a maze of hallways and little rooms, woven rugs and bookcases. On the walls hung painted pictures of landscapes and old photographs.

It was a family home and seeing it made my heart twinge, both for her and for her brother. She'd told me about her parents and the terrible accident.

Turner was taking bread rolls out of the oven when we emerged into a small, cozy kitchen.

"Hello, Julian," he said but didn't look at me, brushing the rolls with melted butter.

"Hi, Turner." I took a seat on one of the high stools. "The bread smells delicious."

"I agree."

They moved in silent harmony around the kitchen, the ease between them obvious. Neither Turner nor Emily needed a lot of words to communicate with one another. Next to the fridge hung a small whiteboard with meals planned out for every day of the week.

For a long while, I just sat and watched them interact. Emily was a firecracker at work, and always around me, but with her brother... she was calm. The ultimate big sister.

"I think the lamb is done. Julian, can you put this on the table?"

I was handed a big bowl of salad and a little jar of sea salt. Despite myself, I smiled as I did as instructed and set the table. There was a homeliness here that I had missed being a part of for a long time. And interacting with Emily in this way... it was enough to make a man dream. One day I'd make sure we shared our lives like this, too. That we had family dinners together on the regular.

Turner wasted no time—questions began the second we were all seated.

"So, you're dating my sister."

"I am, yes."

"Why?"

I resisted the urge to shoot Emily an amused glance. "Because she's a great person. Being around her makes me happy, and I hope I make her happy in return."

He gave a slow nod and reached for the potatoes. "Does he make you happy, Em?"

I watched with great interest as her cheeks flushed. She didn't look at me as she replied. "Yes, he does."

Warmth flooded through me at the response. As if sensing my gaze, Emily's green eyes flicked to mine. A soft smile spread across her face.

"I'm glad to hear it," I said. "I promise I'll never stop."

Turner's cough brought us both back to reality. "I'm also glad you're with my sister, then," he declared. "She's been alone longer than I believe average for a woman her age."

"Turner!" Emily hissed, but I nodded seriously at her brother. His blessing meant a lot to her, and by extension, it did to me too. He was the only proper family she had left.

"I'm glad to hear that. I think the world of her, but I'm sure you do too."

Turner gave a noncommittal shrug as he doused his lamb in pepper. "I think you're also a much better match for her than her last boyfriend."

I couldn't help it—this time I grinned wide. "Is that so?"

Emily put her head in her hands, but Turner only nodded. "He wasn't smart enough for her."

"Really?"

"He didn't have his life in order. Em, will you pass me the bread?"

Emily handed her brother a roll and shot me an amused glance. "Actually, I agree with that. Julian is without a doubt the best man I've ever dated."

I took a sip of my wine and tried to stop a faint blush from creeping up on my own cheeks. This woman had turned me inside out, upside down, and somehow she continued to wield that power. I couldn't remember the last time a compliment like that made me almost bashful.

I cleared my throat. "I heard you're building your own computer here at home?"

Conversation flowed easily after that. I saw Emily glance between me and her brother a couple of times, a private smile on her face, and my chest tightened again. Whatever test this dinner might have been, I was pretty sure I was acing it.

Much, much later, after dessert and jokes and the most intense round of Monopoly I had ever played—the Giordano siblings took the game very seriously—Turner called it a night.

"You're good at that game," he told me.

"Thanks."

"Well, I'll go to my room now. Em, will Julian be staying the night?"

I watched, amused, as she fiddled with the tablecloth. "I'm not sure. We haven't discussed it yet."

Turner considered her response for a moment. "When you have, please let me know. You can text me."

"Okay, I'll do that."

"Good night."

"Night, Turner."

He disappeared around the corner and up the stairs, and a minute later we both heard the soft sound of his bedroom door close.

I grinned at her. "So, am I staying the night?"

She rolled her eyes at me and started clearing the table. "I swear, sometimes… I love him, and I have nothing to hide from you, but…"

"Hey, don't be embarrassed."

"'She's been single longer than normal for a woman her age,'" Emily quoted. "I didn't even know he'd noticed that."

I pushed my chair back and crossed the room, caught her around the waist. Her thick hair tickled my skin as I pulled her close. "It doesn't matter."

She sighed. "No, I suppose it doesn't."

"The food was great."

"Thanks."

"And he's great. I recognize a lot of myself in him."

She twisted in my arms. "You do?"

I nodded. "Sure. He's undoubtedly working away at the circuit board up there right now as we speak. I was the same. I spent most of my high school and college years behind a screen."

Emily's grin turned teasing. "A proper nerd?"

"Now you've found out." I raised my hands in surrender. "Is this the moment you tell me I'm not cool enough to be with you?"

She laughed and tugged at the collar of my button-down. "No, silly. Come here."

I let her tug me down and bent so that our foreheads touched. Her lips were soft and sweet on mine. She tasted of chocolate from the dessert and white wine and *heaven*. My hands found the small area of exposed skin between her top and her jeans, smooth to the touch.

"Mmmm," I murmured against her lips. "Can I stay the night?"

Her arms wrapped around my neck. "I wouldn't let you leave even if you begged me."

"Come on, let's finish up here so we can go to bed. Because if you continue kissing me like that, you'll leave me no choice…"

She raised an eyebrow. "Really? What would you do, Julian?"

"You have a perfectly serviceable kitchen counter," I said darkly. "Use your imagination."

Emily shot me a heated glance but thankfully didn't respond. We washed the dishes in silence, the tension rising by the minute. Suddenly I felt vulnerable again. It was like all the distance between us these past days came rushing in, every minute of absence and fear that she wouldn't come back to me. I wanted nothing more than to twist my hands through her hair and make her moan my name. Bury myself inside of her and make sure she never forgot who I was, who we were together. How good we were together.

"I'm done," she said quietly, closing the dishwasher.

"Your bedroom is down the hall?"

"Yes. The second door on the right."

"Text your brother that I'm staying over," I said. "I'll be waiting for you."

Emily's hand caught mine, warm and dry. "We'll have to be quiet."

"We will be." I bent, pulling her close, my voice against her ear. "We'll have many, many nights in the future to be loud."

32

EMILY

Somehow, someway, Julian convinced me to go camping with him.

My protests had all been shot down. It *wouldn't* be uncomfortable, he promised. He would make sure to take all the necessary precautions against bears. And, as he pointed out, I was a disgrace if I had lived all my life in Northern California and never visited Yosemite.

I had to give it to the man—he was persuasive.

But I also had to admit to not being particularly difficult to persuade. Since our reconciliation, all I wanted to do was spend time with him. Turner was more than OK with me being gone for a weekend, and to my surprise, he announced he was going bowling with some of the coders from Hunt.

Life was good.

During my lunch break, I couldn't stop thinking about the idea Michael had told me recently about franchising his restaurant. It wasn't a bad idea, and his food could most definitely be sold in more places around Northern California. Fresh, Italian food… possibly packaged for lunches. He had the ambition and drive to see it through.

Sasha slipped into the seat next to me in the break room and saw my sketches.

"Is that a grapevine? And... pasta?"

I closed my sketchpad. "Yeah, just something I've been working on."

"Is Hunt branching out into the food business?"

I smiled. "Not unless I've missed something entirely. Are those machines invented now? The ones where you press a few buttons and get whatever meal you want?"

"I wish," she said, waving her PB&J sandwich in front of me. "I don't have time to run out and buy food and this was all I had at home. Josef needs me for a client meeting in ten."

I pushed over the other half of my baguette. "Have some of mine. I'm full."

She smiled gratefully at me and nodded back down at my sketchpad. "So, what's that for? Or is it a secret?"

"No. It's something I'm working on for a friend. Early stages so far."

"Cool, cool." Sasha nodded and tapped her fingers against the table. "Look, I feel like I should apologize for the whole *Burn* situation at drinks last week. I didn't mean to pressure you into doing something you didn't want to."

"Don't worry about it. I know neither you or Rachel meant any harm. I should just have said right away that I'm dating someone, but it was early days and I didn't want to talk about it yet."

Her eyes widened. "Wow, really? That's great! We would totally have understood."

"I'm sure you would have." I shook my head. "It was more my own hang-up."

"Who is he?"

I took a sip from my bottle of ice tea. "I think I'll keep him to myself for a little while longer."

Sasha smiled. "So secretive."

"That's me," I said, winking as I stood. "But I'll tell you as soon as it's official."

"All right, all right. I'm intrigued. See you later?"

"On Monday, actually. I'm heading out of the office a bit earlier today."

"Oh?"

"Family thing." I shrugged. "Have a nice weekend!"

"Yeah, you too!"

I grabbed my notepad and headed back into my office, where my overnight bag was standing prepped and ready against my desk. Its bright colors and striped strings beckoned. Why was athletic gear always so garish? Did neon scare off bears? Was nylon mesh more ergonomic? Some questions just had no answers.

Several hours later, I opened the passenger door to Julian's Jeep and jumped inside. He grinned as he glanced down at my outfit—dark blue jeans, combat boots, and a fleece jacket.

"Very rural," he commented.

"Don't worry," I said primly. "I packed a down jacket as well. And yes, I know I'm the poster child of sexiness right now. Victoria's Secret could basically use me as an ad."

Julian laughed and reached over to rest his hand on my thigh as he backed out of the parking lot. He did the whole thing singlehandedly, long fingers gripping around the steering wheel. Even such a small thing made my skin tingle.

"You are *incredibly* sexy in this getup. Did you bring a flannel and an ax as well?"

"Have a thing for lumberjacks, do you?"

"I think I might." He squeezed my leg. "Or perhaps it's just lumber-Emilys."

I groaned. "You're not a dad, but you've already nailed the lame jokes."

He was quiet for a moment, focusing on the intersection ahead, and a terrible notion crossed my mind. "You're not, are you? Is this the part where you confess that you've fathered five sweet but illegitimate children?"

Julian laughed. In his button-down and rugged blue jeans, he looked every bit the relaxed mountain man from my innermost fantasies. *Damn.*

"No, I don't have any kids. Promise."

"Phew," I said, and pretended to relax against the seat. He laughed again at my dramatics and I smiled at the sound. I had no idea why this beautiful man was with me, but I'd do anything to keep him. "Aren't you going to ask me?"

He glanced over. "If you have any secret kids? I'm fairly certain on that front."

"Maybe, or maybe I'm leading a secret double life. You can never be too sure."

Julian's hand tightened again on my leg, and while his eyes stayed on the road, I heard the warmth in his voice when he replied. "That's a risk I'm willing to take."

As the city around us gave way to open landscapes, our conversation grew into a companionable silence. Julian kept his hand somewhere near or on me for nearly the entire three-and-a-half-hour trip to Yosemite.

Being with him was a new experience entirely for me. There was nothing in him that I could relate to my ex-boyfriend, or to any of the occasional dates I'd been on. There hadn't been anyone who made me laugh or cry like him, or made my heart swell the way he did. And there had definitely never been anyone who touched me like him.

I peeked over at him several times, wondering if dating someone seriously was a common occurrence for him.

"You're thinking," he said. "I can hear the neurons firing from over here."

"Well, you're not very far away."

He smiled. "That's true. Why don't you share?"

I'd slipped off my shoes and crossed my legs, looking at the red, dusty landscape around us. We might as well be on Mars—left to fend for ourselves like the astronaut in that space movie. California was dry this time of year.

There was absolutely no way to ask what I wanted to ask tactfully, so I tried to turn it into a joke. "Have you really been with, like, a thousand models?"

"What?" Julian twisted toward me. "Where did you get that from?"

"The internet," I said. "Sasha. Occasionally Rachel or Josef. My own worst nightmares."

"They love to gossip more than they love their jobs," he growled. "And you shouldn't trust everything you read online."

"I know. That's why I'm asking you."

He ran a hand through his hair and looked flustered, and my nerves immediately spiraled out of control. My worst fears had to be confirmed by his silence. Was there a parade of women he'd gone through before me?

"Hey, it doesn't matter if you have," I rushed. "Truly. I just figured, you know my relationship history, and I was curious…"

Julian put his hand on my knee, effectively silencing me. "Look, it's… there are a lot of photos of me with various women because that's what those events are for. People ask me to take photos with them all the time. Sometimes it's just a random person who wants a picture, sometimes it's a date I've brought, and sometimes—rarely—it's genuinely been someone I was dating. But regardless, the press loves to write about it. It sells copies."

"I get that." I put my hand over his, traced a wide knuckle. "That must make dating really difficult."

"It has. It does. And I'm not going to pretend like I've always been a saint." He glanced over at me quickly, hand tightening on my knee. "There have been more than three for me. But I meant what I said, about not having been with anyone like you before. This… it feels very different to me. So much more."

I leaned back against my seat and glanced at him, his profile and the set of his jaw. This conversation was making him nervous. *I* was making him nervous.

"That makes me glad," I whispered.

Julian nodded. "And it's not always… it hasn't always been clear when women have wanted me, and when they've wanted my money or the prestige that comes with it, you know?"

My heart tore a little at the confession. He so rarely showed vulnerability, and even now, he wasn't looking at me at all. Eyes glued to the road ahead and no charming smile in sight. All the armor was down.

My hand tightened around his. "I can imagine. That must be hard."

"It is."

A terrible thought struck me. "Julian, you know that when I joked about you not being a billionaire, I was a hundred percent just trying to be funny, right? Arguably not very successfully, but still."

He smiled at me. "Yes, I know that. I knew that from the beginning."

"Good." I closed my eyes and stretched my legs out in front, threading my fingers through his. "Because I don't want you for your money. I'm only in it for your unbelievable abs."

I smiled at the sound of his deep laughter filling the car.

We arrived at Yosemite two hours before sunset at a beautiful campsite. Tall trees circled it, and I could hear the sound of a babbling brook close by. We had seen the High Sierra on the way in and I was already riled up with anticipation for the next day. The whole nature thing was growing on me—and we hadn't even finished making camp yet.

"When should we hit the hiking trail tomorrow?"

"The earlier the better." Julian pulled out a massive green bag from his trunk. "If we get up by five we should be able to hit the trail by five thirty. Catch the sunrise."

I struggled to keep my composure and caught the sleeping bag he tossed my way. "Um. Okay, that sounds great."

Julian laughed at my expression. "I'm just joking, you dork."

"Phew."

He pressed a kiss to my forehead, turning us around so we surveyed our lot. He'd managed to get a secluded camping site, no one close by, and the car parked up close. "This is going to be fun," he said. "A fun trip. No have-tos, no musts. We get up when we want to and we do whatever we feel like tomorrow. All right?"

I leaned against him. "All right."

He was right. *It was fun.* Being with him from sunrise to sunset—just enjoying his company—and not worrying about anyone seeing or finding out about us? It was a feeling I could get used to. And though my legs and lungs would ache with the hiking, the views would be worth it. He was worth it.

We spent the whole day hiking. He led the way like a natural, as if he belonged as much to the wilderness as he did to the Hunt Industry offices and the panel discussions. When we made it to the top after several hours of painful walking, he wrapped his arms around my waist and rested his head atop mine.

"Look at that," he murmured. "Isn't this place beautiful?"

I leaned back into him and savored the feel of his body, tall and firm, and the scent of pine and man that clung to him. "Thanks for showing me this."

The wind made his whisper faint, but I heard it, murmured against my ear. "Thanks for being here."

In the evening, Julian set up a campfire and pulled out marshmallows. *You need to get the full experience*, he said, making me a s'more. *I want to get you hooked.*

But when we let the fire burn down and we snuggled in our tent?

He wasn't so sweet then.

"Julian," I whispered, half between giggles and moans. "Julian! We can't. There are people in the tents around us."

"No one's that close," he murmured and turned me over, his hands gliding across the fabric of my camisole. "Plus, this is the best way to ensure we stay warm."

"It's June. I *am* pretty warm."

Julian made a show of reaching down to grab my foot, which elicited a fairly loud shriek from me.

"Julian! I'm ticklish."

"I'd say your toes are pretty cold," he declared. "I can't have you getting frostbite on my watch. I'm sorry, Ace, but I just can't.

I promised to bring you back to Turner with all ten fingers and toes intact."

My laughter died against his lips, slow and insistent on mine. He was right, I thought, luxuriating in the feel and taste of him. The other tents *were* pretty far away.

I grabbed his arms and turned us over, slipping underneath him so I could feel his body against the entirety of mine.

"Mmm," I crooned. "You're the best blanket."

Julian gave an amused huff and bent down to kiss my collarbone, hands pushing my shirt up. I shimmied out of it and his lips soon followed the trail his hands had left. When he took my nipple in his mouth, sucking gently, I had to bite my tongue to keep from moaning.

"Okay," I murmured. "Okay, let's do this. But we have to be quiet."

"I can be quiet," Julian murmured, busy with undoing the laces of my sweatpants. "The question is, Giordano, can you?"

I gave a half-muffled giggle and kicked off my pants. "Only if you promise not to pull some crazy ninja move and sex me out of my senses. Don't go discovering my g-spot or anything, or I'm not responsible for the noises I make."

I could see his wide grin in the moonlight as he tugged off his own T-shirt. "We'll keep it vanilla tonight."

"Good."

But then he bent and tugged off my underwear with his teeth, hands skimming my bare skin, and I had to dig my hands into the sleeping bag to keep from gasping.

Julian kissed me as deft fingers moved over me, inside me. "Vanilla just so happens to be my favorite flavor."

I moaned into his mouth and spread my legs wider, wrapping them around his hips. "Hey, you're still wearing your sweatpants," I protested. "How is it fair that I'm completely naked?"

Julian chuckled silently and knelt between my legs. I could feel his eyes sweeping across me from top to toe, my heaving chest and exposed skin, just barely illuminated in the darkness.

"Only because you look infinitely better clad in moonlight than me," he murmured, "and I am a greedy, greedy man."

I rose up on my elbows and nodded to where the deep V of his stomach traveled into the waistband of his pants. "Let's compare," I said breathlessly. "I'm sure I can make some arguments in your favor."

Julian grinned again and pulled off his pants, leaving me a wide-eyed, lust-crazed mess. It didn't matter how many times I felt him, or saw him, or held him in my arms. I knew I'd always want more— I wanted us close enough to melt into the same person.

He pushed inside me with a slow thrust, setting a deep pace that reached places I'd never shared before with any man. I cradled his hips and let my fingers twine through the silky curls of his hair. The pace he set, the way we held each other—it was more intimate than anything I'd ever experienced before.

He was everywhere and everything, my world beginning and ending with him.

Above us, through the mesh in the tent flap, I could see the sprawling Milky Way in a mixture of stars and galaxies and eternity. A light twinkled as it sped across the dark sky.

"Julian," I whispered. "Julian, there's a star falling above us."

He dropped down onto his elbows and laughed silently into my hair, still inside me. I felt his shoulders shake with mirth. "Ace, I'm giving a *great* performance here."

I wrapped my arms tighter around him and joined in the laughter. "Sorry. *Sorry.* I've just never seen it before."

"I'll just have to compete with the night sky," he murmured huskily and did something with his hips that left me speechless. He covered my mouth with his, brandished me with feverish, quiet kisses and continued to move with excruciating slowness.

The intimacy, the deep pace, it was all too much. I clutched him tight in the darkness as my orgasm racked through my body, the stars silently watching us from far, far above.

I held Julian close as he began to shake, as he groaned his release into my ear and his hips jerked erratically into me. I felt every pulse deep inside and dug my fingers into the taut skin across his back. I felt as if we'd just shared our souls, bared our innermost selves. What we'd had before was sex, what we did in that tent… that was making love.

Julian tucked me close against him and we both basked in the afterglow, our breath heavy. I snuggled closer and relaxed in his warmth. There might have been other tents in the distance, but at that moment I felt like we were the only people in the whole entire universe.

"I love camping," I murmured.

Julian laughed silently. "You know, I have a new appreciation for it too."

I turned over and rested my head on his shoulder, my hand tracing patterns over his chiseled chest and abs. I'd take every part of this man I could, and I'd never give it back. He was mine.

"Do you take all girls out here?" I teased. "Make them giddy with your skills and the stars?"

Julian turned to me, the starlight illuminating him enough that I could make out his gentle smile.

"No, I've never taken a girlfriend camping before."

My hand stopped tracing his chest. "Before? I'm your girlfriend?"

Julian leaned closer and rested his forehead against mine. I could feel the warmth of his breath as he spoke. "Aren't you, Emily?"

I shifted closer so that our bodies were pressed together, not an ounce of space between us, my leg sliding between his.

"Yes," I said softly. "Yes, I am."

33

JULIAN

"Rafe, man, just get yourself a girl."

I heard Rafe's annoyed sigh on the other end of the line. "No, dude. This is the one thing you can't do. You can't tell me that just because you're all loved up. You're not even thinking rationally—you're thinking with your dick."

I couldn't help but laugh. "You know, if there is one person I know who could use a feminine touch, it's you."

"I get enough feminine touches on my own, thank you very much."

"All right, all right. But I'm telling you: one day it'll be your turn."

"Don't count on it."

"We all must fall," I declared. "Alas, today it was me. Tomorrow—"

Rafe hung up. It had been a long time since I'd messed with him so thoroughly, but he'd pushed me hard enough in the gym that morning that he deserved it.

Besides, I felt like spreading some happiness. I had enough inside me to power a small sun. If only that was how energy worked, we could have solved climate change overnight. An endless source of renewable energy, courtesy of Emily.

Looking down at my phone, I saw the photo of Emily struggling to fold the tent poles. I had set the photo as my home screen. I knew it would annoy her when she saw it, and it made me grin every time I looked at my screen.

Tim's voice cut through my office. "Mr. Hunt, Ms. Giordano from marketing is here to see you." His tone was neutral, which was Tim-speak for disapproval. She didn't have a pre-scheduled appointment and I knew that messed with his organizational nature.

But a Ms. Giordano from marketing? I had time.

"Send her in."

Emily slipped into my office with a thick stack of papers pressed to her chest. She smiled at me and I grinned back—I couldn't help it. The reaction was immediate.

"Hey," she said.

"Hi."

With her dark hair in a ponytail and a smattering of freckles across her nose, she was breathtakingly beautiful. I wondered if I'd ever get used to the physical punch in the chest when I saw her.

I highly doubted it.

She put the stack of papers down on the desk but remained standing. I didn't mind, as it gave me an excellent view of her ample curves. A shift dress skimmed over her hips and cut high enough to give me a glimpse of her shapely legs. "You're absolutely stunning."

She smiled and walked around my desk slowly. "I'm ambushing you."

"Oh? What does that mean?" I glanced down at the stack of papers. "Is this business, or pleasure?"

"That's a decoy. They're marketing evaluations from 2009. I think. I found them in the recycling bin."

I grinned. "So you're here on pleasure?"

"If you're not too busy?"

"I'm never too busy for you."

I pushed my chair back and opened my arms wide for her, wanting to feel her against me. But she just shook her head and gave a gentle *tsk*.

No, she did something that nearly gave me a heart attack instead. Gracefully, she sank to her knees in front of me.

"Ace?"

Her hands stroked my thighs and she smiled up at me, with smoldering eyes. "I've thought about you all day."

I gave a half-assed nod, my blood rushing south at the mere hint of what she was considering. What she was so close to doing. "I've thought of you too. What are you doing?"

Emily ran her nails up my thigh and shot me an innocent look. "What does it look like I'm doing?"

"Here?" My voice was pitched at a level it hadn't been since puberty. But Emily just nodded with a sly look in her eye. Her finger traced my zipper and I had to grip the armrests.

Just having her that close to my crotch had me painfully hard. It was impossible to see her and not want her. To have her around me and *not* want to hold her.

"Fuck, Ace. Do you have any idea how much you turn me on? How much I want you?"

She rose up on her knees and unbuckled my belt with slow, torturous movements. "I think so. I can certainly feel it. But to be sure... I'd better take a look."

My breath came in embarrassing huffs as she undid my zipper. Soft hands found my painfully hard cock and I couldn't help the low groan that escaped me. Her gentle stroking was the best form of heavenly teasing, just a beat too slow to give my cock the friction it craved.

She tsked again. "You're going to have to be quiet, Mr. Hunt."

"Mhm."

Then she bent her head and touched her lips to me. I had to bite my tongue to keep from groaning.

"Emily, fucking hell... I can't..." I pushed back her hair, making it easier for her to move and for me to see her movements.

Emily sucked my cock like she'd missed it, as if she genuinely couldn't get enough. As if giving me pleasure was giving her plenty as well. My hands tightened as she swept her tongue up along the sensitive nerve on the underside of my shaft.

Fuck.

And the whole time, she stared up at me with green, earnest eyes. She watched my reactions as if she thrived on them—as if pleasing me made her as mad with want as she made me.

No woman had ever given me a blow job like this. Not reciprocal, not out of obligation, but because she cared about me. She pushed the limits of pleasure to unexplored lands. My heart was a pounding war-drum in my chest and my blood sped through my system fast enough to break world records.

Heaven. She put me in heaven.

"Ace," I warned, trying and failing to articulate full sentences. The part of my brain that housed logic and function had checked out. There was only Emily and her eyes and her warm, warm lips.

I was putty in Emily's capable hands and her skilled tongue. But it was the love in her eyes that undid me. Need and hot tingles started at the base of my spine and spread through my body.

She smiled and kept going, ignoring my vain attempts to signal for her to stop. Her strokes grew faster and her tongue more insistent. I wouldn't last for shit.

And I didn't.

I closed my eyes as pleasure swept through my body. My hips jerked up and into her mouth, and her fingers dug deeper into my thighs as she swallowed. My vision swam.

There was reality and then there was this—hazy vision and tingles everywhere. I was faintly aware of her slow, steady tongue and hearing a satisfied chuckle.

When she'd finished with me, she sat back on her heels and grinned up at me like the cat that ate the canary.

Only, this canary had been very happy to be eaten.

"Ace," I whispered, because words hadn't fully returned to me yet. "Holy shit."

She gave me a final, gentle stroke before doing my fly up. "I'll be right back."

I watched in a daze as she sashayed to the en suite bathroom and I heard the sound of running water. Had that just happened? Who was this woman?

How had I made it this long without telling her I loved her? Because love was all I felt at that moment, my breath heavy and my arms weak. I loved her. The feeling completely overwhelmed me.

She returned with a small smile, completely at odds with the way she'd looked when she'd waltzed into my office, and kneeled beside me. I opened my arms for her again, and this time, she sank down on my lap with a pleased little sigh. For a long while, I just held her close and let her feel the wild beating of my heart.

"What was that for, Em?"

"What do you mean?" Soft fingers played with the hair at the nape of my neck.

"You didn't want us to be together in the office. You said that it didn't make you feel… good."

She pulled back. "You didn't object to this, did you, Julian?"

I couldn't help it: I laughed. "No. Fuck no. That was without a doubt the hottest thing I've ever experienced. You are unbelievably sexy, Ace. I'm just… curious as to what made you change your mind?"

A shy smile spread across her face. "I was just in my office thinking about you… and how I don't think I've been very fair."

"What do you mean?"

Her fingers twisted my hair and goose bumps raced down my neck. "I'm all in, Julian. I'm so in. And I'm sorry that I made you doubt that."

"Don't be." I pulled her closer, wrapped my arms around her waist. "I know you had your reservations, and you were smart to."

She shook her head. "No. Because we belong together. You saw that from the very beginning."

Her green eyes were shiny, and I pressed a soft kiss to her lips. "Anyone can see what a catch you are."

"But I didn't immediately recognize the same thing. That you and I would be good together. And I'm sorry."

"Hey, now." I reached up and wiped away the tear that had escaped. "Where is all this coming from?"

"You're the single best thing that's ever happened to me, Julian. And I don't want to hide it any longer."

I couldn't help the wide smile that spread across my face at her declaration. Her eyes were warm, laughing, as they took in the expression in mine.

"Really?"

"Yes. One hundred percent yes. I want it all."

I pulled her close and kissed her. Her lips were soft and sweet and trusting. This woman was a godsend, and she was here in my arms, understanding me completely. Accepting me completely.

Telling me that I could finally call her mine.

Emily pulled away with a laugh. "There's one more thing."

"Oh?"

"I can't work for you any longer." She worried her lower lip with her teeth, eyes watching my reaction warily.

"Why? I promise to respect your boundaries. I'll never even set foot on the eleventh floor if you don't want me to." I lifted my hands up and away, not touching her. "Look, I'll even institute a hands-off policy while at work."

Emily laughed. "No, dummy. It's not because of you. Well, not entirely because of you."

"Why, then?"

Her hands traced my chest. "Because I know how people will talk about me being your girlfriend. And I don't mind—I genuinely don't, Julian. But I don't want to be in that environment. And I don't want to offend you, but…"

"But…?"

"I'm not much of a techie." Her voice was apologetic. "I love what you do and I have so much respect for it, same with Turner.

And I promise I'll be the most attentive girlfriend ever. I'll listen to you talk about all of your projects happily, okay? And I'll get—"

I broke her off by laughing, shaking her gently by the shoulders. "Emily, don't worry. I always knew this wasn't your field."

"You did?"

I raised an eyebrow. "Honestly, Ace, it's pretty obvious. And it's not only you. Hell, Josef can't even send a document to the printers. And you know those regular lunches Rachel has with the software developers?"

"Yeah?"

"It's just so she can pump them for information. She buys them lunch and they explain all the steps for her." I grinned. "I'm not offended in the slightest."

"You aren't?"

I kissed her again, a slow caress, loving the way she felt in my arms. "As long as you're with me, I don't care if you never want to use a computer again in your life."

Her answering smile was sweet. "I do, you know. Love you."

I pulled her back for another kiss. "I love you too. And while I'm very happy about this new development between us, do you want to tell me what you want to work with instead? Is there anything I can do to help?"

"I have an idea I've been thinking about for the past couple of weeks… it's a bit of a risk, but I think perhaps I've become a risk-taker."

"Oh?"

"Yes. I recently met someone who takes wild business risks and has created some surprisingly successful ventures."

I raised an eyebrow. "You did?"

"Mhm. And without naming any names, he's inspired me to be braver. To go after what I want."

"And what do you want?"

She brushed my nose with hers. "I'm going to start my own press and media consulting company. Small-scale, initially, but primarily with a focus on how restaurants can use social media to grow their audience."

I watched the play of emotions on her face, the hope, the excitement, and the fear. "Ace, that's a great idea."

"You think?"

"Yes. And you already know Michael."

She grinned. "Exactly! There are tons of things I could try."

"You'd be self-employed," I pointed out. "You could work from anywhere. Even a home office."

"Yeah, exactly. Initially, I'll probably have to. I have enough savings to tide me over before I start getting proper commissions."

"You're going to be absolutely great at this."

Sparkling green eyes met mine. "Thanks for believing in me."

I kissed her again. "Always. Thanks for believing in us."

"Always."

34

EMILY

It was a Monday morning and I was feeling *fabulous*. When was the last time anyone could say that? I was officially in a relationship, and I'd spent the weekend with my three favorite people—Turner, Julian, and Denise.

Denise had been adamant that people didn't change their status on social media these days, but I still felt the urge to do it. Once Julian and I had made the decision to go official, I wanted everyone to know. My new business idea and the decision to leave a high-paying job were absolutely crazy, and the Emily I had been months ago would never have dared.

But the Emily I was now? Well, I had a plan for my future, and I was going to do my best to make it come true. It involved a job I enjoyed, a man I loved, and a brother I would cherish through thick and thin.

Julian and I spoke with David at HR together on Friday before leaving the office, just to ensure HR were aware of both my decision to leave the company and our relationship.

David had taken the news better than I had expected, but I noticed the amused glance he shot Julian. "Now we'll have to find another press secretary, *again*."

Julian had been unfazed. "Worth it," he'd said.

But telling my co-workers had been the most difficult part.

Couldn't I just send a memo? *Sleeping with the bossman and will work my last day in two weeks. Thought you all should know. Coffee at five in the break room?*

But no, I had taken the face-to-face route like the responsible adult I was slowly becoming, informing them all at the same time after a meeting.

They had all responded in varying ways. Trent had just given me a little smile and a knowing nod, as if he'd expected nothing else from us. Sasha had squealed, Josef had laughed, and Rachel had been sad that I was quitting. "You are a great co-worker," she'd said. "Can't say I'm surprised, though."

I guess Julian and I must have been less discreet than we thought.

Turner had been first to know, of course.

"So you're quitting your job."

"Yes." I had worried the hem of my blouse between my fingers, unsure of how he'd react. "I want to start working with press more in relation to the food business, but potentially with other businesses as well."

"Being self-employed?"

"Yes."

Turner had cocked his head. "I think that will suit you."

"You do?"

"You've always been very self-sufficient. And I know you know all of this tech stuff because of me, mostly."

"You'd be working at the company without me," I had said carefully. "I only got the job thanks to you, Turner. And I'm super grateful."

He had looked intently at a spot just slightly above my shoulder and shoved his hands in his pockets. "Emily, I'm an adult. I don't need you to work in the same building as me."

"No, I know." I'd nodded and tried to swallow the flood of emotions rising up in me. My baby brother, all grown.

"Besides, I'm working on a side project. It's not like I'll be at Hunt Industries all my life."

"Really?"

"No."

I'd smiled. "I'm really happy you're okay with these changes. The most important thing for me is that you're happy and fulfilled, Turner. That we both are."

"I know." He had looked away from me quickly before his gaze returned, shifting his weight from his left to right foot. "I've always known that."

"Good. Because we're family. And family is all that matters."

"Yes. Does Julian qualify as family yet?"

I had laughed. "Let's give it a bit more time, but I think the answer will probably be yes."

―――

The two weeks until my last day at Hunt moved faster than I had anticipated. They were busy, too—I sat in on interviews with my replacement and finished the projects I had been responsible for.

My spare time was spent building my own fledgling company and contacting potential clients. Michael was already on board, but I couldn't put all my eggs in one basket, even if the person holding it was Michelin-accredited.

My phone buzzed.

Julian: I sent over a spreadsheet for cost calculations. It should help you set up a budget for the first couple of months.

I grinned down at my screen. He'd been more supportive than I ever could have imagined, helping me build this new one-woman business. The opportunity to have *Julian Hunt* as a business mentor was undeniably one ambitious people all around the world would kill for, and here I was, getting his time for free.

God, but I loved him.

Emily: Thanks! But no more helping me until you've written at least 500 words of your speech.

Julian: *Bossy.*

Emily: I've learned from the best. We have to get to the restaurant on time.

Michael and Denise pulled a favor to get us a great table at a place that technically hadn't opened yet for the public. Not only did they serve amazing South American food, but they could also potentially need promotional help...

Julian: We will, Ace.

Emily: But before you go back to work...

I sent him a photo of the long, sleek dress I'd picked out from a high-end store in town. It had fit me like a glove. Denise had given me two thumbs up and scrambled to find her phone to take a photo when I'd come out of the trying room.

Emily: How's this for the awards gala?

Julian: You look stunning. How am I supposed to concentrate on writing this speech now?

I grinned at his exaggeration and the way his praise made me feel. The gala he had invited me to was in two weeks' time, an annual awards ceremony for innovation and app design. Everyone who was anyone in the tech world would be there... and me, with Julian—official and public.

The idea had made me wildly nervous when he asked me, but he'd just pressed a kiss to my neck and told me that we didn't have to go. That he'd do whatever I wanted.

But the idea of being on his arm, of supporting him when he won that award (I didn't have any doubts about that—he'd win)... I couldn't *not* go. Not to mention that Julian in a tux was a very effective incentive.

Emily: I'll leave you alone now. Not another word from you until you have a first draft!

His response was immediate.

Julian: *:D*

I laughed out loud at my phone. Technically not another word, so he wasn't breaking the rules. He could be so silly.

I slid my phone back into my pocket and continued packing the stuff from my office. My last day at Hunt Industries. Who would have known this was where I'd end up?

That I'd only work here for three months?

Or that I would leave, having somehow gained everything I could ever dream of?

35

JULIAN

I cleared my throat and took another sip of wine. Emily's warm hand squeezed mine underneath the table.

"You'll be great up there," she murmured next to me.

I shot her a grateful smile. Somehow she knew exactly when I was nervous, when my ego needed a boost or when I needed to be knocked down a peg.

I squeezed her hand back.

Ryan sat in the seat to my left, the ends of his bowtie already lazily undone. That rascal. He reached for his glass and I shot him a warning glance.

"Take it slow."

"I'm twenty-one," he said.

"Exactly."

He rolled his eyes and took a sip, but I saw the smile hovering on the edge of his lips. It hadn't been particularly difficult to convince the event organizers to give me two extra tickets, one for Ryan and one for Turner.

For Turner, because it was a great chance to network and meet other people in this business.

For Ryan, because Emily had reminded me that if I won it would be great to have family there. It had shamed me slightly that I had to be reminded of that. For so long, I'd thought of

Ryan as my *little* brother, not someone I could lean on for support or hang out with as a friend.

But here he was, looking dapper and grown up next to me. Emily had said that we looked alike when we picked him up earlier in the limo. He'd rolled his eyes but given her a pleased grin, and my chest had tightened. If only my father could have been alive to see how great *both* his sons had turned out.

Emily's hand squeezed mine again under the table and I turned to her. She was a vision tonight, dark hair swept up high and green eyes lined and enhanced. And the red dress… it clung to her skin, even as it rose high to cover her cleavage and extended all the way down to the floor. I'd have to ask her to wear it again for me.

At home.

She smiled at me. "Next category, Julian."

"I know." I leaned in closer, spoke in her ear. "Do you know that every man in here has been aware of you since we came tonight? You're the most beautiful woman here."

I could feel the warmth of the blush in her cheeks. "Julian," she chided.

"I mean it, Ace." I smoothed my thumb over her palm. "And I'm so glad you came tonight. That you're here with me."

"There's nowhere I'd rather be."

Ryan hit my shoulder. "Look alive, man."

I broke away from Emily's gaze to see the gray-haired presenter resume his place at the podium. A respectful hush fell over the room.

"We've reached the end of the night, and with it, our most prestigious award. You've been patient so far, but let me put you out of your misery. This year has seen some truly astonishing new inventions and discoveries. With every passing month, mankind comes closer and closer to solving some of the most pressing issues of our time with the help of technology. I'm honored to be in a room with so many of these thinkers tonight."

We all broke out into applause as the presenter paused, glancing out over the audience. My throat felt dry, despite the fact that I'd told myself this didn't matter. My work did. Recognition came second, or even third.

"With that said, we're here tonight to pay tribute to someone who has shown a tireless commitment to showing how technology can solve real-life problems. This year, he launched never before seen software specifically designed to ensure that health care is more accessible. In a bold move, he designed an accompanying app and delivered the whole thing pro-bono to any hospital, private and public, that wanted to try it."

Emily's hand tightened around mine and I heard Ryan's excited intake of breath.

"I talk of no one other, of course, than Julian Hunt!"

The crowd broke into applause. I stood, and Emily pressed a quick kiss to my cheek before I made my way up to the stage. Someone shoved a large bouquet of flowers into my hands and then I was in front of a huge crowd of my peers. Lights blinked down at me.

"Hi, everyone. Standing here before so many of the greatest minds in our field is truly humbling. I won't lie—this award is both unexpected and wildly exciting."

The crowd laughed, and I wet my lips. "I've always been ambitious. I think the drive to create more and to create better is one of the best things we have as humans. But as I've gotten older, it's shifted. My desire to make great things has eclipsed my desire to simply be great. If we're not making a lasting impact, what are we doing?"

I paused. At my table, I could see my brother, eyes wide as he watched me speak. For the first time in a long while I saw the young kid he used to be and felt like the big brother I wanted to be. Someone worthy of looking up to. Emily's eyes were shiny—I could see it despite the distance.

"I have a lot of people to thank. Not the least everyone in my team, at my company, who've kept me sane for all these years. But more than anything, I need to thank my family. Because none of this means anything without people to share it with. Thank you all."

Applause rained down around me as I walked off the stage. Ryan was already up and ready to greet me. We hugged, the typical slap-on-the-back kind of thing we'd always done.

"Wow, bro. That was... Congrats."

"Thanks."

Emily melted into my arms. I grinned and pulled her back down into our seats.

"Are you crying?"

"No," she sniffled. "You just take my breath away sometimes."

"You might have to get used to it," I said and pressed a kiss to her temple. "I'm going to make you breathless many, many more times."

EPILOGUE
EMILY

Two years later

Opening the door to my home office never failed to give me delicious, happy little goose bumps. It was everything I had ever dreamed of. A huge white desk, a large computer. Fresh flowers and wide windows. The perfect space for brainstorming, hustling, and making my dream business come to life.

After we married, Julian and I moved into a new house together. I'd thought it was silly at the time, since his house was big enough for us both, but he'd been determined—apparently, we needed more space and more security, and a proper lawn.

I had thought he'd been a bit nuts at first… but then we found this place.

Just outside of Palo Alto, we had stumbled across an old, sprawling house with both character and charm. Close enough to Hunt Industries, but with a big enough backyard for a family… it had become ours.

My home office was just another example of how thoughtful he was. It too, had been a surprise, one he'd set up together with that old interior designer of his. I'd been so busy trying to plan our wedding that he outsourced most of the things I was too busy to focus on.

Always efficient, that man.

I fired up my computer and logged in to check my emails. Since launching my business, it had grown steadily, much of that thanks to the success Michael had enjoyed. He'd recently proposed to Denise, and they were both over the moon with joy. So was I, albeit partly for selfish reasons—I was the maid of honor and looked forward to planning her bachelorette party.

I smiled at the email waiting for me from Ryan. He wanted me to look over the marketing strategy he'd devised, and Turner was CCed in the email.

The change that had occurred in both of our brothers was nothing short of astonishing. Unsurprisingly to me, Turner had come up with a revolutionary new line of code and decided he wanted to try his hand at setting up his own company.

I had been worried, but both Turner and Julian were so confident about the whole thing. Julian invested massively but made it very clear that it was because he honestly believed in Turner's idea, and that was that. The launch was only six months away now.

What was more surprising was that Ryan went with him. He'd interned for me and learned about social media marketing for a few months before going back to college and getting credits in marketing. There was something about the social media aspect and the fast-changing nature of the press that really appealed to him.

What's more, Turner and Ryan had quickly developed this odd kind of friendship. Both were blunt and straight. Turner had trusted Ryan from the beginning in his characteristic way, taking his words at face value, and Ryan had risen to the challenge. Having a new friend who knew nothing of his party background had been great for him.

Julian and his brother now had a standing dinner date every week, and I was happy that my husband could enjoy being with his brother in that role. Both of us had been able to abandon the semi-parental authority we'd worn uneasily for several years, and it did us both good.

I smoothed a hand over my tummy and smiled. Especially considering the fact that we were about to become parents for real. I had found out only the day before, taking a drugstore test in our en suite bathroom.

Julian wasn't home—he was away with Ryan, their first camping trip together since their father passed. I had been far too impatient to wait until he returned.

We'd gone off birth control nearly three months ago with the attitude of *if it happens, it happens*.

But judging by the email I'd just gotten from Ryan, they were on their way back. I grabbed a book and headed downstairs, through our large kitchen and out onto the patio.

Julian had been right, as always. A large lawn would be perfect for kids, and there was even space for a pool. Anticipation made my toes curl. This would be a new adventure for both of us.

I spread out a blanket underneath one of the large trees in our yard and settled down with my book. I'd wait for him here. He'd find me... I'd tell him.

It was hard to focus on the words on the page. All I could think about was his reaction, a thousand different responses running through my head.

But eventually, I must have relaxed enough to doze off, because I was jerked awake by the sound of a very familiar, very masculine laugh.

"So this is what you've been doing while I've been away?"

Julian grinned down at me from the patio. I squealed and rose into sitting. He was wearing his old pair of chinos and a rumpled button-down in flannel. His thick hair was mussed and he had a faint five-o'clock shadow.

He looked like sex on a stick.

Of all the Julian Hunts I'd seen, I'd finally realized that there was really only one. This one, the one standing in front of me with a wide smile and sparkling eyes, entirely uncaring about what the rest of the world thought of him. When he was here alone with me, with no expectations on either of us.

When he could just be himself.

"Hi," I said.

Julian walked toward me. "Hi, Ace. You look different."

"I do?" The test showed I was only three weeks along. It was impossible for him to know.

"Yeah. Is that a new dress?"

I grinned. "No, I just haven't worn it in a while."

"Are we celebrating something?" For a moment, he looked distant, undoubtedly running through all our collective anniversaries and birthdays in his mind.

I laughed. "No, don't worry. Nothing like that."

"But there is something." His gaze was warm and intense as he studied me. "Isn't there? You look excited."

I grinned—the man knew me far too well. I stepped close and took his hands in mine, warm and rough and engulfing mine entirely. Nerves raced through my stomach, but I felt the cool weight of his wedding ring against my skin and it gave me strength.

"There is something, actually. I'm pregnant."

Julian's face froze, and for a moment, his look was one of such complete surprise that I wished I had a sneaky camera crew taping the whole thing.

Then he sprung to life and I was lifted up, crushed against his hard chest and spun around and around. I laughed and wrapped my arms around his neck.

"Em, are you sure?"

I nodded into his neck as tears pooled and overflowed, running down my cheeks. "I took three consecutive tests, so pretty sure, yes."

Julian held me at arm's length, eyes glued to mine. A wide grin stretched across his face and my heart felt so full of love I couldn't speak.

"Wow," he said faintly.

"Wow," I echoed. "You're going to be a dad, Julian."

He blinked. "And you're going to be a mom. The best mom. You'll have to make sure I do okay."

I laughed. "I won't know what I'm doing either!"

"No, you will. You'll ace it like you do everything."

I pulled him closer and pressed my lips to his. "And so will you. We'll figure it out."

He kissed me back gently, hands tracing patterns along my sides. "We will," he said. "Together."

―――

Thank you so much for reading Arrogant Boss! I hope you enjoyed Julian and Emily's story as much as I did writing it.

Do you want more forbidden office romances? Perhaps between a billionaire single dad and the feisty new intern?

Read on for the first chapter of Think Outside the Boss, a page turning romance filled with steamy banter and sizzling stakes...

CHAPTER ONE
FREDERICA

I'm sorting through junk mail when my fingers gloss over a thick golden envelope. My address is handwritten on the front in sprawling black letters, but there's no name. Mentally, I run through all my friends who might be getting married... no, no and no.

Golden envelope in hand, I sink onto my kitchen chair and flip it over. It has a black wax seal. Stamped into it is a mask, the kind people wear to fancy masquerades in movies. I've never received anything like this.

If this is junk mail, it's gotten very classy.

Can it be to the previous tenant? I've only lived in this studio for a month. Best to make sure... I tear the envelope open with a kitchen knife and pull out a card-stock invitation with gold, printed lettering.

Dear Rebecca Hartford,

It's a new month, and that means new sins to explore. Join us at the Halycon Hotel at ten p.m. the following Saturday and wear the accompanying mask as proof of invitation.

Don't forget that secrecy is fun, phones are not (no one likes a tattle-

tale), and everyone looks better in lace. Or disrobed. But we're getting ahead of ourselves…

Yours in pleasure,
The Gilded Room

Oh God.

I read the invitation twice to sort through all the innuendos.

The Gilded Room? Everyone looks better disrobed? Rebecca Hartford, you minx!

This might be the most elaborate practical joke I've ever been on the receiving end of. Peering into the envelope, I find a mask lined in delicate black silk, two feathers curling above the cutout eyes like eyebrows. Black jewels crust the bottom half, and three words are written in gold cursive along the edge. *United in pleasure.*

Okay.

Maybe not a practical joke.

I open my laptop and type the Gilded Room in the search bar. A bunch of newspaper articles have been written about the organization, but not a single one of them features pictures. I click open the one entitled *A night in the elite's world of pleasure.*

What I read makes my eyes widen. The Gilded Room is one of New York's best kept secrets, primarily because those in it don't want to be known. They don't want to be seen, heard, and especially not pictured. The Gilded Room guarantees anonymity to its high-flying members, many of whom pay over twenty thousand dollars for their yearly memberships.

I scroll down, my eyes scanning paragraph after incredible paragraph.

Rules are simple. No one is invited that isn't rich, beautiful, or both. Anyone caught with a phone is immediately expelled… and women have all the power at these parties. There are whispers of politicians attending Gilded Room parties, football players, billionaires and media tycoons… but if they have, the journalist couldn't find anyone willing to talk. It seems this is the only venue among New York's upper echelons where name-dropping *isn't* the norm.

I close my laptop and stare down at the mask and invitation, now lying on my sofa table. Who had Rebecca Hartford been, to be invited to a party like this? I know for a fact that the previous tenant had left the country, my landlord telling me she'd been offered a job in Hong Kong. Contacting her about this feels out of the question.

What if I go myself?

The idea makes me smile. Secret sex parties for the rich? I'm not rich, nor a partier. I am sex-interested, though. It's been a long time since I last...

What am I thinking? Of course I'm not going.

I toss the invitation and the mask in the paper-basket and the lid closes decisively behind them. Besides, I have things to do, like preparing for the internship of a lifetime. I'd worked too hard to get accepted into Exciteur Global's Junior Professionals program, and my first day as a trainee is on Monday.

I have things to do before then.

Get three new pairs of stockings to go with my professional outfits. Unpack the last of the moving boxes. Schedule a time at the DMV to update my driver's license to New York instead of Pennsylvania.

Attend secret sex party is nowhere on that list.

I make it almost an hour and another moving box unpacked before I fish the invitation and mask back out of the paper-basket. Standing in front of the bathroom mirror, I put on the black, feather-adorned mask.

I look moderately pretty. Thick, dark hair, and more than my fair share of it, thanks to my Italian mother. Quite short, but I like to think I'm just petite. Eyes that are a muddy sort of green. It did say you had to be rich or beautiful to get in...

I tug at my ratty old T-shirt to make a V-shaped neckline. Courtesy of an unusually large chest, I never wear anything that revealing. But I had just unpacked the black dress I got on sale last year. The one that showed a lot of cleavage... Could I pass for Rebecca Hartford? Or at least beautiful enough to gain admission?

"An adventure before the real one starts on Monday," I tell my masked reflection.

I once heard it said that women have three forms of showers. The first, a quick body wash. The second, a quick hair and body wash. The third? That's the date-shower, where things get scrubbed and shaven and deep-conditioned.

As it turns out, I've discovered a fourth shower, the help-I'm-going-to-an-elite-sex-party shower. It has a lot of elements from shower number three, like shaving and scrubbing, but includes a few minutes of panicking on the shower floor.

My mind clings to the words I'd read online, that women have all the power. If I don't like it, I'll leave. The Halycon Hotel is one of the nicest in the city, so it's not like I'm walking into an organized crime syndicate.

At least I tell myself that.

It's nearly ten-thirty when I arrive at the hotel. My high heels click on the floor as I walk to the reception. My invitation and mask are both safe and secure in my clutch, ready to be whipped out in lieu of an ID.

"Good evening, miss," a hotel attendant says. His eyes dip to the deep V of my black dress before returning to my eyes.

And *that's* why I usually wear high necklines.

A flush rises on his neck. "You're here for the private party?"

I tug my coat shut. "Yes."

"The elevator to your left," he says, "and straight up to the thirty-second floor. Have fun, miss."

"Thank you." And because I can't resist, I add, "I plan to."

I ride alone in the elevator, my eyes tracking the ever-increasing number of floors on the display. It's become a surefire way to keep my fear of heights at bay. Focus on the floors I'm passing and soon enough, it's over. I still breathe a sigh of relief as I step out.

Showtime, Freddie.

I put the mask on and tie the silken strings together, ignoring the way my heart runs amok in my chest with nerves. The scene that awaits me is exceedingly normal. An empty corridor and an open doorway with a pretty, dark-clad woman in front, her face radiating calm professionalism.

She tucks an iPad under her arm. "Welcome, miss."

"Thank you."

"One performance has already concluded, but the next one should be starting just now."

I nod, like I understand what she's referring to. "Terrific, thank you."

She holds her hand out with an expectant look in her eyes. "Right," I say, digging through my clutch to hand her my invitation card. *Don't ask for ID, don't ask for ID...*

But she just looks it over and gives me another smile, this one more friend-to-friend. "Welcome, Miss Hartford. Don't forget to check your phone in on the right, after you enter."

"Of course."

She pushes aside the curtain blocking the door. The contrast is sharp from the bright corridor outside to the dimly lit, smoke-filled rooms beyond. A scent hangs in the air... something thick, like magnolia and incense.

A man dressed only in a pair of black slacks and a tie, no shirt to cover up the broad chest on display, welcomes me. "I'll check your coat, miss."

"Yes, thank you," I say, shrugging out of it. He hangs it up and returns, a hand extended. "Oh! Right." I hand him my phone.

His answering smile makes me think I'm not masking my nerves as well as I thought. "I'll put your phone right here," he says, opening one of a hundred identical security boxes. "The code is automatically generated, and you'll get a printed receipt with it... here you go. Only you know this. Don't lose it."

"All right," I murmur. "Awesome."

He gives me another encouraging smile, this time tinged with humor. "Enjoy yourself, and remember that we're here at any time if you need help or you have any questions."

"Thank you."

Gripping my clutch tight, I walk into the main space. The first impressions strike me in flashes. White lace and high heels. Drapes of black silk from the ceiling. Men in impeccably fitted suits and dark masks.

People mingle, some standing, some reclining on sofas. A beautiful woman strolls past me in lingerie. It's the imposing kind, with garters and thigh-highs.

"Champagne, miss?" a waiter asks, holding out a tray of flutes. Just like the man working the coat check, he's shirtless.

"Yes, thank you," I murmur. Walking through the throngs of people in a dazed sort of wonder, I think I see people I recognize. It's difficult to tell with the masks, but not impossible, and a few have discarded theirs entirely. One woman is a news anchor and I've seen her on TV dozens of times. A tall, broad-shouldered man has the face of a football player. If I'd been more sports interested, his name would have come to me, but as it is I settle on furtive glances his way. Bottles of champagne with golden labels line an entire wall.

This is wealth like I've never seen it before. It's a rich person's playground, a study in how the wealthy amuse themselves.

Then I see it.

The performance.

There's a raised stage in the middle of the room, and what's taking place on it makes my high school drama club's rendition of *Macbeth* look like child's play. Two lingerie-clad women circle a man on a chair, his hands in cuffs behind him. One runs proprietary nails over the man's sculpted chest, the other sliding her hand up his bare thigh.

My eyes are glued to the scene.

And yet all around me, guests of the Gilded Room continue

to mingle in varying states of undress as if three people aren't currently engaged in *very* public foreplay in front of us.

A masked woman in her mid-forties walks past me, pulling a man along behind her by his tie. She shoots me a triumphant look. "The next performance should have pyrotechnics," she says.

I give her a weak smile. "Just what this party needs. Fire."

"I like you!" she calls over her shoulder. "Feel free to join us later!"

Join them, wow. I smile into my champagne and look across the room, hoping to spot more famous people. There is no way my friends will believe me, but I still want to make sure this night turns into the best anecdote possible.

My gaze lingers on a man on the other side of the room. Like most men here, he's in a suit, but he's one of the few not wearing a mask. Not speaking to anyone, either. He just leans against the wall and watches the performance with arms crossed over his chest.

Looks like he's sitting this one out.

I turn in my empty glass of champagne for a full one and lean against the wall opposite him. There's nothing familiar about him, and yet I can't seem to look away.

His gaze snaps to mine, and the laser-focus makes it clear he's well aware of my staring. He raises an eyebrow.

My lips curve into the universal sign of *hi, there.* It's the smile you give a man in a bar to let him know you want him to come over. It's brazen.

A group of guests stop in the middle of the room and it sunders our eye contact. I look down into my champagne with a heart that's suddenly pounding. I'd come here to observe, without any plans of participating…

But a girl can flirt, can't she?

When I see him again, he's no longer alone. A woman runs her hand down his arm in a manner that would be easy to read even if we *weren't* at an elite sex party.

I push off the wall and take a lap of the room. There's a

steady, pounding beat emanating from the speakers, heady in its power. More than a few of the mingling guests have moved on from simple conversation, and I pass by a man taking off his partner's bra while discussing New York real estate.

I find a dark corner of the space to retreat to, far away from the couples in varying states of undress. I've never watched other people… well. Perhaps it's time for me to declare this little adventure finished.

That's when he appears by my side, a crystal tumbler in hand.

Brown hair rises over a strong forehead and the square of his jaw covered in two days' worth of stubble. Up close, it's even harder to look away from him.

He raises that eyebrow at me again, but says nothing. He just leans against the wall beside me and we gaze at the crowd in silence.

I take another sip of my champagne to keep my nerves at bay. Who is he? A media mogul? A celebrity I don't recognize? The scion of a political family? For the night, he's a stranger, just like me.

"So?" I ask, watching him through the slitted eyes of my mask. "Are you planning on introducing yourself?"

Keep reading in Think Outside the Boss!

OTHER BOOKS BY OLIVIA
LISTED IN READING ORDER

New York Billionaires Series

Think Outside the Boss
Tristan and Freddie

Saved by the Boss
Anthony and Summer

Say Yes to the Boss
Victor and Cecilia

A Ticking Time Boss
Carter and Audrey

Seattle Billionaires Series

Billion Dollar Enemy
Cole and Skye

Billion Dollar Beast
Nick and Blair

Billion Dollar Catch
Ethan and Bella

Billion Dollar Fiancé
Liam and Maddie

Brothers of Paradise Series

Rogue
Lily and Hayden

Ice Cold Boss
Faye and Henry

Red Hot Rebel
Ivy and Rhys

Standalones

Arrogant Boss
Julian and Emily

Look But Don't Touch
Grant and Ada

The Billionaire Scrooge Next Door
Adam and Holly

ABOUT OLIVIA

Olivia loves billionaire heroes despite never having met one in person. Taking matters into her own hands, she creates them on the page instead. Stern, charming, cold or brooding, so far she's never met a (fictional) billionaire she didn't like.

Her favorite things include wide-shouldered heroes, late-night conversations, too-expensive wine and romances that lift you up.

Smart and sexy romance—those are her lead themes!

Join her newsletter for updates and bonus content.
www.oliviahayle.com.
Connect with Olivia

- facebook.com/authoroliviahayle
- instagram.com/oliviahayle
- goodreads.com/oliviahayle
- amazon.com/author/oliviahayle
- bookbub.com/profile/olivia-hayle

Printed in Great Britain
by Amazon